Alberto's Dream

By Philip J. Braun

Copyright © 2004 by Philip J. Braun

ISBN 0-7414-1966-1

Published by:

INFINITY
PUBLISHING.COM

1094 New Dehaven Street
Suite 100
West Conshohocken, PA 19428-2713
Info@buybooksontheweb.com
www.buybooksontheweb.com
Toll-free (877) BUY BOOK
Local Phone (610) 520-2500
Fax (610) 519-0261

Printed in the United States of America
Printed on Recycled Paper
Published April 2004

Table of Contents

Prologue

A big buck sergeant lined you up in a windy, tar-papered barracks in Del Rio. You stood there, your body jerking and itching like hell in olive-drab. On your left slumped a gaunt, pockmarked guy from a hick place in Arkansas called Calico-Rock. He was nervous as you and smelled of hay and manure and had the gait of 20 years in the furrows. On your right stood a shifty-eyed, razor-headed guy from Kansas city who held a half-smoked weed between two yellow-stained fingers. He stared at the ceiling and down at the cracks in the floorboards. The buck sergeant had big paws on his hips, his bulk rocking on a pair of size 13s, his eyes pendulum-like at raw, green men to whom the sudden command "ten-shun!" was a half-heard, unregistered call in the dark . . .

* * *

Waking to a Neapolitan dawn with a thump and grating of windlasses turning, chains dropping, to the cries of deck hands, and the snorting of nearby ships in the harbor. A light fog offshore as you brush a thick blackout curtain aside and step to the rail amidship. Already the other olive-drab are watching gray ships move sluggishly in the bay. Ahead lies the city, beaten, dejected, creeping like brown lava over the hills. The sea all scum and oil and debris with an occasional gull nosing in an ill-colored mass, coming up with a squirming, ivory-colored fish, then with a wheeling motion rising with its weight and lost itself in the red-blue sky.

Sepia-colored craft fly torn red sails manned by dark-skinned kids, the little boats pushing their way in among the Liberty ships. The little boats grope and plunge like still-wet pups reaching hungrily for their mother's teats. Your ear now catches the phrase you'll hear over and over again whenever black-eyed youngsters tug at your uniform. "Hey, Joe . . . Hey, Joe . . . cigarettos . . . cigarettos . . ."

* * *

Always the same—moving up, up to the line. Seeing the strewn "C" ration cans, the "K" boxes with the half-moon cut in them, the rusting rolls of barbed wire, the torn-up earth from artillery fire . . . And if there's any sense of security at all in this mud-slogging push up the boot in Italy it's seeing those cans in the mud, those boxes in the wet earth, because somewhere up ahead there's another olive-drab, grinding it out, hunkered down, killing Krauts, and just maybe you aren't alone . . . just maybe . . .

* * *

Sixth day on the line—rain, mud and monotony—in a week-old shell-hole serrated with cannon fire. Piedigrossi is bossing in the piece, the ground so fucking hard you blast it to lower the Bofors . . . cursing never stopping . . . The SCR593 is on at a machine gun pit, a red alert out . . . an October day near Luneville, the leaves a waxy red and gold in the wetness, 155's belching in the valley, three Spits at 6,000 feet. They nose down, waggle wings, scoot up towards Rambervillers . . . A Piper Cub is up spotting for the artillery. . .

They're on you, three of them. Three ugly, yellow-nosed ME109's, busting at you from tree-top level. Over the treetops and down past gun section 8, sending the Cub diving . . . Eager sharks hunting prey, sweeping down on the 155's, our 50's chattering, slugs curving skywards, the pong-pong-pong of the Bofors, the hail of lead from surrounding gun positions. . .

* * *

A scarlet cock crows on his manure pile, proclaiming the surge of dawn, the rain falling lightly, silently, gathering in pools in the cobblestones. Beside a doorway, an olive-drab yawns, shifts his rifle on his shoulder, stares at the morning. From the north comes a muffled roar and the electrifying wham of incoming mail tunneling in the wet sky.

Inside a limestone house an old woman busies herself around a small stove, sips her ersatz coffee, stares at the grayness outside her window. An olive-drab rises wearily from the stone floor, rubs an arm across red eyes, looks around his scarred resting place, sees a brown wall with pictures of Bernadette and the "White Lady." He sees a crucifix on a side wall as from the hollows comes the crescendo of battle. He stares heavily at the crucifix and wonders. . .

* * *

This is your war, everyone's war . . . ugly, monotonous, hardness and sweat and melancholy in the evening., whistle of death in the wind . . . Oil, machinery, warped science in hard labor, masses of once-free men following like children, the Pied Piper from Mars. False emotion percolating to a boil, heated by the forces of greed, the heretics of civilization. A war of rapid humanity, cart-filled roads—gutted with the despairing. Civilization streaming down a dark passage. . . White crosses in arrow-straight diagonals, stretching toward the sunset.

* * *

There is nothing beautiful in a man's vomit.
The Pole hadn't eaten in some time, his stomach swollen . . .
You don't put down in black and white
What the Germans did to him.

> He wasn't a man. A piece of vermin, squirming
> Upwards from a dark prison.
> Up towards a shaft of warm, earth light
> Closed for four years.
> We gave him eggs . . . he went at them
> like a mad dog.
> We saw him beside the road . . . vomiting.
> Vermin in the light.

* * *

A Bavarian.
With a green felt hat
And a white-flowing feather
Perched in it . . . brown leather britches
Covered with a woven Edelweiss pattern.

He cycles along the asphalt track from Munich to Dachau
It's May of '45.

He admires the strength and beauty of his native soil.
The bright, new May flowers, the rugged
Oxen tugging the farmer's carts.

Twenty box-cars
Filled with inferior races
In various states of decomposition
Covered with lime . . . stand on a side-track
Around them spring the sweet flowers of Germania.

The Bavarian rests his cycle on the grass,
Picks some of them for his frau, smiles
At the goodness of the day . . . mounts his cycle,
Passes the box cars.

Chapter 1 — Three Young Men

Section 1.01 Alberto

The dream came back in the early morning hours as the sun touched the ramparts of Acoma. It was the identical dream Alberto had had as a boy of eight when he was being initiated into the kakale rites preparing him for manhood. In this recurring dream, Alberto's father stared at him from the granite face of Mount Hasasu, his features carved into the solid red rock. Felipe Campione gazed down at Alberto, his son, across the wide valley that stretched between the great mountain and his home on the mesa called Acoma.

The dream. What did it mean? Why was his father staring at him? Was it an omen? Why had the dream come back after all these years? Why was Felipe's face carved into the great mountain? Was it telling something to Alberto, something he should know, something that was important?

He must tell Felipe about it this morning as they rode to Laguna in the wagon. Alberto lay on his bed and pondered the dream and its hidden meaning. Thoughts from the dream drifted in and out until he fell asleep.

* * *

Alberto breakfasted with his family and then said good-bye to them. He wouldn't see them or his home again until the Christmas holidays. He was on his way to the famous high school far away in Santa Fe and it pleased him to think that he was the second young man from his mesa to go to St. Catherines. The first had been some years ago—Juan Romero. Juan had never come back to Acoma after he graduated from St. Catherines. People on the mesa said he was trying to make it in the white world.

Alberto felt good about himself. Felipe told him that he had been chosen to go to the school because of three things: his athletic skills, his art work, and his academic standing. His father also told him that it was an honor to represent Acoma because St. Catherines picked students from all the reservations and pueblos in the southwest.

His mother packed an old cracked, brown valise for him and she put in some of his charcoal drawings that had won prizes at the All-Indian show in Gallup. His two sisters kissed him and made him promise to write. He then walked down the mesa with his father and Henrique, his boyhood friend, to where the mules were hitched to the wagon. He would miss Henrique because they had grown up together on the mesa, had many times run together on the hard-packed desert, and had camped out at night under the stars. Alberto looked north across the desert toward Laguna, thirteen miles away. Here he would catch the bus to Santa Fe.

He told his father and Felipe about the dream and they couldn't figure out what it meant. "Maybe you'll be a sculptor some day, Runner," Henrique said. "Maybe you'll put your father's face on Mount Hasasu." The three Indians looked at each other and laughed.

Alberto turned around in the wagon and took one last look at Acoma. Far up on the rim of the mesa he could see people. He thought of how, hundreds of years before, his people had bravely fought against the Spaniards. For days they stood on the mesa above and poured boiling oil on the invaders, but they couldn't win against the power of the Spanish cannon. The conquerors took every male Indian over fourteen and cut off his right hand and made slaves of his people. Now he was going to school in the old town that had been the Spanish capitol for hundreds of years. Now he was about to enter the white world in Santa Fe, a world he knew nothing about.

At the bus depot he said good-bye to his father and Henrique. As the bus pulled out of Laguna, he reached into his pocket and pulled out a bear fetish. An old woman had given it to him years before during the kakale ceremonies. It was made out of onyx and had been carefully carved and shaped by the old woman until its curved surfaces seemed to glow in the light. It fit into Alberto's right hand and had been rubbed many times through the years. Hoping for good fortune, he rubbed it now.

* * *

Alberto entered the dormitory room assigned to him at the St. Catherines Indian School. He was greeted by a short, thin, wiry Indian with a pock-marked face and a hawk-like nose.

"My name's Charbonneau, Dennis Charbonneau. What's yours?"

"Alberto Campione. Call me Runner. My friends do. I'm from Acoma."

Charbonneau picked up a pack of cigarettes from a study desk and stuck one in his mouth and lit it. He held out the pack to Alberto and he declined to take one.

"Acoma? Pueblo, huh?" Dennis said. "I know where that is. Never been there. Where'd you get your height? You must be over six. I've never known Pueblo Indians over five six. You're old man tall?"

Alberto walked over to a chair and sat down. "I'm six feet two. My father is only five eight. The elders on our mesa think the gods blessed him with extra seed."

Dennis sucked on his cigarette and blew a smoke ring as the room turned blue.

"I'm Sioux; a half-breed. Got some French in me. They were the first whites in that part of the north. A lot of my people up there have French-sounding names. I'm from Pine Ridge. That's in South Dakota." Then he added, "Seen Sister Margaret yet?"

"I'm to see her at one."

"Well, I'll tell you what you're in for. She'll sit you down and give you her two-dollar, character-building speech."

* * *

Alberto knocked on Sister Margaret's door and waited. He knocked again. The door opened and a short, elderly nun with pink cheeks looked up at him from behind her desk.

"I believe you are Alberto Campione," she said warmly.

He took a chair opposite her desk. To his left a window looked out upon a large military cemetery stretching up a hillside, white crosses following the curve of the land.

"They died during the great war," she mused. "They were too young to die." She paused. "Now then, as you know, I'm Sister Margaret. We're a small school. We don't have a Mother Superior. I'm in charge."

Alberto looked around the room, it was empty of all pictures save a single wooden cross in a silver frame behind her desk. The only other furnishing consisted of three green metal filing cabinets, her desk, and the old wooden rocker on which she sat. On her desk was a thin manila folder.

She opened the folder and looked at Alberto.

"God has given you much. You're strong and athletic. You're also possessed with some artistic ability. But I caution you. Your academic studies are your first priority. Do I make myself clear?"

"Yes, Sister."

"Tell me about yourself."

He searched for words. No one had ever asked him about his life.

"This is my first time, Sister. My first time away from home."

She leaned forward in her rocker.

"Tell me something I don't already know, Alberto. You're the fastest runner in your village. You're an accomplished artist. Tell me something new. I want to know about you."

He gazed around the room. The silence persisted and he started to sweat. Sister Margaret leaned back in her chair. Her hands were clasped expectantly, waiting for a response. Finally she prompted, "What do you like to do, Alberto?"

"I like to run with the deer."

Her eyes widened and she urged him to tell her more.

"I was hunting with my father and Henrique, my friend. We were on Mount Hasasu. We had to break through many cedar windfalls. We wanted a deer because winter was coming on and we needed the meat."

Alberto stopped to look at Sister Margaret. She had an approving look on her face. "Go on, Alberto. Tell me about the deer."

"We broke through a tree line and came into a meadow. On the other side of the meadow were the rock walls of the mountain. There was snow on them. There were some birches at the edge of the meadow and in the center we saw a big stag. He was feeding on some bark and his antlers stirred as he moved his head. I reached for my bow."

Again Alberto hesitated. "What happened next?" she nearly demanded.

"I was too late, Sister. He antlers shot high and he streaked across the meadow. I tried to catch him, Sister. I dropped my bow and arrows and raced after him, trying to keep up with him. I did for quite a ways."

"Then what?" she asked.

"He suddenly stopped and faced me no more than fifty feet away. He snorted and pawed the ground. I just stood there, Sister. I can't describe it. It was like the deer and I were going to meet sometime again, some time in my life. Like I was somehow tied together with him in some way. I told my father later and he said that perhaps I had a kinship with the deer."

"Remarkable!" Sister Margaret uttered. "What a wonderful thing to happen! What did happen after that?"

"He shook his head and disappeared into a heavy thicket. I ran into the thicket but I couldn't go on because of the brambles that tore at me. I stood there until my father and Henrique came up to me."

"What did they think? What did they say?"

"Henrique gasped and said to my father, 'Alberto has earned a new name. He will be called Runner because he runs with the deer.' "

"Do they all call you Runner on the mesa?"

"Yes, Sister."

She stood up and put her hands on her desk. "Alberto, perhaps your father is right. There may be a kinship with that fine animal. God moves in ways we sometimes cannot perceive. You had an experience that few will ever have. And what do you think that magnificent animal was thinking himself as he stood there facing you? We'll never know that but it is an interesting question, isn't it?"

Sister appeared to have lost herself in her own thoughts and then she said, "Now, I must ask you. Did you bring your drawings with you from Acoma?"

"I have some in my room, Sister."

"I'll want to see them." She sat down again. "You know, Alberto, our little school is going to afford you a window on the white world. I know too well the way our white culture invaded that of your people. I'm familiar with many of your problems on the mesa. Your people are little more than pebbles in a body of water that sweeps over them more violently each day. Every day the current in the water changes like the tides and your people are moved in a different direction. Your clan cares little for the whites and many of their advancements in science, in medicine, in many areas. On the other hand, few whites appreciate your culture which is distinct. Your dances, your customs, your kiva rules mean nothing to them. You'll face adjustments here to your thoughts and actions as you get further and further exposed."

She twirled a pencil on the top of her desk. The sharp point traced fluid gray lines on a tan blotter that covered her work area.

"Your roommate can help you, Alberto. At heart, Dennis is a firebrand and that doesn't bother us. He believes deeply about issues. There is much Sioux in him. He doesn't wear the world's harness gracefully."

Sister Margaret rocked in her chair. "You'll have the opportunity to ask all the questions you want to while you're here. Questions are just as important as answers. We want your mind and your thoughts to be as wide and open as the beautiful valley that surrounds you mesa." She leaned forward again. "We listen to our young people; we learn. Both the mind and the heart are revered here, Alberto. How these apparently opposed forces are harnessed is our greatest challenge."

She put her palms flatly on the blotter and stood up.

"It is also," she said, "life's greatest mystery."

He found it difficult to speak.

"Alberto, always remember that my door is open to you. May God be with you."

* * *

When Alberto returned to his dorm room, Dennis challenged him.

"She gave you that 'life is suffering' speech, didn't she?"

Alberto ignored the sarcasm. "I like her."

"She shoves the cross at us every day."

"I liked what she said. It made sense."

"She crams religion down your throat!"

Alberto thought of Father Manuel, his priest at San Estaban Rey in Acoma where he'd been an altar boy. At first he'd been awed by the candle flames that floated like magic during mass and the smell of the incense that permeated the old building. After a while, he became disinterested with the routine, and Father Manuel had assigned another boy to his labors.

"Her cross won't hold me back!" Dennis said vehemently, lighting another cigarette. "I suppose," he sneered, "you have to deal with the Bureau of Indian Affairs at Acoma, just as we do."

"We have to," Alberto answered, "but not any more than we can help it. We're run by a clan and by their rule in our kiva. Our leader, our cacique rules with a tight fist. Sometimes I think we could learn more from the Bureau."

"Bullshit! They're leeches! They suck you dry."

Alberto, who had been standing by his desk, turned and directly faced his roommate. "Give me some credit, Dennis. It's tough to work with the Bureau. Most of the time we don't even try. Acoma has no use for the whites."

Alberto was beginning to see what Sister Margaret said about Dennis.

"Our cacique isn't always right, Dennis. The same can be said of our war chiefs and our medicine man. I get steamed when I think what they did to my family."

"What was that?"

"It's a long story. I'm not up to it today."

"Suit yourself. The BIA are bastards. They make all the rules, take it or leave it. We're treated like children in Pine Ridge. All they harp on is our laziness, our drunkenness."

Dennis' words were bitter as he went on.

"The fucking Indian agents and the politicians tell us everything is wonderful. Wonderful, my ass! My people are in deep shit and nobody gives a damn!" He took a long drag. "Out this gate is white man's territory. You either make your mark in it or you're back on the reservation. Forget your dances, your painted pots, your medicine men. Forget your cacique and your chiefs. They don't mean shit! The world is white from asshole to eyeball!"

Alberto put up his hand. "I'll take your word for it."

Dennis rattled on. "When you're through here, Runner, don't go back to Acoma. It'd be a mistake."

"Not much to go back to," Alberto responded. "We lose people every year. We're getting smaller and smaller. When I was a boy, we had eight hundred on the mesa. It's down to five hundred now. It's tough to make a living. I hope I can make it with my drawings."

"You got drawings?"

"Yeah."

"Let me see them."

Alberto reached under his bed and pulled out the old valise. He opened it and laid the drawings on his bed.

Dennis walked over and looked at them. He picked one up, put it down, picked up another.

"Christ!" he exploded. "These are good! They're a helluva lot better than the stuff I see in the Plaza downtown. You can sell these!"

"And if I do, they end up over some white man's sofa."

"So what? You got the money. That's the equalizer, Runner. That's what it's all about."

* * *

The next few months were hard for the Indian boy from Acoma. The sisters taught him and they were strict. Many of his studies were difficult. Slowly he began to fit into the academic work and to make some progress. He went out for cross-country and the baseball team, much to the excitement of the coach. Alberto quickly set a record in cross-country. A coach from Santa Fe High came one day and asked him whether he'd like to go to college and run track. Alberto said he would prefer to keep on with his drawing. The coach was miffed. In baseball, St. Catherines played Indian schools in Colorado and Arizona and the team rode in an ancient orange bus that had an Indian headdress on its sides and one of the sisters drove the bus. Alberto hit over 400 and played first base because of his size and reach. Even with his bulk, his speed let him steal second and occasionally third on a left-handed pitcher. Many of the locals came out to see him and felt he could make the big leagues.

Each day as he studied, he thought about Acoma. He saw how his mesa was cut-off from the world. While at Acoma, the only whites he saw were tourists. All they desired were the heralded painted pots.

In the late afternoons after school, if he didn't run track or have a baseball game, he and Dennis roamed the streets of Santa Fe. Walking downtown one day, Dennis said to Alberto, "What do you do with all your time on the mesa?"

"The same as my people did five hundred years ago. We tend sheep and raise food in the valley, make pots for the tourists, bake our paper-bread. The problem is the clan won't buy from the whites. They don't trust them. All we have to work our irrigation ditches are picks and shovels, most of them we made ourselves. We need tractors and backhoes."

"You saw all those big watering machines outside of town on the way in from the south?"

"Yeah. I couldn't believe what I saw. I get mad as hell, Dennis. We're still back in the stone age. I argue with the clan, argue with my father. It doesn't do any good."

"Maybe your people ain't so dumb, Runner. My people, the Oglala, made a mess of it when we got stuff from our great white father in Washington."

"When was this?"

"Oh, Christ. Many years ago. The BIA sold us on the deal. We ended up spending all our tribal funds. We got tractors, plows, cultivators, backhoes, you name it. We had them coming out our ears. But we didn't know how to maintain them or we didn't care. Hell, Runner, the Oglala ain't farmers; we're nomads. Horse riders. All we every knew were horses. When the Spaniards brought horses to this country, we adapted to them and were the best on them. As far as all that equipment was concerned, all the stuff we bought ended up busted and ruined. Worth ten cents on the dollar. The BIA didn't care; they got their cut, their pieces of silver."

"I still think we should try to work with the BIA. We could get what we need and improve our irrigation and have much better crops. Our desert-land is so hard-packed."

"Bullshit!"

Dennis took another drag. "The more I think of it, the better Uncle Sam looks to me."

"The Army?"

"Yeah."

By now they stood in the central Plaza in the park. "I don't want the Army," Alberto commented. "I'd like to make it with my drawings but I'm not sure if I can."

"You ain't even tried yet. I tell you, Runner. You can sell your stuff. You just got to start. It'll be like a job and you gotta work at it. That's our problem up in Pine Ridge. We got eighteen thousand people and eighty percent of 'em ain't got a job!"

"A lot of my people at Acoma draw from the government."

"My people live on welfare and booze," Dennis said with a grim face. "They die on booze. Take my mother. Her liver is a lost cause. It's just a matter of time. I got two sisters. They're on booze."

"There must be jobs some place," Alberto countered.

"Sure. White jobs. Look around here in Santa Fe. You see many Indians working?"

They walked out of the park and stared at a window in a store showing men's suits. Alberto had never tried on a suit of clothes.

Dennis sucked another cloud into his lungs. "I'll tell you, Runner, when you get out of St. Catherines, you got two ways to make it. The first is the tough way."

"What's that?"

"Get the hell away; as far away from your own people as you can. Give up everything that has to do with where you came from. Let the old ways die. Get a trade. Get good at it. Real good. Become so fucking good at it that you end up taking some white man's job."

"And the other way?"

"Uncle Sam; the easy way. And another thing. The way things are going right now, we're gonna be up to our assholes in the biggest, frigging war you ever saw."

11

"How do you know that?"

"Read the papers. Hell, I'm not some dumb Indian with a reservation mentality."

"That's not for me."

"You might not have any say in the matter," Dennis responded. "And it ain't too bad. You eat three meals a day."

"I eat three times a day now."

"Yeah; and when you're through here, you'll go home to beans and corn, beans and corn. You'll sit on your frigging ass and marry some fat Indian squaw who sits all day firing pots."

* * *

They walked down San Isadora Street and passed an old church, its adobe facade gleaming in the afternoon sun. Alberto gazed at the gangly spires that reached up into a brilliant sky.

"Ever hear of Crowfoot, Runner?"

"Yeah, he was a chief."

"Right. A Nez Perce. You see that church. Made me think of him. The church tried to teach him the white man's religion. Figured if they converted him, they'd get the whole tribe in the bargain. Ole' Crowfoot was too smart for them. There was this Catholic priest and this preacher. They were competing for Crowfoot's soul. Crowfoot let them talk. Finally he says to them while they're arguing which faith goes to heaven, 'You two go ahead and argue it out. When one of you converts the other, you come and get me. I'll convince my people then.' You see, Runner, he had them! Right by the balls, pecker and all. Religion is nothing but hypocrisy and exploitation. Nothing else."

"No Dennis, you miss the point. The ones that go to church are the same ones who don't practice what they preach. That's where the problem lies."

"You don't buy the exploitation? Look how the church sucks the money out of the poor. What about that?"

"I'll buy part of it. Some of the poor have only the church to hold on to. I don't know. You're too analytical for me."

Presently they stood in front of the LaFonda Hotel, adjacent to the Plaza. From inside the old four-story adobe building came waves of music.

"Let's go in," Alberto said.

"No way," Dennis answered.

"Why?"

"I'm off the hard stuff."

"Let's go in anyway."

Dennis faced Alberto. "They probably wouldn't stop you. You look a lot older than sixteen. You listen. I've had it, all I want of it. You start on whiskey, you're in deep shit."

* * *

Dennis' warning was all Alberto needed. He had to find out for himself. A few days later, he talked to Paul Wing, a Navajo on the track team.

"Yeah," Paul exclaimed, "I have been to the LaFonda a number of times. Good whiskey."

"How'd you get in at your age?"

Paul reached into his muddy jeans and pulled out a card and handed it to Alberto.

"It's a fake ID. A guy in Galisteo makes them. You wouldn't need one, Runner. You're too big. Nobody will question you."

Alberto studied the card. "Let's go tonight, Paul."

That night they entered the hotel and stood eyeing the busy lobby and the crowded newsstand. In one dim corner of the lobby, a fat, dirty Indian sprawled, his jewelry on display. Alberto crossed over and looked at it. He figured most of what he saw was cheap stuff. Nearby, a young Indian strummed a guitar. His well-worn hat lay on the floor. A few dollars were in it.

"The booze is great in the bar," Paul said.

They entered the bar, sat in a back booth, and watched the people.

"They say if you sit here long enough, you'll see everyone you ever met. It's the busiest place in Santa Fe. You see all kinds here: nuns, priests, bums, whores, pimps, cow-punchers, politicians, millionaires. What'll it be, Runner?"

"I'll have what you have," Alberto replied boldly.

"Okay. I like Early Times."

After Paul headed towards the bar for the drinks, Alberto looked around. Spanish music came from a juke box. Couples sat in booths along one wall and beside tables in the center of the room. Waitresses moved among the tables serving drinks, their green uniforms bearing the insignia of the LaFonda. Occasionally one would stop at an empty table just left by patrons and pick up the glasses and wipe the table clean.

"Here you go," Paul said, coming back with a bottle and a pitcher of water. He poured some whiskey into a couple of glasses and added some water. Alberto took his glass and drank it straight down. The whiskey burned as it went down his throat, and it warmed him in a way he couldn't understand. He hacked and coughed and sat back unsteadily.

"Drink often?" Paul asked.

"Few times," he lied.

"Take it easy."

"It burns, doesn't it?"

"Add some water."

"Gimme another drink."

"Don't rush it."

He downed the second and his insides began to float. Then he had another.

* * *

He was barely conscious when they left the hotel. His legs felt heavy and his head was spinning. He had never tasted whiskey at Acoma. There was one bar on the mesa and it was off

14

limits to those under age. It was pitch dark when they came to the gate at St. Catherines. The gate was locked and Paul started to climb over it.

"Come on," he said, urging Alberto over the gate. The big Indian looked like a rag doll doing a dance. He started to climb but fell back.

"Hurry up, Runner, hurry up!"

Alberto lay his head on the cool desert floor. He wanted to stay there. It felt so good just to lie there.

"They find us out here," Paul said, "we're kicked out of school!"

Alberto finally made it over the gate and fell heavily into the sand. Paul grabbed him and hauled him up and helped him stagger behind the school gym. Shadows followed them as they stole through a garden filled with the remains of last summer's flowers. They came to the boys' dorm and Paul opened the front door with a key and shoved Alberto inside. He helped him down the hall and pushed him into his room. Alberto crawled into bed with his clothes on.

* * *

Someone shook Alberto. He tried to focus his bloodshot eyes.

"Wake up, Runner! Wake up!"

Dennis hollered at him and shook him.

"For Christ's sake, get up! The Japs bombed Pearl Harbor! We're at war!"

Dennis half-pushed, half-shoved Alberto to a window.

"Look down, Runner! Look down!"

Through blurry eyes, Alberto looked down below to the school yard. Sister Margaret and some other nuns were down with a number of students gathered around a radio. The students huddled like cattle, trying to protect each other from a raging storm. Snow filtered down from a solid gray sky and an occasional gust of wind unfurled the American flag. The red and white stripes streaked above everyone's head as if to say that the world they knew the day before had not suddenly collapsed; that they still had refuge in the coming storm.

* * *

Late that Sunday afternoon, Dennis and Alberto walked up the hill behind the Administration Building and entered the military cemetery. Alberto still felt shaky from the night before. He felt even strange thinking about the bones beneath his feet.

"First thing tomorrow, I'm gonna enlist," Dennis said. "I called my old man this noon in Pine Ridge. Told him what I was gonna do. He was in the big one, Runner, back in '18. He fought at a place called Chateau Thierry. Still has ribbons in a drawer. I used to line 'em up and pin 'em on my chest when I was a kid."

"I'll enlist with you."

"You're too young. They won't take you."

"We'll see."

"They'll probably ask to see birth records. Anyway, you had too much fun last night at the LaFonda. You don't want to give that up now."

"How'd you know?"

"Christ Almighty! You smelled like a sewer. You slept in your clothes. Paul told me. I almost decked him. Boy, you got a lot to learn. You think you can handle it. It'll handle you."

"I had enough last night," Alberto said uneasily. "I don't know what the big deal is over whiskey. God, I feel terrible. That was enough for me."

"Don't kid yourself. You'll be back down there the first chance you get. I ought to know. I got so bad last year, they had to dry me out. I got to drinking. I couldn't stop and they had to put me in a hospital. While I was there I took a swing at an attendant and broke a glass panel in a door. If it hadn't been for Sister Margaret, they would have sent me back home for good. She hung in there for me and convinced me to stop. I haven't had any hard stuff since. Just a beer now and then."

Alberto changed the subject. "When you go to enlist, what will it be in?"

A grin lit up Dennis' face. "They'll have to fight for me. After all, ain't I irresistible?" Thin-like, wiry, pock-marked Dennis Charbonneau beamed his confidence. Both of them stood up and laughed.

16

"One thing about the service, Runner. Nobody gives a damn about you, who you are, who you were, where you came from. It's the only place where a half-breed like me can be invisible."

* * *

Down at the recruiting station, which was filled with young men waiting to enlist, Alberto and Dennis sat by a raw-faced young cowpuncher smelling of horse and leather. Every few moments he tilted his head and spit tobacco into a bottle. Next to him sat a smaller version, his younger brother. Thin trails of tobacco leaves moved from the corner of his mouth to his stained shirt. On the other side of Alberto was a dark Mexican he recognized who lubed cars across the street from St. Catherines. His face held no emotion and his body was still like a rock, his dark eyes looking straight ahead.

Alberto felt funny realizing that of all those young men in the building, he was the biggest. Yet, because of his age, he couldn't get in the service.

Dennis' name was called and he disappeared into a room. Twenty minutes later he came out with a burly sergeant who had battle stripes on his sleeves. Alberto noticed how excited Dennis looked. They walked out on the street and Dennis exclaimed, "This sergeant handed me this form after my physical. The physical was a laugh. Nuthin' to it. This sergeant says to me, 'Kid, you ain't nuthin' but skin and bones. What'll it be, Army or Air Corps?' I said, 'Who has the best grub?' and he says, 'The Air Corps. Besides, they're looking for runts like you as tail gunners on the big bombers.' I said, 'Sign me up, Sarge.'"

* * *

On the way back to St. Catherines to pick up his gear, Dennis was in high spirits. "I'm in the U-nited States fucking Air Corps!" He wiped his brow and took a deep drag on his cigarette and hollered, "How about that!" Pale gray smoke blew across his face. Suddenly he threw the cigarette onto the pavement and a thin red arc flew in the sky.

"Jesus H. Christ! I made it!" he yelled jubilantly.

Two hours later, after saying good-bye to Sister Margaret, Dennis stood beside a Greyhound bus, its motors revving. He shook hands with Alberto and quietly said, "Runner, listen to me. Don't let whiskey spoil it for you, man."

He stepped onto the bus and into World War II.

* * *

Alberto had mixed emotions. In three days he'd be on a bus, headed south to Acoma for Christmas. School had been hard, but he liked it better than home. He enjoyed roaming the streets on his free time. Already he missed the biting wit of his roommate and he wondered where he ended up for Basic Training.

The day before his bus was to leave, he had all afternoon and evening free. He decided to try and sell some of his sketches, just to see if Dennis was right, that they would sell. He walked downtown to the Plaza and set one sketch on a cheap tripod he had bought in one of the stores. Within an hour, he sold his first rough piece for twenty dollars to a tourist. It was a lot of money and the drawing wasn't that good. He'd done it the year before at Acoma showing two elderly women standing over their metates as they ground corn. As he pocketed the money, he thought of how the two old crones had rolled the corn through their dark hands and how he had drawn the small kernels that lay like pebbles between their gnarled fingers.

One hour later he sold another sketch. He had more money in his pocket than he'd ever made in his life. He wondered whether his father, Felipe, had ever carried forty dollars in his pockets.

* * *

Alberto sat alone in the back of the bus as it moved toward Laguna. He kept seeing images of St. Catherines, of Dennis, and of his running cross-country with the team. He found himself looking down at everyone clustered around the flagpole the day of Pearl Harbor. That made him think of how drunk he had been the night he went with Paul to the LaFonda and he wondered what there was about whiskey that appealed to so many of his people. He didn't want to go back to Acoma, but he did want to see his family and Henrique. He felt that somehow, things would never be quite the same.

Henrique and Alberto's father met him with the wagon. They were glad to see him. He greeted them warmly but didn't say much. His silence spoke of things unknown to them.

Everything seemed smaller. The hills he passed were smaller than four months before. The wide expanse of the desert didn't seem as important to him as before. In the distance he saw his mesa at Acoma rising from the desert. Its three hundred foot thrust over the valley now was dwarfed for him by the power and grandeur of the great Sangre De Christo that hung over Santa Fe. In his mind, he even minimized the days long ago when his people had held Acoma against the onslaught of the Spaniards. Then his home rose in front of him, its reddish-brown hue reflecting the afternoon sun.

He walked down the dirt streets of Acoma with Henrique and his father and his thoughts were of the Santa Fe he'd left. The pull from the old city far to the north was strong and he couldn't get it out of his thoughts.

"See you in the square," Henrique said uncertainly.

"Yeah, okay," Alberto answered as he carried his old valise into his house. He kissed his mother and was hugged by his two sisters who started to bombard him with questions about St. Catherines and were there girls? He passed through the mud-covered walls and told his sisters he would answer them later.

Maria, his mother, wore a heavy silver necklace that rested lightly on her neck. Thin streaks of gray filtered through the dark sheets of her hair. She looked longingly at Alberto and her rich, dark caramel eyes revealed how much she loved him. He left her for a few moments and took his valise to his bedroom and sat down on his bed. He sat there for a while with Santa Fe filling his head. Finally he got up and walked into the great room to sit with his family. The questions came from all sides.

"What is it like? Did you meet some nice girls? Are they pretty? What are your friends like? Who are your teachers? Do you like them? What do they teach? Is the work hard? Can you go downtown? Have you been in the Plaza? Have you bought things? What are the whites like?"

Juanita and Francesca peppered him with these questions as he stared at the wooden vigas in the great room. They held bright red chilies grown the last summer. Next to them hung dried beef that his father and he would take the next time they hunted on Mount Hasasu.

Finally the numbing barrage of his sisters faded as he tried to answer their questions. He told them more about St. Catherines and Sister Margaret and Dennis. As he spoke, it made him long for his school far to the north.

Fatigue from his journey finally hit him like a cold fog. He needed fresh air. He left the house with his father and they walked as was their custom every night before retiring. They often walked the length of the mesa, stopping to view the dark valley below and the cold stars piercing the sky. The air was crisp. Winter breezes embraced them as they passed through the village beyond San Estaban Rey and the church graveyard. Quietly they stood at the far eastern end of the mesa. They gazed far out into the desert. A humpbacked orange moon rose and cleared the horizon as Alberto's father spoke softly.

"You have seen much, son?"

The words sailed on the night air.

"It is as you said, Father. You said to me before I left that I would see many things."

Felipe waited; he knew Alberto had more to say.

"It is very powerful. I don't know where to begin."

His father broke in. "Don't tell me what you told your mother and your sisters. Tell me what you're thinking."

"It's like I'm a different person up there."

"I understand that."

"There is so much. Many things. Things forbidden here. The whites . . ."

"What about the whites?"

Felipe's tone grew hard.

"They have everything. Cars, trucks, houses, inside toilets, all kinds of clothes. They don't have to wait forever for things to be ordered and delivered."

There was iron in his father's response.

"Those things don't make a better person."

"I know that."

Alberto knew his father was trying to control himself.

"How is your school work?"

"Some is very hard. I have to work hard to get my grades. I study under nuns."

"White nuns?"

"All the teachers are white, Father."

"How do the whites treat you?"

"Good. I haven't met many yet outside of the school. I see tourists in the Plaza downtown. I met a few storekeepers."

"These storekeepers . . . these whites. They overcharge you?"

Alberto was getting angry. His face began to tighten. His father's question was typical of one from Acoma. Here was the deep chasm between Acoma and the outside world. Here was an attitude that pervaded everything that Acoma did or thought.

"I didn't buy much," he said. "An easel one day; some drawing pencils. They didn't overcharge me. You know, you're suspicious of anything that has to do with the whites. I'm not going to live that way."

Below the father and the son, the moon's icy light revealed the scarred lines on the earth. The land in the valley looked wasted to Alberto when he compared it to the evenly plowed rows on the farms around Santa Fe. Alberto said to himself, *This is the way my people have lived for hundreds of years; using mules and hand tools; refusing to admit that there is a better way. All because of their contempt and distrust of the whites.* Alberto shivered in silence as the wind picked up. He asked his father, "Did we get the motorized plows for next spring?" He knew the answer before his father spoke. "We didn't get them, did we? They were supposed to bring it up to a vote in the kiva!"

"The clan voted it down."

"That's bullshit, Father!"

Felipe Campione faced his son. "Who are you to say, Alberto?"

"Father, I see farms around Albuquerque and Santa Fe. Some are Indian farms. I see water in the fields. I see corn, good fat ears. I see green rice fields with big irrigation ditches and watering equipment. Then I look down below, here in the valley. All I see is hen-scratching. It isn't fair. It isn't enough. I know I have a lot to learn but I also know that having good food is a hell of a lot more important than firing pots for the tourists." Felipe turned away from him, but Alberto continued. "All around us they're growing crops with modern methods while we sit on our asses chasing witches!"

"Stop it! You will not talk like that!"

"You can't deny . . ."

He faced Alberto, his face livid.

"Let me tell you something. I believe in our ways; the way that was good enough for my father and his father before him. When you're here on our mesa, you'll do as the clan says. You'll live as we live! You'll live and die by our rules!"

Felipe glared intensely at his son. "The whites don't give a damn about us! They don't care what we believe! All they want from us are our secrets. Anything they can take and sell and make a profit. You give them what they want and they'll take everything else. They'll tell us what to do and how to do it. We're better off without them.

"If you can't see that, God help you!"

Felipe walked to the edge of the mesa, his back toward Alberto. His silhouette stood in stark relief against the moon. Alberto could make out his aging frame as he shivered in the cold desert air.

Alberto spoke. "I eat a lot better at St. Catherines. I sleep on sheets that are changed once a week. I use a flush toilet. I don't have to use a lousy two-holer that leaves crap all over the mesa! I don't have to do that and my family shouldn't have to. You know I'm right! You're too proud to admit it! You won't change your attitude toward the whites and you're afraid of the clan!"

Felipe turned slowly and fixed a stare on his son; then walked away.

* * *

The next morning at breakfast, Alberto's father was silent, his face set and stern. Alberto's insides churned when he thought of his words of the night before. There was no use in saying anything now because it wouldn't be accepted. He left the house after breakfast and met Henrique in the Plaza.

"He walked away from you?" Henrique asked in disbelief.

"I said what I wanted to say and he walked away."

Bile rose in Alberto's throat. He could see his father, standing at the edge of the mesa, first listening to what he had to say, then walking away.

"Why'd you bring up the part about chasing witches? That probably corked him off."

"I had to say it. I get so god-damned mad about the clan turning down the plows."

Henrique put his face close. "You told him he was afraid of the clan? What were you thinking of?"

The two young Indians walked down the street, kicking up dust. Alberto's stomach growled and his head ached. "I love my father. We've been close since I was a small boy. We've stayed out in the desert together, we've hunted."

"Apologize to him."

"I won't do that. He knows I'm right."

"Be miserable then."

Three teen-age girls crossed in front of them. They giggled as they ducked into a house.

Henrique punched Alberto playfully. "You get laid in Santa Fe?"

"I haven't even had a date."

"How come? There must be a lot of good stuff up there."

"You know what," Alberto retorted. "You got it on the brain. You've been screwing since you were fourteen. Nobody's safe around here."

Henrique laughed and pulled out a pack of cigarettes.

"When did you start that?"

"Couple of months ago."

"I did get to the LaFonda Hotel," Alberto countered.

"A whorehouse?"

"No. A hotel near the Plaza. I had some whiskey."

"Hey, maybe when I take you back to Laguna to catch the bus, we can get a drink."

* * *

Alberto sat in his bedroom, a drawing pad on his desk. He was surrounded by the smells of Christmas. The scent of paper-bread and cooked meat and chilies. After a few attempts at a sketch, he walked into the great room where his mother was placing a small cross in a dark blue bowl. It was a ritual the family had observed over the years. It was her way of reflecting on the seasons of the year and what they meant to her. Many times she thought about a particular joy or sadness. Alberto wondered if she felt the tension between his father and himself. He felt she did and he knew she wouldn't ask her husband about it until the Christmas celebration was over and he had left for St. Catherines.

Juanita and Francesca clucked over him like a couple of hens, wanting to know more about St. Catherines. He tried to shush them as he gave his mother a bright red shawl.

"You are now more noticeable, Mother," he said. "More noticeable than our red peppers hanging over our hearth."

He gave his sisters similar shawls, more muted than his mother's.

He failed to smile as he presented his father a hand-tooled rawhide belt. "I found this in Santa Fe," he said, "and the white man I bought it from didn't overcharge me."

Felipe Campione didn't look up as he mumbled a barely discernible "Thank you."

Alberto received some nice gifts of warm clothing and a belt which was for Dennis. He'd mail it to him when he received his address.

The family ate breakfast in silence, mixed with a few giggles from the girls. "Are you taking Alberto to Laguna?" his mother asked Felipe. The answer was cold. "No, Henrique will. I have things to do."

A look of resignation settled on Maria's face.

Alberto stood up, walked into his room, and collected his valise.

"We'll walk with you down the mesa to the wagon," she said stiffly.

She motioned for the girls to follow her and they left the house. They walked through the streets and down the only route to the valley, the rough steps leading to the valley where Henrique waited with the two mules and the wagon. Maria and the two daughters kissed Alberto and urged him to write. They expressed hope for a good school year. Nothing was said about the father. Alberto said good-bye and waved as the wagon pulled out. They watched with affection and sadness. Alberto turned his face to the north for the thirteen mile ride to Laguna. To him, the old farm wagon and their two decrepit mules was another link to the impoverished past of Acoma.

* * *

Back at school, Alberto received a letter from his mother. She wrote that when she and her daughters returned to their house, her husband still sat there. She sat beside him for a long time and no words were spoken. Much of the festive air and light of Christmas had faded. Finally, Felipe stood up and said, "I have lost my son." When he had read the letter through for the second time, Alberto sat at his desk and wrote to his mother. In his letter, he tried to explain what had happened when he and his father faced each other at the eastern terminus of the mesa. He didn't apologize but made his case for improvements needed for his people and left it there.

A week later, he was called out of class and asked to report to Sister Margaret. He wondered if someone had finally reported him and his drinking at the LaFonda. That had been weeks before. When he knocked, and was asked to step in, she greeted him with a smile and notified him that she had been able to arrange for some art classes for him. "Alberto, I'm pleased and I hope you will be. The Cerillos Indian School is a very fine art school right here in Santa Fe. You can take some classes there which will benefit you and you'll get full credits toward graduation here. You'll have to work hard. You'll find much competition, but I feel it will be a real step up for you with your talent." It made Alberto proud that he had been accepted and he thanked Sister Margaret.

One afternoon after classes, he walked alone downtown. One of the graduates of Cerillos had an exhibition of his work at the Museum of Santa Fe on the Plaza. It was a sculpture done in alabaster and marble. Alberto was wrapped in his own thoughts and not paying much attention to the people at the entrance of the museum. The smell of roses drifted to his senses. It was the middle of winter and flower scents were unusual for that time of year. It had to be a woman's perfume. He turned slowly to locate the source. He saw a small woman of about thirty standing behind him. She was above five feet two and had long black hair that hung over her shoulders. The necklace she wore had to have come from one of the pueblos. It was silver with heavy turquoise stones. It complemented her eyes and her hair.

She was a very beautiful woman. A warm wave, not unlike his first taste of whiskey passed over him and settled in his groin. He found it difficult to look away from her. She looked at Alberto as he turned toward her and she smiled and said, "You must be Alberto. Alberto Campione. Am I right?"

She held out a delicate hand and Alberto took it. When he released it, he noticed that her fingernails were short and graceful like a child's. A sad smile caused thin lines to form around her eyes and mouth.

Nervously he stammered, "Yes."

"I saw you at St. Catherines. You were running on the track and Sister Margaret pointed you out to me. I'm Sarah. Sarah Sato. I teach photography at Cerillos. Sister Margaret told me about your drawings. She feels you have great promise."

"They're just charcoal," he said, scanning the ground with his eyes.

"Are you here to see the exhibit?"

"I wanted to see the sculptures."

"You'll love Creekwater's work. He was in one of the first classes at Cerillos. He's not thirty yet and he's doing marvelous things. May I go in with you?"

Alberto was speechless. He couldn't believe this was happening to him. The words he wanted to say to her lay in his belly like iron balloons.

"I'm glad I ran into you," she said as she took one of his massive hands and brushed hair out of her eyes.

He felt his senses quickening as they entered the gallery. Fifteen of Creekwater's sculptures were arranged on wooden pedestals. One large rock had been cut and sanded into wild curves. The form suggested a rattlesnake wakened from sleep by a wandering wolf. The images fashioned from stone revealed more life to Alberto than any painting or drawing he had ever seen.

Another work showed a sun slowly rising from a mountain. As he turned away, it looked as if the sun was setting behind him. Another sculpture depicted a sidewinder striking out at two chicken hawks. The artist had caught the sweeping motion of the birds and the deadly intent of the snake. The menace of the rattler penetrated Alberto's thoughts as his eyes drank in the scene. He was struck both with the power and the beauty of Creekwater's effort. They were far more intense and exhibited much greater power than his charcoal sketches. He knew at that moment what he wanted to do with his life.

Sara Sato broke his look of utter astonishment.

"You're consumed with what you see. I can see it in your face. These sculptures are like a great symphony. You're not satisfied when the music dies."

Deep within him came his reply. "This is what I want."

She stared at him. "If this is what you truly want, I can help you. The curator here is a good friend. Edgar Huling. He's one of our biggest supporters at Cerillos. Let's go see him about your interest."

He heard himself saying to her, "I would like that."

"I won't be but a moment. I'll see if he is here."

As Sarah turned a corner, she paused briefly and pointed at the sculptures, indicating he should study them some more. He had hardly started to look some more when she was back.

"Good news. Edgar tells me that Frederick Creekwater is looking for an apprentice. We'll talk to Sister Margaret."

He wanted to thank her but she stopped him. "I've always been fascinated with Indian culture. Tell me about Acoma."

It annoyed him. Her remark sounded like the tourists who came to Acoma who really didn't care anything about his people.

"We're pretty poor and backward," he replied, his voice suddenly flat.

She pushed her hair out of her eyes and said, "Your mesa has a great history. I know about the terrible days under the Spanish."

"Our history hurts us now."

Her voice became soft and low. "I don't understand. What do you mean?"

"We live in the past." His voice was stronger now. "We have a dictator. Everyone fears him. We don't get anything done."

"That would be the cacique, wouldn't it?"

Alberto hesitated.

"He's all-powerful, isn't he?"

"Yes. My father, Felipe; he's one of our three war chiefs. He takes his orders from the cacique. Nobody challenges the cacique. We have little work on the mesa, other than firing pots for the tourists and making our paper-bread for ourselves. Our clan won't buy good farm equipment from the whites. They won't listen to the Bureau of Indian Affairs. No one trusts the whites. We just get old and people leave the mesa."

She touched his hand. "I want to hear more. I can tell you feel strongly for your people. I must go, Alberto. I promised some photographs for next week's class. Why don't you bring your sketches to my class next Monday since you'll be coming to Cerillos. We'll show them to Edgar at the museum."

"Where will I find you?" he asked. His voice sounded like a small child wanting its mother.

Turning quickly, her long hair swirled around her neck, and her movements were graceful. Her dark eyes gleamed at him. "Ask for me. They all know me."

* * *

Sara Sato was gone. Henrique's voice filled Alberto's mind. "Did you get laid up in Santa Fe?" His chest pounded as he stood at the entrance to the museum. He stared across the busy plaza at the dull brown storefronts. He looked down at the gray-blue slate in the Avenue de Peralta and felt his hands shake. His back muscles tightened as a warm wave came over his body. A beautiful, charming, magnificent lady had touched him and suddenly she had disappeared. In his fantasy, he suddenly stood in her bedroom and she invited him into her bed. Her skin was soft like a fawn and her body moist and warm and eager. A fire spread rapidly through him and it consumed him.

Pigeons whirled at his feet and two lovers passed by, their arms entwined. A young woman lifted an infant out of a carriage and held her as she whispered gentle words.

His life had changed dramatically; a woman had changed it. A woman had walked with him and had reached out and touched his hand. His hands still shook and his breathing came hard and fast and he felt a sexual hardness. He needed a drink. He crossed the Plaza and entered the LaFonda.

* * *

Runner-England is the greatest! I got a bird over here that thinks I'm the greatest thing since sliced bread. They call women, birds over here. Things couldn't be better. Nobody gives a shit that I'm an Oglala Sioux. When I left Santa Fe, they sent me to MacDill Field—that's near Tampa, Florida. They call it Alligator Alley. We shot sharks on the sandbars in the Gulf after we had range target runs over the water and were clearing our guns.

I'm a hotshot tail gunner on a B-17. I got three missions under my belt already. They sure ain't no walk in the park. The kraut planes come like hell at you. When we get back to our base, the first thing we do is check our balls and pecker. What a way to fight a war! Thirty thousand feet up, looking down on the world.

Write soon, now you know where I am.

> Your best friend,
>
> Dennis Charbonneau
>
> The invisible one

* * *

Alberto couldn't think of anything but Sarah. He wanted to be with her, to make love to her. Finally the day came when he took his drawings to her at Cerillos. She liked what she saw and they walked to the Museum to meet Edgar Huling.

As they walked along, Sarah seemed hesitant about something. Finally she said, "Alberto, I met with Sister Margaret to arrange a time for you to meet Frederick Creekwater." Walking beside Sarah made him feel good, made him want to reach out and take her in his arms. It also made his chest hurt and he was getting hard.

"Is it okay?" he asked.

"Yes," she said. "It's fine. But something bothers me."

"What's that?"

"Sister asked me to sit down. She wanted to tell me something."

He waited, not knowing what was coming. Perhaps he couldn't stay at Cerillos, but Sister hadn't said anything to him.

"She's concerned about you, Alberto. She says you've started to drink liquor. She told me you were in the bar in the LaFonda and they served you whiskey. Said if you weren't careful, you'd destroy yourself."

"It's only occasionally, Sarah. I don't make a habit of it."

"It does bother me. You have such a future ahead. I'd hate to see you spoil it."

"It's no problem, Sarah. I can handle it. I've only been there a couple of times."

She had more to say and he was afraid it might mean he would get kicked out of school. "She told me it was the toughest of all problems for young Indians, that she'd had to confront many of her students because of it."

He was reflective. "If it will please you, I'll stop."

"That would please me."

They entered the museum and proceeded to Edgar Huling's office. They faced him in a room filled with a jumble of maps and books. Edgar Huling was a thin, sandy-haired man of sixty, an archeologist who spent much time at the pueblos along the river. He was well respected by the pueblo people.

"I'm glad to meet you, young man." He shook Alberto's hand and smiled at Sarah. "I'm pleased to have you bring me your work. I've heard good things about it."

Alberto handed his drawings to Edgar, who spread them out on a large table. Alberto waited anxiously for Huling's response, searching for some answer in his eyes. Finally Huling turned to him and cleared his throat.

"I must be frank," he said in a soft voice.

Alberto's hopes dropped. It was like getting hit in the teeth.

"These aren't bad. You capture certain aspects of your subjects. But they lack something; a certain discipline. There must be more depth, more feeling. More of you, Alberto. That's very difficult to come by."

Alberto felt like a raw beginner starting in school for the first time. "I want to understand you," he replied weakly.

"You must do more, Alberto. You have to go beyond where you are."

"I can work hard, Mr. Huling. I want to study sculpture."

"Sarah told me. Call me Edgar. I call you Alberto."

Huling touched Sarah on the shoulder. "You have a believer in this fine lady. Cerillos is the place for you; you'll find excellent instruction."

Huling took off his glasses and wiped them with a handkerchief.

"It's a matter of dedication. You're going to have to take all the tradition and ritual of your people and put it strongly in your work."

He picked up one of Alberto's sketches and studied it intensely. "This world outside your mesa. It must respond to what you do. Your work must be distinctive, creative. Must pull people to you. Creekwater does that. Very well. He finds a common thread in his culture and the white culture and he develops that. For someone not thirty, he's astounding. And he works hard. And yes, I'll admit to you; much of the success achieved in the world of art is just plain luck. I hate to say it but it's true."

Alberto began to feel better.

"I want to be a sculptor, Mr. Huling."

"Edgar."

As Alberto spoke his last words, he felt strong, more sure of himself. He felt that he could lift a mountain.

"All right," Edgar said. "We'll see to it that you meet Creekwater. He needs a good apprentice."

Alberto was elated. Sarah stood beside him. They both wanted to help him. It was a wonderful feeling. First he had taken a kick in the pants, but Huling had then encouraged him. He liked the way Huling talked. He talked straight. Alberto wished that his father had been there to meet Huling. His praise hadn't been strong, but his knowledge was great. Any accolade to Alberto was like pennies to a beggar.

Alberto thought of his father, Felipe. Tending sheep, sitting as a war chief in the kiva, taking orders from an old, arrogant cacique, staring out into the desert where the sheep camp was, flickering lights showing where men patrolled against an occasional wolf. His father never had the chance that Alberto now had, never had the luck. Never felt real exultation beyond viewing a herd of sheep or seeing the great stag that day on Mount Hasasu. His father would spend the rest of his days on the mesa.

Suddenly the image came back strong and clear to Alberto of his father's face, a face carved into a mountain. Was this tied to Alberto's wanting to be a sculptor? Could this be a sign?

* * *

A few days later, Alberto was again called out of class and asked to report to Sister Margaret's office. He wondered if now she was going to lower the boom on him for his drinking. When he knocked on the door, a strange voice answered,

"Come in."

Sitting behind her desk was an Indian dressed entirely in dark green. His hair was cut short and Alberto could see the thin white lines that formed the scalp underneath the dark, shiny bristles of hair. As he walked toward him, the man stood up. He wore a long, dirty wool coat that scraped the ground like a lazy broom as he moved to shake Alberto's hand. As the man got closer, Alberto noticed that the coat wasn't really dirty, but covered with a thin white dust, like chalk. The same dust coated his hands and outlined his fingernails like the beginning of a sketch. He slumped his shoulders slightly and looked as if he was disinterested in everything. He raised his head to introduce himself and Alberto was astonished at the darkness and depth of his eyes. They were raven-like with very little white.

The man held out his thin, dusty hand.

"I'm Frederick Creekwater."

* * *

Madrid was buried carelessly in the side of a mountain fourteen miles southeast of Santa Fe. At one time it had been a vibrant mining community. The only monument to its past was the gray-brown slag heaps that stood now like angry beasts guarding empty coffers. Fewer than a hundred people lived there, mostly squatters. They had taken over decaying, rat-infested former houses of miners who raped the hills of all their strength. During the hot, dusty days, the squatters congregated in front of a lone, scrubby store, its begrimed, half-empty shelves housing dented food cans. At the front entrance, a mangy red dog lazed, as dusty as the air he breathed, insolent to all passersby.

Alberto stood in awe at Creekwater's studio. Sarah had told him earlier that Creekwater felt a kinship for this down-in-the-mouth place and had no desire to leave its aura of decay. Using his surroundings he found peace and solitude as he carved incessantly. He used a sturdy metal shed as his studio and lived alone . . . unmarried, unencumbered, unfettered on the edge of a wasteland. His studio was a place of chisels, saws, and hammers which his skillful hands used to reveal the latent beauty in the rock. People came from miles to marvel at his creations.

Frederick said to Alberto, "I take the hidden beauty, Alberto. I transform it. I make it into something that I understand." Around him were structures in various phases of completion, all the culmination of delicate and time-consuming labor.

Standing was a lovely Zuni maiden, her black hair in whorls. Nearby, a vibrant sun rose behind a lonely mountain. Beside it, a proud eagle grasped a young rabbit in its carved talons; in a nest were two hungry eaglets, stretching their necks for dinner, their jaws extended.

"Sure this is what you want?" Creekwater's staccato voice hit the metal shed.

"Yes," Alberto answered nervously. "Can I ask you something?"

"Fire away."

"When you start, do you know what the stone will be?"

"Good question. In any form of art, there are hidden truths. You can't force them to come out."

Creekwater caressed a rough block of marble with his white-sooted hands.

"You struggle, everybody struggles. The truth comes. It comes slowly. The form emerges like a long dream from the rock's sleep."

Alberto liked that. He walked over and put both hands on the marble and imagined what he could do.

"I treat the rock gently," Creekwater said. "Like I'm trying to wake it. Like foreplay with a woman. I listen. With my heart. It helps tell me what to do next."

The words of Creekwater circled Alberto's head like a hot desert wind.

"Where do the rocks come from?"

"Friends of mine. South of here. Down near the Mexican border. Apache. Mescalero. I barter with them. I give them sugar and flour and tobacco. They give me the stone."

Frederick's hands wandered over a section of granite, seeking out the secret places where he would work it.

Alberto listened carefully to what Creekwater said. It was like being parched in the desert after a long hunt, then getting down on all fours and drinking pure, clear water from a flowing well, letting it run over your face and down your clothes.

"Sarah spoke to me even before Edgar," Frederick remarked. "They think well of you." As he said it, his long, muscular arms curved around a stone as if in an embrace.

"They've done a lot for me. I don't want to let them down," responded Alberto.

"That's good enough for me," Creekwater answered. He hugged the stone and peered intently into its veined surface.

"I won't let you down," Alberto said. "I'll work hard."

"Sister Margaret will let you spend some afternoons here after school. Weekends too. I'm at it seven days a week."

Frederick picked up a heavy drill and looked around the shed for his goggles. "When summer comes, I go east. I look for commissions. New York, Philly, Washington, Baltimore. What do you say?"

Alberto broke out in a grin as he shook hands with Creekwater. "I'm the lucky one. This is what I want, Frederick. You tell me when to start and I'll be here."

"Welcome, Alberto," Frederick Creekwater responded.

* * *

Now the days become slow like a tired lizard. Alberto had not heard back from Creekwater as when he was to start. He was anxious to begin. Some days in his school work, he found himself thinking of Madrid when he should have been studying. And then there was Sarah. He wanted her in the worst way. During the night, he woke up drenched in cold sweat and had to relieve himself. He imagined every curve in her body and fantasized his making love to her. At Cerillos, they told him she had gone into the desert for two weeks on a photo shoot.

He decided to make something for her. He went downtown one late afternoon after school and bought some firing clay and paints. Back in his dorm room, he started to mold the clay, shaping and forming the smooth gray pieces. They had to be special. As he formed ten inch high pieces on his desk, he found himself breathing heavily, as if he'd been running hard. He was excited at the prospect of setting them in front of Sarah. He knew when she saw them, she'd come into his arms and declare her love for him.

By the weekend, he stared proudly at the forms on his desk. First there were two deer. He spent time, feeling the form of the deer, visualizing the antlers of the males, the strong body movements of the animals. Near them were two old men, modeled on men he had known in his village, men with lined faces and long, thin arms, their bodies copper from countless days in the sun. He put on them the headdress of the male deer which they were in the summer Deer Dance. Standing by them were the Koshare, the village clowns, who had the sacred duty of separating the two deer from the rest of the herd.

35

Alberto picked up one of the pieces and examined it carefully. His heart pounded with love for Sarah and he couldn't wait to start on the remaining members of the dance. He was consumed with what he was doing. So much had to be perfect for Sarah. So much had to be just right! He sat at his desk and peered at his creation and felt anxious. Anxious to finish the pieces, anxious that Sarah would love them, that she would come into his arms.

By the end of two weeks, he had twenty dancers, each modeled after someone he knew at home. Some leaned on sticks that imitated the forelegs of the deer. He knew that when he was finished, he could take the pieces to the kiln in the museum and pay to have them fired. Now he had the two deer, the two old men, the koshare, the women in their buckskin robes, the men in white robes, and children playing under turkey feathers. Except for the coloring, the forms were complete. The glazing would require patience, as much as the forming, and tedious work lay ahead.

* * *

Runner—If I get through this frigging war in one piece, I'm going to marry my bird and bring her back to the states. When you get in the service, make sure it's in the flyboys. Don't pick the Army or Navy. When you get in, be invisible like me. Stick in the rear ranks, stay in the lowest grade, and don't volunteer for nothing. Don't let them promote you. Stay low, don't get noticed. Just ride the war out that way.

I got a bad letter the other day. My old man was greasing a car and he rolled over and died. He was the best, Runner. He got me into St. Catherines. When I get back, I'm going to stand over his grave and say a prayer and then get out of Pine Ridge for good.

Your invisible buddy

Dennis Charbonneau

* * *

Easter Sunday came to Santa Fe. Snow hung on the Sangre de Christo and crisp air blew in from the desert bringing with it the summery smell of dust. Catkins showed by the willows along the yellow Rio Grande and purple lupin spread out on the high meadows. Alberto saw the Sangre from his dorm window as two eagles soared in lazy circles. They swooped and twisted in the air as light flashed on their wings.

He stayed in the dorm over the holiday to give him a chance to finish his clay pieces and to glaze them.

He wrapped them carefully and put them in a big box, and took them to the museum. Edgar was in his office, papers spread all over his desk, his heavy glasses hooked on his nose.

"Can someone help me fire some clay pieces, Mr. Huling?" Alberto asked. "I can pay for the firing."

"What do you have there, Alberto?" Edgar twisted his glasses until they rested on the tip of his nose. Alberto set the box on the table and began to unwrap the pieces. Edgar came over to the table, his glasses now thrust in his breast pocket. He looked at them intently.

"Is this the first time for you in this medium?"

"Yes."

"Excellent. You have your heart in this, Alberto."

"They're for Sarah. The Deer Dance."

"I've seen it many times, son. One of the best rituals of your people. Let's go down to the kiln. This is for Sarah, there won't be any charge."

* * *

Two sunsets later, after the forms had cooled and dried, Alberto picked them up at the kiln and headed for San Isadora Street. Edgar had told Alberto where Sarah lived. Alberto didn't let her know he was coming, wanting to surprise her. As he strode past quiet streets sunk in shadow, his heart pounded and sweat formed on his body. He was nervous wondering what her reaction would be. Would he be ready to tell her how he felt about her? What if she turned him down? What if she wasn't home? What would calm him down, make him relax?

The light was strong on the Sangre. Bold shadows fell from the crosses in the old city cemetery on the little hillside north of the Plaza. They formed bands like ebony necklaces and as the bands faded, the sky turned blood red. It was a sight he could use in a future sketch. Now he was torn with anxiety. How could he act with Sarah?

He found the bungalow about a mile east of St. Catherines. The window boxes were lined with bright blue wild violets that must have come from the desert. Her blue door was typical of Santa Fe and it had a small stained glass window. The central figure in it was a single rose.

He was struck by the lightness and beauty of the little house.

Sarah opened the door and was surprised to see him. It appeared to him that she had been crying. She wore the light blue sweater she had worn when he first met her at the museum. She dabbed at her eyes with a handkerchief and asked him to step in. He carried the heavy box in and set it on a table. She excused herself and told him to make himself at home. Alberto looked around as she left the living room. Her home was filled with a number of photographs and many Indian artifacts. One whole wall was lined with bookshelves.

A plate stood in a holder on the top of her upright piano. It showed a young man chasing a deer, his hair flowing behind him as the deer pulled away from him. He recognized it immediately. She came back in the room and he asked her, "May I look at this?"

"Yes," she said uncertainly.

He carefully picked it up and saw the small cross on the bottom with a circle "M."

"My mother made this, Sarah."

"I know," she said, trying to smile, but not succeeding. "It came from Indian Market last August. I knew it was a Maria Campione piece from Acoma but I didn't know about you then."

"What a coincidence," he remarked.

Sarah began to cry. She went over and sat down and was silent. He was uncomfortable and didn't know what to do or say. Then she looked up and asked, "Tell me about your mother, Alberto."

"She's looked upon as the best potter in our village. She tries to teach my two sisters, but they're more interested in getting married."

Sarah brushed some tears from her eyes.

"You never mentioned your sisters."

"No."

"You never talked about your family. Do you have other members?"

"I had a brother. He died several years ago." As Alberto spoke the words, memory of that terrible time came back. He tried to block it from his mind.

"I'm so sorry," she said.

"I get angry thinking about it."

"You do? Why?"

"I really don't want to talk about it."

"All right. What's in the box?"

His anger faded and his excitement grew. His hands shook a little as he slowly took the clay pieces out and unwrapped them. As he did, he looked at Sarah, his heart pounding. Sarah's obvious astonishment made him feel like a god. He was elated and he wanted to reach out and hold her.

He put all the figures in their proper positions. First came the two heavy women who led the Deer Dance. Each was wrapped in buckskin robes and wearing boots. He had carved the boots in great detail and was proud of his work. Hanging from the back of the women's necks was the carefully formed breast of a duck. Following the women were three men wearing white robes fringed with green. The glaze had fired beautifully and it was radiant on the figures. Near the three men were several small children playing under a pile of turkey feathers. This, he thought, was the best part of his work and he looked at Sarah.

She was smiling now and her eyes had a sparkle that her tears had masked.

"Wonderful, Alberto! You made these, didn't you?"

"It's the Deer Dance, Sarah. I made them for you." He could scarcely breathe as he said the words.

Her hands came up to her face. "For me? They are so beautiful. The glaze is exquisite. They should be in a museum."

He leaned over and tried to kiss her.

"Alberto, please, no."

From deep inside he blurted, "I'm in love with you." His voice broke as he said it.

She sat down and covered her face with her hands. Her hands trembled and her body shook. She took her hands away and started to cry. He was at a loss at what to do. Finally, she looked up sadly and said, "I'm married, Alberto."

Married? He couldn't believe her worlds. His anguish showed in his face. He felt sick to his stomach. He tried to steady himself and stared at her left hand. "I didn't know." She wore no ring.

Tearfully she replied, "I don't wear a ring." She wiped her eyes again and sat in a chair. Alberto felt lost. He had counted so much on this moment. He buried his head in his hands.

"A ring brings up too many questions. I don't want people asking where my husband is and wondering why I don't live with him."

From his slumped position he turned and said, "Where is your husband, Sarah?"

She twisted her handkerchief, smoothed her dress, and stood up.

"He's a prisoner."

"A prisoner?"

"In a detention camp. His name is Jimmy Sato."

He started to say something, then thought better of it.

"He's Japanese-American. A tuna fisherman. We lived on Terminal Island, off Los Angeles harbor. He had a boat, a fishing boat, the Sato II." She sighed and wiped her face. "When the Japanese bombed Pearl Harbor in Hawaii, our government confiscated the boats. We had to sell almost everything by government order. Our house, our furniture, all of my husband's fishing equipment. Everything we owned. Fishing was his life. Now he and his family, his sister and his father are in a horrible place called Desperado. It's about thirty miles west of here in the mountains. I get to see him once a week for two hours. Yesterday I went and when I arrived, they wouldn't let me in. It's quarantined because of an epidemic of flu. Now I don't known when I can see him."

She flung herself down on the couch.

Alberto felt lost. His chest hammered and his breathing was hard and he heard himself say uncertainly, "I didn't know, Sarah."

"Jimmy did nothing wrong," she said. She stood up and left the room. She came back quickly with a stack of photographs and thrust them at him. "Look," she exclaimed, "look how they have to live!"

The photographs were dog-eared and brown. He saw people standing in a field with guard towers over them and barbed wire surrounding them. Soldiers with rifles stood on the towers.

"That's him," she said, pointing to a picture. A small man worked in a field with a hoe. Sarah put her hand on her cheek and said, "I miss him terribly."

His heart was broken. He couldn't say the right words and his feelings overwhelmed him. "I'm sorry," he mumbled and moved uncertainly to the front door and left. A few minutes later, he sat in a booth at the LaFonda and downed several bourbons.

* * *

Creekwater watched his pupil work on a slab of marble. Frederick's eyes were like black onyx, and his face was covered with white grinding dust.

"Keep at it," he encouraged.

Alberto followed the milky rivers embedded in the stone and waited for Frederick to speak.

"You're trying to capture the world as you see it. Everyone sees things differently; you'll never quite catch it as it is. A lot of artists exist that way; doing that and nothing else. You're better than that, Runner. If you weren't, I wouldn't bother with you. You have to go beyond that and you will eventually. You have to move past what you think you're seeing and get to the very essence, the spirit itself."

Frederick took a marking pen from his pocket and made some marks on a rough section of a large piece of alabaster. He ran his hands over the piece and stepped back to view it.

"Say you draw a deer. Everyone sees it as a deer. But they don't know what that deer means to you. You don't stop there, Runner. You capture the tranquility, the grace, the speed, the grandeur. In drawing that deer for what it means to you, and no one else, you may choose to draw a circle. Maybe a square. Maybe an apple. But the splendor of what you are working toward comes from deep inside you."

"What if no one cares for it?"

Creekwater stared hard at Alberto, as if suddenly he could take his bare hands and rip him apart. It was a look so strong, so passionate, that Alberto knew nothing in the work could keep Creekwater from what he was doing with his hands.

"No one. No one will care for it, want to possess it, travel thousands of miles for it, if you don't care for it yourself. That's why you must go beyond what you see. In time, you'll understand what I mean."

"Did Sarah show you what I made for her? The ceramic pieces of the Deer Dance?"

"Sure."

Alberto hesitated. "Did you like them?" He had to raise his voice so Frederick could hear him.

Frederick came out of the shed with two cold beers.

"Here," he laughed, his dark eyes sparkling. "Hell, yes, I liked them. Now relax and enjoy this. You have to pay for it at the LaFonda."

* * *

It was late spring and time to go back to Acoma. All Alberto could see ahead was tending sheep and repairing worn irrigation ditches. All because the clan was too proud, too set in its way. It made him set his teeth in disgust and bitterness.

And there was Sarah. She wouldn't go away. It was utterly hopeless but he wouldn't let it go. He saw her now only at Cerillos and she gave him no encouragement. When he wanted to tell her about his work with Frederick, she was gone before he started. His love for her tore him apart. There was only one consolation. He drank. He kept a bottle in his room, hiding it from the cleaners by putting it in the toilet tank. To now satisfy his craving, he sold more drawings. They weren't first-rate; but they sold.

Semi-circles of water formed under his glass at the LaFonda. He put his glass down, picked it up, tried to make the circles complete. The color in the glass reminded him of the color of the great stag he chased on Mount Hasasu.

* * *

Runner—Sorry to hear about Sarah. She must really love that little Jap. If you're smart, you won't mess with that situation. You do and you're in for nothing but trouble.

This war ain't any fun any more. You drink with a buddy, the next night somebody else sleeps in his bunk.

If I don't make it, Runner, don't ever forget me. We had some good times.

Take my advice. Stay the hell away from booze. It'll kill you.

I got a bad feeling you ain't listening to what I'm saying.

The invisible one

Dennis Charbonneau

* * *

Hot winds scoured the valley as Alberto tended his herd of underfed and mangy sheep. He couldn't leave for Creekwater's until the second week in August. Frederick would be east until then. All he did was think of Sarah and his lousy job in the valley. To bury his thoughts and to taste the hot, sweet run of whiskey, he and Henrique took the wagon up the long, dusty trail to Laguna.

The days were endless, rain like a drop in a teacup. Up at dawn, he was down in the fields, working the agate-hard ditches, his hands bleeding, the sun a fury in his face. Again he spoke to his father about better equipment. It was like talking to a deaf man. In this inferno of heat and despair, his bitterness grew and his resolve hardened.

"You act like an old man," Henrique said. "What's eating you?"

"I can't get Sarah out of my mind."

"Get on the bus and go see her. Make your move."

"I can't do that. She's married."

Alberto threw down his shovel. "I get so fucking mad, I'm ready to tell the clan to go fuck themselves."

Henrique answered, "Let's go to Laguna."

* * *

One day a summons was delivered to the Campione house by one of the war chiefs of the clan. It was a command to perform in the upcoming Kachina dance. Everyone in the village was involved in some way and it was considered mandatory to take part if summoned by the clan. Alberto had performed in the dance since a small boy and also his sisters. Their parents always eagerly awaited the day when they could watch their children in this ritual dance. Each year when he'd received his summons, he had gone to the kiva and entered it and had taken his mask from where it regularly hung. It was made of thin, curved wood, painted corn-color and ocher. In the Kachina Dance, he wore moccasins trimmed with skunk to chase the bad spirits. Around his waist was a white leather belt with long dangling tassels. His chest was bare and he shook dry gourds. The sound they made imitated rain falling on the corn in the valley.

His resolve fortified with whiskey, he didn't bother to pick up his mask. No longer would he fear the punishment the clan might order for declining to dance.

The day of the dance came and Alberto walked down into the valley and built a great roaring mesquite fire. He sat in front of it far into the night, asking himself many questions as the flames licked the sky. Will I ever see Sarah again? And if I do, what will come of it? Will she let me walk with her? Let me come into her house? Let me make love to her? He knew the answer to his questions before he asked them. What of her husband? Does he know anything about my visit to Sarah's house? Did she tell him? Then his thoughts switched to Acoma. What of the clan? What will they do to me? Will they bring me to the kiva and flog me with a horsewhip? Will I be banished from Acoma if I persist in disobeying them? Bitter smoke circled his body as he agonized his latest decision.

Sometime after dark, he heard someone coming and knew it would be his father.

"Let's walk into the desert," Felipe said nervously, his ebony eyes furious, his profile strong against the fire light.

"Whatever you have to say to me, say it right here."

"You've set yourself up for trouble. You've angered the cacique."

"I made up my mind. Nothing's going to stop me."

Saying the words gave Alberto some relief. It was as if he'd been in chains in a dark hole and suddenly the shackles had been removed and he was a free man. He sensed his father's body tighten. It was as if his father was a coyote about to leap. Felipe's features appeared tense in the light from the fire.

"You won't listen to me," Alberto hollered. "About our crops! You won't talk to the clan. You won't try to make things better!"

Felipe Campione started to say something in rebuttal, his face thrust forward, but Alberto stopped him.

"My brother didn't have to die!"

"Stop it, Alberto! That was a long time ago."

"No, you listen to me! When Louis was sick, you wouldn't listen. To my mother, to my sisters, to me. You listened to the clan!"

Felipe's face appeared pinched and withered. He looked old and helpless, like a leaf caught in a whirlpool.

"We wanted a doctor. Instead, you went to the kiva. They sent our medicine man. He said Louis was infested with witches. I heard him say it. He shook his eagle plumes and rattled his gourds and Louis died! You didn't do anything. You let the clan decide."

Alberto heard his father softly say, "It was his time." It was as if Felipe Campione had repeated this phrase a thousand times, trying to convince himself of its truth.

Felipe stared at his hands as if there was blood on them. He looked like he might suddenly crumple to the ground.

Alberto became overwhelmed with his father's pain. He realized how hard his words had been. He believed every word he had said but he still loved his father very much. Quietly he said, "Let's walk now." He put his arms around him.

They walked into the desert and the years rolled back and Alberto was a boy again. He was walking with his father on his first rabbit hunt. He carried an old shotgun that had been given to him by his father as a present. Together they searched the desert floor for the big jackrabbits that burrowed into the soil. His father spoke, interrupting his thoughts. "You've been away a year now. You aren't the same person we took to the bus station."

Suddenly Alberto wanted to tell him everything, like a dam bursting and spreading what it was holding all over the land. He wanted to share his feelings for Sarah and his uncompromising hatred toward the clan and the cacique, all the things that brought bile up in his throat.

"Do you remember, father, the night, years ago, when we walked in the desert? You spoke to me about what it might be like, going away."

Felipe nodded, his stride now more confident, his back straighter.

"Much troubles me," Alberto said. There was a rustle off the path and Alberto imagined it to be a big jack, emerging from his burrow, his heart beating rapidly as they passed.

"I remember," his father said. "I said that there would come a time when you felt you were no longer one of the fish in the stream or the deer in the forest."

Felipe stopped, rubbed his hands, picked up a pebble from the desert floor.

"When the bird is on the nest, it's taught to fly. It's fed. When the bird leaves the nest, it has its own sky, its own place to alight, its own food to find. It's the same with everyone, Alberto. You do these things or you don't grow. It's hard for me to realize you've left the nest."

He took the stone and flung it far into the desert. "Your time came and you flew. On the way you met some bumpy currents and they tossed you in many directions."

Alberto thought. *I have to tell him about Sarah, how I'm driven crazy thinking of her, the nights he lay awake thinking of her, the miserable feelings he had. His father had to know how Alberto felt about the clan and their unbending ways. The only thing he wouldn't tell him was about his drinking.*

"I met a man, father. Frederick Creekwater. He's in Madrid, south of Santa Fe. A sculptor. I worked with him some afternoons. He likes my work and wants me to come the middle of August. I want to be a sculptor.

"A sculptor. You mean with stone?"

"Yes. He works in alabaster and granite."

"Can you make a living?"

"I'm sure I can." As Alberto said it, he knew he could.

"Fine," Felipe said, putting an arm around his son's shoulder. "Is there more?"

Haltingly, Alberto said, "There is a woman." The moment he said it, his good feelings vanished and his heart jumped.

"A woman?" Felipe faced Alberto, his face questioning.

"A white woman."

Alberto's chest began to hurt and his legs felt weak. He breathed in and out in heavy gasps and he couldn't calm himself. He sat down and his father stood over him.

"A white woman? What's this all about?"

"She's married. Her husband is in prison. In the mountains west of Santa Fe. In a place called Desperado."

"Why are you telling me this?"

"I love her, Father." Alberto was on his feet and his stomach was like a hot iron. He shook and he gasped for breath. He sat down again and covered his face with his hands.

Felipe waited. Finally Alberto got up again and stared into the desert.

"How did this happen?" Felipe asked.

Alberto brushed at his face. "She's a teacher. She helped me meet Creekwater, the sculptor."

"But her husband? What about her husband?"

"He's a Japanese-American. After Pearl Harbor, the government rounded up all these people on the west coast and put them in detention camps away from the ocean."

Felipe threw up his hands. "You cannot. You cannot have her!"

"But I love her!"

"It's impossible!" Felipe put his hands on his face and rubbed it. "You cannot!"

Alberto's head felt like it would blow apart and his stomach was tight. He wanted to lie down and fall into a deep sleep. To forget everything; to forget Sarah. Forget an empty life without her.

Felipe put his arm around him. The only sound in the darkness was Alberto's heavy breathing.

Felipe finally said, "Let's walk some more. Their air is good now."

Stars appeared and a thin moon cut a path across the desert. Alberto found no more words.

"Much has happened to you," Felipe said. "Too much and too fast." He reached into his faded jeans and pulled out a carved deer fetish, one that Alberto had seen him hold many times. Felipe rubbed it and held it in his hands. "I must say this to you again. When you disobey the clan, there is punishment. It could be the lash or worse. I will go to the cacique and tell him it won't happen again. As for the woman, if you keep on, I see nothing but sadness ahead of you."

Alberto had calmed down. "I have to decide; I know that."

Felipe ran his hands through his hair. "I must speak to you about another matter."

"What's that?" Alberto asked.

Felipe cleared his throat and spit out some phlegm. "Listen to me, son. When I fell in love, I was older than you. She was from our mesa. She had warm feelings for me and I wanted her for my wife."

They reached a place in the valley where cottonwood trees lined a dried stream bed. They sat down with their backs to the trees and looked up at the stars and the moon that sliced through the sky.

"There was a festival in Laguna that fall. We went with others in the wagons. This woman, she had dark eyes. Darker than a cloudless night. She wore her hair very long. When she walked beside me, I felt powerful and full of life. In Laguna, we sat and watched the festival and we were served whiskey. I had money I'd saved. I had several drinks. She didn't like it and tried to get me to stop. She got so angry at me that she went back with friends. I got drunk and wound up in jail."

As Alberto's father spoke, he took a gnarled stick from the ground and drew circles in the sand. They reminded Alberto of rain clouds forming in the sky.

"That was your mother, Alberto. That was Maria. A year passed before her father allowed her to speak to me. When she did, I courted her. She gave me a choice; give up whiskey or give her up. It sounded at the time like an easy choice. It wasn't. Whiskey almost won."

His face was close to his son's now and he said, "I know about your drinking. I know about the LaFonda. I know why you go up to Laguna with Henrique."

"I don't touch it much," Alberto replied, but it wasn't convincing.

Felipe became angry. His eyes snapped and his face tightened. "I know better. Sister talked to me. Look, when a man is gone on whiskey, he can't find any truth in himself. He lies to himself. He thinks because he's young and strong, he can handle it. It doesn't work that way. It'll handle you."

He took the stick again and rubbed out all the circles in the sand, then flung it into the desert. He stood up. "The woman." As he said it, he glared at his son, his hands on his hips. "God help you."

* * *

Alberto felt better after talking to his father. Bringing up Louis' death was good for both of them. It released some poison that had been in their systems a long time. And yet, he knew his father wasn't going to change. And his father couldn't help him with Sarah. But he had listened and had said what he thought. And his father couldn't change the clan. Nothing would change. So Alberto made his resolve. No more would he take orders from them. From now on, the only voice that counted was his own.

* * *

Runner—I never told you the name of my bird. It's Diana. Diana Claypool. She's nineteen and a real looker. She's nuts about me, which you can understand. Diana had a steady but he was killed at Dunkirk. I never told you about our hot-shot pilot. Name's Archie Brown and he hails from Wichita, Kansas. He's a major and a damn good one. We have this ritual now when we land after a mission. First, he gets out and kisses our plane, then the rest of us. I ain't heard from you in a long time. Still fussing around about Sarah? What's up?

Your invisible buddy
Dennis Charbonneau

* * *

Hot, sweltering August brought the Deer Dance ceremony to Acoma. It was the biggest event of the year on the mesa and every member of the village had some part to play. Henrique and Alberto had been for years the fighting bucks in the Dance. Again they were chosen.

Alberto knew his answer. His friendship with Henrique would be sorely tested. Their long mock-battle in the dusty streets was always eagerly awaited and crowds lined the streets. The two young men fought for hours, street to street. Finally, as in the script, Henrique fell and Alberto became the dominant buck. For his prize, he was given the best doe.

Always before the Deer Dance was the rabbit hunt in which all the men and the older boys participated. Alberto looked forward to the hunt and decided to be in the hunt, but not the Dance. He enjoyed trapping the fleet-footed animals and he relished the companionship of Henrique. The hunt lasted three days before the Dance. The two young men built a lean-to in the desert and stayed out from the village the three nights. By the end of that time, they had four fat jacks who sat with their arched backs in their traps. The last night, they skinned the jacks and sat in front of their lean-to as the coals from their pinonwood fire skittered out on the sand.

Alberto broke their contented silence with words that heavily damaged their boyhood friendship. "I made up my mind some time ago, Henrique. I decided to have it out with the clan. I'm not going to fight you in the Deer Dance."

"You're what?" Henrique roared as he stared at Alberto, unbelieving.

"The clan can go to hell!"

"Are you out of your mind? What about you and me? Our fight in the streets? Are you kidding me?"

"Look. If I don't dance, they'll make me come to the kiva. Everyone will be there. I'll take some punishment, maybe the lash. But I'll be able to state my position and stick by it."

Henrique looked at his longtime friend sitting by the fire. It was too much for him to understand. He was well aware of Alberto's disgust at the clan's repeated refusal to deal with the whites, and Alberto's feelings on mechanical farm equipment, but to do this. It was too much.

"You're crazy, Runner. They'll whip you! They'll kick you out of the village!" Henrique's eyes blazed and his temper rose. "You don't know what you're doing. What's got into you?"

"I know what I'm doing. I've thought about this for months."

Alberto pulled out his bear fetish and rubbed it. "Look, I'm tired of this crap. Tired of digging ditches with broken shovels. Tired of seeing crops whither like old men. We could have good corn, good rice. We could have fat sheep. But the god-damned clan won't accept the fact that we have to deal with the whites. They've got five hundred years of bitterness up their ass and they won't change. God-damn it, Henrique, we both know we need machinery. We've bitched about it many times. If the clan got off its butt and spent the money, things would be better. I have to show them. And I'm not afraid to do it. We're wasting away here. Nobody gives a damn! Tradition is killing them and they won't admit it!"

Henrique's face was purple. "You're throwing your life away! I don't know you any more!"

Alberto Campione's best friend turned and walked away.

Three Young Men: Alberto

* * *

Alberto slept uneasily, knowing what faced him in the morning. The dance would begin and the cacique would hear about him and summon his father. They'd bring Alberto to the kiva. His heart began to beat faster and he started to sweat. Soon he saw his father coming down the path. Felipe offered no comfort to him and was short on words. "The time has come. We must go to the kiva." They began their walk out of the valley and up the hand-hewn steps leading to the mesa.

Twelve steps led down into the underground home of the clan. As Alberto took them with his father, he wondered, *Will this be the last time I'll enter here?*

The kiva was filled to capacity as men and boys sat around the old adobe walls, occupying pine benches. Alberto knew them all; many had played under turkey feathers with him as a boy and had run with him in flag games.

It was hot and steamy in the kiva and a red fire blazed. Alberto looked calm but his insides shook. Inside his mind raced the thought of the pain of the whip as it cracked again and again into his flesh. He saw the lash given to a thief years before and he remembered how he winced every time the man was struck. He wondered whether he could stand the lash if it came to that. Punishment by the clan in the kiva was called "The Judgment." It was always pronounced by the cacique and carried out by the war chiefs. He looked around the smoky room and saw the medicine man, the same man who had stood over his brother. The three war chiefs stood near the cacique. The old man himself stood by the altar. It had been carved into the rock and the soil and it rose dramatically from the mud floor. Alberto felt weak as the cacique motioned him to stand facing the altar. Sweat formed on his face and body.

The old cacique was a thin, wizened man of more than eighty years. His skin was dark from years in the sun and his arms small and frail. Veins showed heavily in his flesh which hung limp and flabby. Alberto felt no sympathy for him because of his haughty treatment of the villagers and his iron-clad stubbornness toward the whites which was dooming Acoma. The cacique began to speak and the villagers leaned forward to hear him. The once powerful voice had weakened with age.

"My people," he said, "I speak to you today of the great mountain to the north, or own Mount Hasasu. I remind you of our ancestors and the terrible days under the Spanish." Men and boys strained forward on their benches. "Our people were forced under the gun to carry great timbers down the mountain, timbers they had to cut. They carried them across the valley to Acoma. On the way, they were whipped by the oppressor and the lash cut their skins and blood flowed into the timbers. Those timbers are part of our beautiful San Estaban Rey, our church. I remind you of how the conquerors took each Indian male fourteen and over and cut off their left hand." As the old cacique's message filled the kiva, the men and boys were silent. They knew the story which had been drilled into them over and over.

The cacique went on. "A time came when we rose up and fought the Spanish and defeated them. We cast off our chains of bondage." The audience knew that when the cacique was through and the three war chiefs had briefly spoken, that the judgment would be made. This is what they had come for.

Alberto stood facing the cacique and he tried to calm himself. The image of the great Sangre de Christo came to him and he saw its power and its vastness. He said to himself, *This place where I stand is insignificant.* He reached into his jeans and rubbed his fetish. It was cold and hard and it gave him courage.

The cacique finished and it was time for the war chiefs to speak. By tradition, the oldest chief spoke last, this being Felipe Campione. The cacique introduced each war chief with a flourish. The youngest spoke first and was enamored with his voice which soared to the ceiling of the kiva. "My brothers," he began, "our great leader has spoken words of wisdom. He believes in the strength of our people. I affirm what he said. We must follow our laws and be loyal to the clan. We must be loyal to the rule of the kiva." The young chief sat down.

The next war chief was short in stature but powerfully built. Alberto knew him from the many wrestling contests he had won. His message was vigorous, parroting what the two before him had said. "I have lived here. I live by kiva rule. I am strong because of the clan. My duty is to my people." He strode in front of the cacique and raised his arms, his muscles rippling beneath his shirt. "Always remember our leader and what he means to Acoma." He shook hands with the cacique and he was finished speaking.

A hush fell over everyone. They knew how difficult it must be for a father to speak of a defiant son. Felipe Campione came forward and a chill ran through Alberto. Felipe faced everyone and his manner was serious with a look of sadness.

"My brothers, my heart is deeply troubled. I have lived my life on this rock we call home. I was born on the mesa and here I shall die. I have hunted the valley below and our great mountain with my own father, and with my sons. This is what I know."

Alberto found himself back that day on Mount Hasasu when they came upon the great stag and he had run with the animal. Now his father stood in front of the multitude and his features were ones of strength and serenity.

"My father taught me the ways of our people. I taught my sons these ways." Felipe's eyes moved over the crowded kiva and settled on Alberto. "There are truths men live by, truths that come from our ancestors. We live our lives by them." His voice became stronger, a voice that held everyone. No one moved or said a word.

"I was told many times that we must not change. That we are strong because we do not change." A murmur of approval swept the kiva. This is what the villagers were used to hearing, and what they lived by.

"I was told that if we listened to those outside our mesa, our people would wither like crops without rain." Again the audience echoed their approval. Alberto's father's eyes now seemed to focus on some point millions of miles away.

"Now I am deeply troubled. My own flesh and blood stands here before you and he questions our ways. He has been in the white world. He feels he is better for it." Shouts rang out for the first time. "It is a world we choose not to see. A world we have not wished to see because of our own culture. Now he tells me there is a better way. He has seen it and has lived in it."

Alberto's heart beat faster as his father formed a picture of a larger world.

"I do not approve of his attitude, but I cannot condemn his thoughts." Something was coming. The crowd was suddenly taken aback, their voices stilled.

Felipe Campione came closer to those seated and his arms came out and up in a gesture as he exclaimed, "Are we so proud that we think the world revolves around our beliefs? Are we that vain?" Now he had to almost shout because of the commotion his remarks caused. "It made me think. Who is it with too much pride, my son or us?"

The youngest of the war chiefs angrily motioned to Felipe and said, "You've said enough." Alberto's father brushed him off. Faces were troubled; faces were angry. Some were dumb-stricken. Men looked at each other and wondered what came next.

"My son has flaunted our rules. I believe in our rules." A sigh ran through the villagers. "Our rules make me feel secure. Now the clan must decide if my son is to be punished." Some men and boys were on their feet.

Felipe went on, hitting hard. "This mesa needs strong young men, men with pride, pride in themselves, pride in their own beliefs. Not just our beliefs. Alberto has that pride. He has the courage to show it even though you disagree."

Most of the villagers now tried to sort out what Felipe had said. Some told their sons to sit down and keep quiet. Hatred blazed on the old cacique's face. His hands quivered and his arms shook and his face was dark with rage. The other two war chiefs stood beside him and they were stunned by Felipe's hard-hitting message. He had momentarily shocked them into bewilderment.

Alberto heard his father say, "Look around you. Some here have little spirit left in them. Some can hardly survive anymore. Many have left us and have gone into the white world. There was nothing to keep them here, no work for them. There was not enough food, because our crops were poor. Think about this, my brothers. Think long and hard."

Felipe hadn't finished and his voice rose stronger than ever. "We need new voices here. We need young, fresh thinking. We must change our ways."

He sat down. Alberto couldn't tell whether the crowd was for him or against him. Whatever happened, his powerful words had been said. Alberto's heart went out to him and he was immensely proud of him. His father had shaken many and he had made an enemy of the cacique.

The cacique leaned heavily on his brightly feathered staff and slowly climbed the four steps to the altar. His arms quivered and his steps were erratic. No one had ever spoken like Felipe in the presence of the cacique. He had been seriously challenged. He turned from the altar, his words muted, but still carrying authority. "Alberto Campione," he said, "you have been brought before our ruling body because you flaunted our tradition. Not once, but twice, you refused summons to our sacred dances. Do you have anything to say for yourself?"

Now was the chance that Alberto had waited for. Now he could say as strongly as possible the many things that had made him bitter. But he looked at his father and knew that enough had been said.

"Nothing," he said forcefully. "My father has spoken. His words carry much wisdom and should be acted upon. I am proud to be his son." Alberto trembled as he said the last few words. The expectation of the lash made him sick. He hoped he could go the distance as a man.

The old man raised his staff over his head and he chanted words ancient to the clan as his face became pale. It was dotted with silver beads of sweat that reflected in the yellow flames of the altar fire. He appeared like a weary old coyote surrounded by hungry wolves. Slowly he pointed with his staff to a bullwhip hanging on the wall. Alberto's punishment was at hand. Four times it would descend. Four times it would tear into his flesh. Some in the kiva yelled their approval but most were silent. The words of Felipe had sunk in and made them turn matters over in their minds. The youngest chief removed the whip and made Alberto remove his shirt and kneel in the dust.

Everyone was on their feet. The smell of blood was in the air. Now a mob of men and boys tensed as they waited for the whip to descend. Now, however, there were many who were realizing that Felipe's words had aroused them and made them question what they were about to do.

The whip tore at Alberto. Searing torture racked his body. The whip descended again. Pain ripped at him and he fell over in agony. The two war chiefs other than Felipe pulled Alberto again to a kneeling position and the whip cracked for the third time. Alberto exploded in a bellowing rage. Animals were all around him; animals out for blood, animals with senseless traditions that would carry Acoma to extinction. The whip cracked for the fourth and final time. Alberto shrieked and fell over and tried to right himself. As he did, he saw his father standing alone against a wall. Suddenly the wall and his father were one. A mountain rose against a barren desert. Its face was like polished marble. By it, a young Indian with thick black hair stood on a scaffold, carving his father's face into the mountain. Alberto was looking at himself.

He placed his hand on the cheek of the sculpture as his consciousness faded beyond the reach of pain.

* * *

Alberto's mother stood beside his bed as she applied some ointment to his back. Alberto heard his father's voice for the first time since being in the kiva.

"I have good news for you. You're allowed to finish your schooling in Santa Fe and are welcome on the mesa."

"How did it happen?" he asked, turning his head from his pillow to speak to his father. Felipe sat down beside him and lightly touched him on the shoulder.

"Last night there was a meeting in the kiva. There is a split in the views now. The cacique hasn't spoken to me."

"You made an enemy, didn't you?"

Felipe ran his hands through his hair. "Our people aren't open yet in their views. Time will bring more out. What they choose not to talk about is as important as what they discuss."

* * *

In three weeks, St. Catherines started. Alberto rested four days at home, then took off for Madrid. The afternoon he arrived, Frederick put him to work moving blocks of granite. Alberto's side and back still pained him but he didn't complain. Late that day they sat outside the shed.

Frederick handed Alberto a beer. "I got about three words out of you today." He took a drink from a dusty canister and a wet line formed around his mouth. He wiped it on his sleeve.

"I'm not going back to Acoma."

"Figured as much. I hear you took the lash. I have some stuff for your back if you need it."

"How'd you know?" Alberto asked. "I could use something. It itches like hell."

"That's a good sign. It's healing. How'd I know? Edgar told me. He knows everything that goes on in the pueblos."

Creekwater walked into the shed and came out with a small jar. "Take your shirt off." Alberto complied and Frederick examined the wounds. "They did a good job on you." He applied the ointment. "I know why you're not going back."

"What's that?"

"You can't get a drink."

"What's that supposed to mean?" Alberto countered, getting irritable.

Frederick rubbed the ointment off his hands. "I know about your nights in the LaFonda. I know your quick sketches give you drinking money."

He walked over to a block of granite. "Edgar filled me in. I figured out Sarah by myself."

He sat beside Alberto. "Give it up," he urged. "The booze and Sarah. If you don't, you'll hurt you both. She has enough trouble already without worrying about a lovesick Indian with a hard-on."

Creekwater stood up and worked his shoulders with his arms. "Another thing, as long as I'm mouthing off. You have this notion you can help your people. You want them to have a hell of a lot more than prayer sticks to bring rain."

Frederick wiped his hands on his jeans and took a swig of beer.

"I'm twelve years older than you, Runner. I used to be like you. I wanted to right all the wrongs done to my people, the Nez Perce. They weren't interested. You have to remember, people aren't rocks or paper. You can't shape them or cut them to fit your vision."

He sat down again, his back to the shed as he surveyed the brown slag-heaps of Madrid. Running his finger over a slab of alabaster, he removed a red pencil from his breast pocket and drew a diagram on the slab.

"You're witnessing your civilization crumble. The white man is here to stay. Every day I look at the decay in the pueblos and I record it on stone. The whites flock here and buy the stone. You have to do the same thing. And Runner . . . don't end up a drawing machine in Santa Fe for a few bucks for whiskey."

Alberto looked out to the west. A long line of purple thunderclouds was building up. He knew Frederick was right.

* * *

School started. On the first weekend, he took off for the Plaza, ignoring Creekwater's warning. He set up his easel and put on a quick sketch and waited. Someone tapped him on the shoulder. It was Sarah.

His heart leaped. She looked wonderful standing there, her eyes sparkling and a smile on her face. He'd been in a wasteland all summer long with his emotions boiling over, the miles denying him any chance to see her. It tore him up knowing she belonged to someone else. Her hair was in a bun and a brilliant turquoise necklace hung around her neck. She shook hands with him. "Come for lunch, Alberto."

He was overcome and elated, thinking he'd never see her again, sit close to her, touch her. He took the sketch off the easel, folded the easel, and they started to walk. Her next few words made him sick to his stomach.

"I'm happy, Alberto. Jimmy is being released." Her face was radiant and filled with joy.

"You'll be with him?" he asked plaintively, his face showing anguish.

"Three days. That's all. Then he goes in the Army. It's an all-Nisei outfit that's formed. I'm so proud, but I'm scared too."

So that was it. This might be his last chance to see her. She'd follow him, be near him, by his camp. His mind whirled like twisting blackbirds in the sky.

He managed to say, "I'm happy for you" even though it was a monumental lie.

They sat in her living room and he was silent, not knowing what to say. He felt like a wet rag. He reached into his jeans and pulled out his fetish.

"May I see the fetish?" she asked.

She held it in her hands.

"Have you had it long?"

"Since I was eight. An old woman made it for me."

Sarah was close to him now. All he had to do was reach out and hold her, never let her go.

"Tell me about it," she said.

He didn't want to hear that. He wanted her to say, "I love you, Alberto. I've always loved you. Take me in your arms." It was like a bad dream, one where he sank into a bottomless pit. No one was there to save him, to see him, to reach out, to pull him to safety.

"It's difficult for me," he said. She didn't understand. And he said to her, "Sarah, the old woman. My dream. I never told you."

"Told me what?" she asked.

Alberto sat down and she sat across from him.

"Sarah, when I was eight years old, the kakale came for me. They're the men in our clan who initiate small boys. It's part of growing into manhood."

"Tell me. I'm interested."

"It was my time, Sarah. I remember that day. My mother had tears when they took me. I was led through the streets to a house. I was kept there until after dark. Most of the time I sat in a room by myself and nothing happened. Then in the evening, my parents came for me. This was repeated for four days. The number four comes up many times in our ritual. One day the kakale made me drink a mixture of cornmeal and grasshoppers. I saw them mixing the hoppers and the meal in a mortar with a pestle. When I drank it, I threw up. They mixed it again and made me drink it. Another day they made me smoke a cigarette. I couldn't stand that. Each day after they left, an old woman came. She must have been ninety. I saw the heavy veins in her arms and her face was furrowed and drawn. She sat beside me and combed my hair and sang songs I'd never heard before. Then she rolled a cigarette with her hands and smoked it. The smoke made tears roll down her cheeks.

Sarah seemed enthralled with what he was saying.

"At the end of the fourth day, Sarah, after the old woman left, the head kakale came. He walked with me to the far eastern end of our mesa. It was dark by then and you looked down and saw the sheep fires burning in the valley. We stood there and he reached into his pocket and pulled out this bear fetish. He handed it to me and said, 'Keep it. Always. The old woman made it for you. Cherish it. Never be without it.'"

"And you've had it all these years?"

"Yes. Most of us carry fetishes. But there's more, Sarah. This is so strange to me. When I got home that night, I had this dream. I saw my father on Mount Hasasu. Someone carved his face into the mountain. I saw his face clearly. What is so strange is that the first night in the dorm at St. Catherines, I had the identical dream."

"One that comes back in the same form?"

"Yes. Then, three weeks ago, I was punished in our kiva. Afterwards, as I knelt in front of the altar in the kiva, I witnessed my father on the mountain. It was amazing! I couldn't believe what I was seeing!"

"Tell me; what did you see?" she asked.

"I saw a young Indian with long dark hair working from a scaffold. He was cutting my father's features into the face of the mountain. He turned from the scaffold and looked at me, and it was me, Sarah!"

"My God!" she said softly. "What did they do to you in the kiva?"

"I was whipped. I took the lash; four times."

"Why?" she asked.

"Because I objected to their attitude toward the whites, and I wouldn't take part in their ritual."

Sarah sat back as if in shock, but didn't speak. Alberto stood up and walked to a window and looked out. His feelings were getting the best of him. His chest burned and his shoulders ached. Suddenly she sprang up and exclaimed, "Of course; don't you see!"

She faced him excitedly, her face flushed, her eyes sparkling. Sunlight came through a window and put ribbons of gold in her hair. "You're going to do it! You're going to sculpt your father's face on that mountain. You are, Alberto. I know you are!"

They sat in her dining room and had lunch. Sarah was still excited about what he told her and happy about meeting her husband. She didn't seem to notice that Alberto said little and excused himself as soon as lunch was over. He said he had to go back in the Plaza and sell his sketches. She cheerily said good-bye to him and he walked back downtown toward the Plaza.

His thoughts were dark, his hopes for love torn to pieces. Never again would he see Sarah, he felt. His steps were slow and unsure as he headed for his one sure relief, the LaFonda.

* * *

Sarah beckoned to him from an empty whiskey glass as he sprawled listlessly in a booth and mumbled something to a waiter. His arms seemed to have heavy weights on them. Things were a blur. As he stumbled to his feet, knocking over a bar chair, someone shouted at him. Sarah lay in his arms and they made violent love. Jimmy Sato stood by the bed and he grabbed Alberto and they struggled. He smashed Jimmy to the floor, reached down and hit him, knocked him against a wall where he slumped to the floor. Alberto went after him again. More people were around him and there were noises, flashing lights, and shouts. Then a whistle blew.

* * *

Bitter metal lodged in Alberto's throat and his shoulders and side ached. He lay on a hard, damp cement floor that smelled of stale urine. Deep pains shot through his chest. He tried to roll over and sit up. Gradually his eyes became accustomed to the weak light coming in a barred window and he realized he was in jail.

He struggled to his feet and remembered what his father had said about waking up in jail in Laguna. He stumbled to a cot suspended by rusty arms to a cracked ceiling. Bile and copper burned in his throat and green mucous crusted his eyes. As he brushed his eyes with his sleeve, he heard a gruff voice say, "Here's your grub, Indian." A tray of food was shoved under the door to his cell.

He wearily rose from his cot and picked up the tray. The tepid oatmeal lingered in his throat and his stomach growled. Memories of the past few weeks crowded in: the whip of the lash, the days with Creekwater, his warning to Alberto, Sarah telling him about her husband, his feeling in the pit of his stomach that he'd never see her again. Telling Sarah about his strange dream that kept coming back. The whiskey at the LaFonda after he left her house. Then everything blurred out. Did he go back to her place? What had happened? He remembered hearing Sarah yell, "Get out! Get out! You smell like a sewer! I want you out! I want you to leave! Right now!"

"I don't want to leave! I want you, Sarah! I want to be inside you!" He ripped her dress and saw her breasts. She ducked under him and screamed, "Get out! Get out! I'll call the police! Leave me alone!"

He lashed out at her and she whirled and he ripped books from her shelves. She ran to the front door. He grabbed her shoulder and spun her around. Something hit him on his cheek and blood flowed down his face. He held up a hand to his face and it was bloody.

Sarah was outside screaming and he ran after her. He cried and said he was sorry. Arms grabbed him. He broke loose and ran to her again. A flashing, rotating light blinded him and he was knocked down. He smashed at a face and another face appeared. He was tackled and handcuffs put on his wrists.

"Jesus!" someone hollered. "He's a big sonofabitch!"

Alberto got to his feet and rushed someone and he was hit on the head. Whirling lights came through a flashing red shroud.

What day was it? How long had he been in jail? He lay back down on the cot and lost track of time. His back and sides hurt and itched.

Someone was coming. Sister Margaret and Edgar stood outside his cell with a short, dark-skinned man dressed in a light gray suit. Disappointment showed in Sister's eyes and anger in Edgar's. Alberto walked over to the bars and asked why he was in jail.

"You tried to rape Sarah," Sister answered. It was as if she gave an answer to an algebraic equation.

"I'm so sorry," he said. "I feel terrible. I didn't mean any harm."

Sister came closer. "I should have stopped you, Alberto. Should have stopped you from drinking."

"Can I see Sarah?" he asked sadly. "Can I tell her how sorry I am?"

"She doesn't want to see you," Edgar snapped.

"Did I hurt her?"

"You betrayed her!" Edgar countered, his eyes cold and flat.

The other man dismissed the guard and came closer. Alberto recognized Juan Romero, whom he had known for years at Acoma, and who had graduated from St. Catherines and never came back to the mesa. He wore an expensive suit and carried a black briefcase. His hair was cut short.

"Remember me, Runner?" he offered.

"Sure, Juan."

"You've friends, Runner. Good friends." He smiled at Sister Margaret and Edgar. "Sister hasn't seen me since I left. I'm in practice here in Santa Fe. Right now I'm a public defender. You're lucky. In most cases like this, you'd be found beaten and dead with no questions. I'm here to cut a deal. The D.A.'s office is overworked and underpaid. They don't need another Indian incident."

"I don't understand," Alberto said.

Romero spelled it out. "You're going to get out of Santa Fe and stay out."

"Get out?"

"The charges of attempted rape have been changed to a misdemeanor. Uncle Sam wants you, Runner. You're old enough now. I checked your birth record. The recruiting station is three blocks away."

"I enlist?" Things were happening so fast that Alberto was confused.

"Five hundred dollars springs you. Your friends here arranged it. You'll be on a bus headed out of town before nightfall."

"The money?"

"The school advanced the money. They keep all your drawings."

Sister Margaret nodded, her lips compressed.

"My folks?"

"It's arranged," Edgar said. "You had no choice. You'll get a leave to see them."

Romero thrust his hand through the bars. Alberto looked at a poor Indian from Acoma who had made it in the white world.

* * *

He took a shower and they gave him some new clothes. He was sick at heart, sick to his stomach, sick of what he'd done. He'd never see Sarah again. His folks must feel terrible at what he'd done. His whole world was collapsing and he was drowning in remorse.

He passed the physical and the bus was to leave at noon.

No one saw him off. He sat in the back of the bus with gall and bile and emptiness as companions. Looking back up Galisteo Street, he saw the Sangre de Christo hanging over the town. Thunderclouds built up in the heat and an occasional rumble was heard.

Then he spied her. Sarah stood in a doorway. She didn't move. She didn't wave.

* * *

Section 1.02 Steve

The whistle blew in Plant 10, its long, continual wail a signal the shift was over. Frank Nagy winced as he hoisted his last flywheel of the day and heaved it on the moving belt. The light in the old plant was gray-blue and the air heavy with steel dust. Welding sparks cast prickly light in the gloom.

Frank straightened up slowly, his weary body aching. He took off his heavy gloves and started to walk toward his locker. He opened the green-gray locker and reached for his old brown overcoat and felt hat. Walking to a partition in the building, he punched out on a time clock and turned wearily toward an exit. He stared at the falling snow, buttoned tight his heavy coat and started up St. John Street. Frank chuckled to himself, which was unusual because of his well-known frown. He said to himself, *I told that union steward to go screw himself when he tried to sign me up. The union can go pissup a rope!*

The snow was wet and heavy and there was no horizon. All the cars across Leith Street in the main parking lot were covered. The weatherman predicted another four inches by morning. That much could tie up the town, halt production. He'd seen it happen before. The big trucks coming with parts jackknifed on some of the hills near town. The snow removal rigs got behind and some people left their cars in the middle of roads. Figured they'd get them when the snow stopped and the rigs got the streets in order. Already he could see traffic was snarled by the shift coming in.

Thirty-four years he'd been in Buick Plant 10. Every day except Sunday. Every day he punched in and stood at his work station and lifted. Every day he bent over, bent his knees, strained his back as he put another flywheel on the belt. Every day he lifted thirty flywheels every hour, each one weighing fifty pounds. On Saturdays, he got overtime.

On the fifth of May, in 1934, at one in the afternoon, as he tried lifting a flywheel to put it on the belt, he doubled over in pain. They took him to the company doctor. One week later, a steel brace on his back, he was back on the job. The week they fitted his brace, he stewed at home. He worried he wouldn't get his job back. Buick was in high production. Maybe they'd give his job to a younger man. When he got his job back, he thanked General Motors for their generosity and breathed a sigh of relief. From that day on, he never missed a day. Now it was the winter of '41 and he walked with a stoop.

Every day he walked the same twelve blocks to where he lived. Every day he passed Bokors where he traded, Little Joe's where he stopped in for a shot, and the Catholic church where he sat with his wife in the same pew every Sunday. Every day Sophie Nagy peered out her front window on Tilden Street as she had for the last thirty-four years and watched her man come in the gate. She helped him with his coat, took off his sweaty shirt, massaged his tired back with Bengay. Then she said, "How was it today, Frank?"

"Okay. Them union bastards tried to get me to sign again. I didn't give them squat."

Over and over she rubbed his worn body as it shook from the exertion of lifting. Every day she saw her man fight the monster that was the rhythm of the job. Frank Nagy made eight dollars a day, paid for his groceries at Bokors on St. John Street, had money taken out of his pay for the mortgage, kept a little for the mass at St. Luke's. He didn't complain. He worked for the best company in the world. They built his house, got him a mortgage, got him started on a savings plan, even had a recreation center where he and Sophie could watch movies, see prize fights, enjoy softball teams on the four diamonds.

So he kept on working, every day except Sunday. Lifting, heaving, sweating, straining, his back brace cutting into his flesh, his back and legs forming a permanent stoop. He didn't complain about the iron dust that hung in the air in the plant, about the thick smoke, thick as gruel at work stations. About the factory air blue and gray. About the clang and bang of machinery that made him deaf, the stink of machine lubricants and cutting compounds that permeated his clothes, coated his worn-out body, followed him home as he trudged between Plant 10 and the river. A job was a job and the union could go piss up a rope.

* * *

Steve Nagy and Benny Kowalski stood talking as the whistle blew in Fisher 8. They finished clipping steel bands from a heavy bundle of flat sheets of steel weighing six tons. The steel was one-sixteenth of the daily consumption of Fisher 8, the steel made into body fenders. Each day except Sunday, over and over again, Steve and Benny lifted a heavy flat sheet of steel from a pile and placed it in the jaw of a giant die machine. Benny pushed a button and the machine came down on the steel. When it came back up, a raw, unfinished fender lay in its lap. They removed the stamped fender and handed it to two men next to them on the line. The men punched bolt holes in the front section of the fender with another machine, then lifted the fender onto the moving belt.

Today Benny was pissed about the line speed-up. The super wanted more fenders per hour. The men talked about it on their short break and put in a complaint to the shop steward. Benny figured it wouldn't make any difference; GM was too strong. Steve agreed and felt the union was getting the run-around. He wondered if they'd really accomplished anything in the sit-down strike in '37. They'd held Fisher 1 and 2 and Chevy 4 and brought down the wrath of most of the citizens of Flint, the condemnation of GM, the fight with the county sheriff and the local police. Even the National Guard had been called out. The famous—or infamous—Battle of the Bulls resulting, depending on which side you were on, and for what? It was five years later and things seemed to be as bad as before. Maybe one exception. There were locks on the line so a super couldn't turn up the speed if a gap developed in the belt.

Plant conditions weren't any better. You still put up with steel dust and smoke and noise and the stink of cutting compounds. You still couldn't get any place with your grievances unless you struck. And a strike was a tough way to go. A hell of an effort with time and planning, knowing there were mouths to feed and bills to pay and no money coming in except a pittance from the union. So what happened in the meantime? The local played the waiting game and looked to the contract year, for a few chips at the bargaining table. A few crumbs. Not enough to make a meal.

Steve thought of all the time he'd heard the nasty word, *speed-up*. Of the uncaring, unknowing factory lines that moved inexorably. Of management constantly trying to enforce speed-up. Of the line pressures every day and night. Speed-up was a science. If you wanted work, you didn't fight it. Sure, the local fought it, in every plant in town, in every factory in the country where it was practiced. Speed-up was an obscene plan of productivity hard to cope with. Over at Fisher 2, before the sit-down, workers argued they should produce the same number of door panels on each shift. That made sense. When GM tried speed-up, some men took panels and hid them in racks below the belt, covered with rough stock. Spies hired by management found the panels and the men that hid them were out of a job.

GM spent endless hours figuring ways to get speed-up. Above the din and commotion of the factory floor, white collar workers sat in air conditioned offices free of dirt and grime and charted man hours and efficiency. They calculated hour after hour the advantages of speed-up. In cool, clean offices, charts revealed where lines crossed. Those crossed lines meant the maximum, the ultimate use of the moving belt. Up where the air was clear, men put pencils to paper and let the numbers show bottom-line results that illustrated profit or loss. Up above the factory din, men controlled the outcome and let the profit side be the master, making paper statistics come into irrevocable conflict with human needs below. Down on the lines, where aching backs and tired legs and robot-like arms performed over and over, there was no semblance of time; nothing to think about but the steady, unwavering function; the work output that ate men's souls.

Steve was pulled out of reverie by Benny as they punched out and walked to an exit.

They stared at a winter storm raging outside. Benny said, "Christ Almighty, here we are mucking around, just like we were that night five years ago in old Fisher 2. I can still see ole' fat Sheriff Wolcott yelling at his deputies to go get us and break us up! That was one of the best fights I ever got into. We sure showed 'em we wouldn't take shit from 'em!"

"Yeah," Steve came back, "I wonder whether it was worth it."

"Hey, we made GM recognize us. Sure it was worth it. You're goddamn right it was!"

"I dunno."

Steve thought of that December of '36. He and Benny couldn't find work at Buick. They pooled their gas money and drove across town to the old plant on the west side. They'd graduated from Flint Northern High School where they'd played football under Virgil Heston. He was trying to help them get athletic scholarships to college. While they waited to hear from different schools, they had to find work.

Fisher #2 was a run-down plant along the Flint River where it made a wide loop after working its way downtown. The river passed the graying buildings in a deep hollow formed by coffee-colored bluffs. A hundred years before, red men watched early settlers come down the river on flatboats.

Steve and Benny were greenhands, so they took what they could get. They were lucky and got on a night shift building storage bins. One night, during a break period, a workman noticed some plant dies placed in boxcars in the railroad siding that ran by the factory. He reported it to a union shop steward and they talked about the dies. They reasoned that if the dies were shipped to some other plant, the parts for the cars could be made elsewhere. That might cause Fisher #2 to close its doors and they'd lose their jobs. Rumors had flown for some time that because the plant was old and falling apart, it might be torn down or replaced.

Seeing the dies on the siding happened the night of December 30th, 1936. The steward reasoned if the workers went home after the shift change, the dies would be moved. Steve Nagy knew the local had talked of striking. He overhead the conversation between the steward and the man that saw the dies on the siding.

"You won't get anywhere if you strike," he said to the steward. "They'll move the dies. You've got to keep them from moving the dies. The way to do that is to lock the plant up."

"What's that?" the steward said, looking at Steve.

"Stay in the plant and protect the siding. Don't go home. Close the factory down. Lock the gates. Kick the supers and the plant guards out and take over the building."

"What the hell you talking about? We can't do that!"

The steward was right. You couldn't do that. The law would be on you in no time. What kind of crazy talk was that?

The shop steward knew it was absurd. You couldn't take over something that didn't belong to you. But he kept thinking about it as Nagy stood there. Finally he went looking for two of the union leaders in the plant. After some discussion, a meeting was called in a second floor lunchroom. At some point, after much vigorous discussion, the union went to work.

The line stopped.

Foremen and plant protection men and guards were ushered out. The workers inside had a choice: they could go home or stay to take over the plant. A handful of men left.

It was a monumental moment in labor relations. A tremendous step for a small union local. Something still talked about when union men got together. A show of hands in a lunchroom and there was no turning back. A pivotal moment, one of destiny for the auto union, one that led eventually to recognition of the upstart local by the Goliath of the automobile industry, GM. Recognition from the biggest industrial corporation the world ever knew.

Gates closed, not to open for weeks. Weeks of bloodshed and strife, separation from families, weeks of waiting, of boredom, of belt-tightening, women's brigades responsible for food for the workers, weeks of wondering what was finally going to happen. Would they win from GM?

Word spread around the globe about Flint, Michigan and a band of factory workers. The town was on the map for everyone to see. The local and the national and the international press were on the scene.

Steve remembered how his dad had come into the plant after the second day. A short, pale-faced, bent-over man in work clothes came to the main gate and asked to see his son. He was admitted and taken to the same lunch room where everything had happened and he faced Steve.

"I reported in sick at Buick so I could see you," his father said. "I took a chance. What the hell's gotten into you? You realize what you're doin' here, son? You get your god-damned gear together and come home with me right now!"

"I can't do that, Pop."

"Whatdoya mean you can't do it? I'm giving you an order. I'm telling you to get the hell outta here!"

"I'm not coming, Pop. Not 'till it's over."

"You believe this crap the union's giving you? For Christ sake. This is your father talking to you. This is bad, real bad! You know what's goin' to happen. You won't get work anywhere! Think of me and your mother. When they find out you're my son, they'll fire me! Think about your mother. She's all torn up over this!"

"I'm sorry, Pop. I really am. But I believe in what we're trying to do and you don't. You've told me enough times how you felt about the union."

"Look. If you don't come home right now, there won't be no home for you to come to. I mean it. You stay here with these scumbags and you can find another place to live."

Steve towered over his father. "Look what we're trying to do. Justice in the workplace. Our fair share and decent working conditions. That's what we want, Pop."

"Don't Pop me. You and me are through."

Frank Nagy turned and left the room, bitterness churning inside his worn-out body. That night he railed at Sophie and paced the floor and stared out the front window. His head ached and his mind whirled when he thought of what the union was doing to his only son. Sophie

Nagy sat at her kitchen table, her head in her arms, tears streaming down her face, tears for her boy and her man.

Frank Nagy couldn't believe his own flesh and blood was a party to the union take-over. His feelings were shared by most of the people in town. What right did a bunch of factory workers have to take over a factory, to take something that didn't belong to them?

Some seven hundred men had cast the die and waited to see how it rolled. They had to live for weeks in a factory and be responsible to one another or it would have been simply anarchy. Steve remembered how they formed a council who gave orders, made kitchen details, makeshift police and guard service, a first aid station, set up a barber shop, figured out what they needed in the way of food and supplies, figured out where men were to sleep. Most of the time, he and Benny slept on the stopped belt in a couple of unfinished cars. Then he thought of the time that a reporter from the Flint Journal interviewed him in the plant about Steve's comments that the only way to keep the dies in the plant was to lock up the plant. The story was printed in the local paper. He remember how his mother had told him months later how her husband had seen the story and had rammed his fist through the paper and stalked out of their kitchen. She said she was so heartbroken over everything that her only solace was to walk daily to church and light candles for both her man and her son.

Benny and Steve trudged down St. John Street in the falling snow and met their friend Timmie Noonan at the gate of Plant #6. The three of them headed for Little Joe's Bar. The area they walked through sat between the Buick plant and the river and was known to the locals as "Little Europe." It consisted of twenty blocks of tightly packed two bedroom bungalows built by General Motors and sold to the thousands that came from the old country to work in the auto factories. Poles, Hungarians, Slavs, Russians, Montenegrins, Macedonians, Greeks, Turks, Rumanians, Bulgarians, Italians, even a few Mexicans. They all mortgaged their homes, worked for GM, and most were glad to be employed. They needed a job to live and raise a family. It was for this reason as much as any other that these arrivals to the United States weren't easily recruited by the unions. What they made, they hung onto. To pay their bills, raise their families, have some for church, and enough to make beer on weekends and enjoy the little free time they had.

Steve looked forward to the evening because there was a truce of sorts with the old man. Rainy, Steve's girl, who Frank loved, would be at the house for dinner, a dinner Sophie would fix with sauerkraut and pig's knuckles. Afterwards, they'd dance at Knickerbockers and Benny and his date would join them.

Kowalski wadded up a snowball and threw it and Noonan asked him, "You started to tell me about the night they called it the 'Battle of the Running Bulls.' You gonna tell me or not?"

"Yeah," Benny answered. "Well, it was like this, Timmie. Me and Steve were made plant guards during the strike. We had to watch any place where the police might get in or the sheriff's men. That particular night was cold as hell. You gotta remember too, it was the middle of winter. Steve and I were up on the roof overlooking Chevrolet Avenue. GM turned off the heat on us that night. So we were twice as cold. Anyway, we're looking down in the yard. Our guys are going out to get the food containers."

"That was the women's brigade?" Timmie asked.

"Yeah, they fixed a lot of the food. It came from all over the country, from several unions. Then there was a little restaurant up the street where they fixed most of the food and brought it to the gate in these big metal containers. That night the police barred their way. That had never happened before. So we had no heat, and maybe no food."

"Whajado?"

"Along comes Vic Reuther in a sound truck. He gets on the horn and tells our guys to insist the gates be opened so they can get the food. The cops didn't budge, so a lot of our guys came out and forced the gate."

"That's when all hell broke loose," Steve said.

"Like what?" Noonan asked.

"We hear someone yell, 'They got tear gas!' " Benny answered. "You saw police squad cars coming over the bridge just south of the plant. They started firing tear gas into the factory. Steve and I had some door hinges up on the roof and we threw them at the cops. Somebody inside the plant shot cold water from the fire hoses. Pretty soon everybody was mixing it up."

"Benny and I came down from the roof and got into it," Steve said.

"Then here comes old Sheriff Wolcott," Benny said. "We turned over his car and he got hit on the head with a hinge. You could hear ambulances coming. It was a god-damned battleground!"

"Who won?" Noonan asked.

"Nobody won!" Steve retorted.

"Bullshit! We won!" Benny declared. "We showed 'em they couldn't roll over us."

"No," Steve came back. "The whole town was against us. Guys got laid off after it was settled. Production went down. Business was bad. We didn't win."

The three young men entered Little Joe's Bar and sat in a booth, their lunch pails on the booth table. Benny whistled at Trudy and she thumbed an obscenity at him. When their beers came, Benny suddenly stood up in the booth and said to Noonan, "Some guy sat down in the plant after the Battle of the Running Bulls and wrote a song to the tune of 'There'll Be a Hot Time in the Old Town Tonight.' I'll sing ya a chorus." Benny Kowalski, two hundred and twenty pounds, belted out the words:

> Cheer, boys, cheer
> For we are full of fun,
> Cheer, boys, cheer
> Old Parker's on the run
> We fought last night
> And I tell you boys we won,
> We had a hot time in the old town tonight!

Steve Nagy pushed Benny down in the booth as they both laughed. As Steve pushed Benny, he remembered the day after the Battle of the Running Bulls. A visitor came to the plant and asked to see him. It was his mother. She hadn't seen him since the strike had begun weeks before. He felt a lump in his throat as she waddled toward him on her short bow legs. She reached up to him and put her arms around him and with tears in her eyes said, "Stephen, your father won't talk to you anymore. He thinks he's gonna lose his job over you. I can't reason with him. He's as stubborn as you are and says he's lost his only son." Steve found a chair for her and they sat and talked for an hour. She told him how she had endured the wrath of her husband by baking one day for the Women's Brigade, the wives of the men on strike.

She'd received a call from Trudy of Little Joe's. She didn't feel she could turn it down. When Frank found out about it, he refused to eat his dinner and went into the bedroom and wouldn't come out. She pleaded with Steve to come home. He explained to her as well as he could how he felt about the strike and that to get justice for the workers, he had to stand up and fight for their rights. Finally, Sophie stood up and her last words lingered in his mind, "You are my son, Stevie. You are always welcome to our home, to your home. Don't you worry what your father says."

He thought of the last burning argument he had waged with his father in their home before the strike. Room by room, word by word, a rampaging dialogue had taken place about the little auto union and its many attempts, most of them ill-conceived, to organize the workers in the auto plants. The heavy, harsh words on both sides were laced with bile and bitterness.

"You don't know what you're talking about!" his father yelled.

"What do you mean I don't know, Pop? How come you work for peanuts? Other unions in other industries are getting better wages for their people. Why can't it work here? You take all that shit from Buick and you don't open your mouth. Lifting flywheels all day long, your back killing you!"

"You got a lot to learn."

"Yeah, I got a lot to learn. Like about the lousy air, the machine cuttings, the long hours with short breaks, the speed-up, the goons spying on men on the line. No. You let things ride. You know why? Because you're afraid if you open your mouth, you'll get fired!"

Sophie Nagy stood in her kitchen, her hands covering her face, fear rising in her. She'd heard it all before. It never got finished, never got laid to rest. Her only son was like a flame shooting out, taking on her Frank, pushing for the union. She stood there and took it. She knew she couldn't leave. Where would she go?

"Now you listen to me, goddamnit. I've heard just about enough from you. I'm gonna lay it out for you once more, and you better hear me out. Don't you try and stop me!" Frank Nagy stepped closer to his son who towered over him.

"You get your union in your plant. That's what you want, hothead. Then the union makes waves. I've seen this for years at Buick. It never changes. They make their demands. The corporation fights them. Year in and year out it fights them. Each time the union makes more demands. I know. I've seen it happen. The day comes when GM and Ford and Chrysler get damn sick of it. They're trying to make cars with workers howling this is wrong and that is wrong and give me this and give me that and give me more. Nothing the corporations do for the workers means anything. They give the unions more and more and it never satisfies the big union bosses; the ones at the top that have to ask for more to keep their cushy jobs. Then the union gets its contract. What happens? Now this I knew from what happened right here at Buick. Don't tell me I don't know what I'm talkin' about. You have to pay more in union dues. First it's a dollar more a month, then two, then three, then five. Christ, Steve, it happened right in my plant! Where does that money go? Into pockets at the top. You never see any results."

"Pop . . ."

"Don't Pop me. I know what I'm talkin' about. A strike comes along. You get socked more money to the union. Money you need for food, to pay off the mortgage. Finally, the Big Three get fed up. What do they do? They raise the price of the car. They add on whatever the union gets and the public be damned."

"Pop, you're having a smoke dream. All we want is a fair wage for a day's work. Clean plants. Clean toilets. Get rid of the smoke, the grime, the filth. Get rid of speed-up."

"That's what they all say. Then they never tire of bucking for more, of increasing the ante. Let me keep my job and they can go fuck themselves!"

Steve's long dialogue with his father made him think of old Charley Maxwell, the dean of the union workers who talked to him one night while they were on plant guard on the roof. "I suppose," Charley said, "you're discouraged because we don't seem to be making any headway. I got a book in my locker that'll spell it out. When we go off in a couple of hours, I'll let you read it. It'll open your eyes." Charley Maxwell was one of those little stringy guys that didn't have an ounce of fat on their bones, who looked like he could be blown away by a good wind. He'd been in the plant along the river since he'd been a nineteen year old. When not keeping the motors on the line oiled and in good repair, he constantly talked "union" to anyone who would listen. One of the first believers and organizers, he was respected by the rank and file. When they went down from the roof, Charley went to his locker and handed Steve a well-worn book, its pages yellowed with age.

"You read this book by Taylor, you'll see what I've been telling you. He's the one who gave Henry Ford the idea for the production line. Taylor was a time-study man. He studied the functions of workers."

With time on his hands, Steve settled down one day in the bowels of a half-completed Chevrolet and read the book. Gradually it reinforced his thinking that the labor movement was an essential cog in the wheel, an element not to be sidetracked from its destiny. Taylor's thesis was that productivity in industry was accomplished by repeated functions, where the worker obeyed without any questions asked. He made no decisions and had but one single job to perform which became a small part of the whole. This job he did repeatedly, and rapidly, without any variation. In effect, Steve realized, he was a robot, mastered by a system that put a premium on efficiency. When Steve finished the book, he sought Charley out and said, "The guy was a genius."

"Sure he was. You see, there's no human factor. That's what we're fighting for. We want to bring humanity back in the factory. Management looks at one thing: the bottom line."

Steve was brought back to reality as he sat in Little Joe's by the squeaky voice of Timmie Noonan. "You guys been talking about that strike. I seen in the Journal where that old Judge died. You know ... the old guy that owned all that GM stock, the one that signed the injunction during the strike. The old bastard won't get to take all that stock with him where he's going." Then he added, "There won't be no wakes for him in Gracelawn!"

Trudy Fenstermacher was a thin, cadaverous, battle-scarred woman in her seventies who had run her bar with her husband since the late twenties. During the sit-down strike, she helped organize the famous Food Brigade, serving countless canteens of hot soup and sandwiches to the embattled men behind the barricades. Her wonderful "sit-down bean soup," which she still served in Little Joe's, was known far and wide. Beloved by the residents of "Little Europe," she possessed a biting wit and an irreverent tongue. A woman with a short fuse that blew at the slightest provocation, it burned now as she stood an inch from Timmie's red nose.

"Noonan," she retorted, her gray face close to his, "you Irish punk. You ain't got the decency to let a man die in peace. That judge was no friend of mine, but the son-of-a-bitch is still entitled to a decent burial. No shanty-Irishman like you speaks ill of the dead while I'm around!" Trudy's face was flushed and purple as she whirled from him, slammed the bar gate and went back to work. Noonan stared at her as the silence deepened.

"You got the short stick," Kowalski laughed. "You mess with Trudy, you come up dry."

Nagy chuckled as he stared at Noonan's tomato-red face. Timmie had been on the cross country team at Northern. Steve was amazed at the Irisher's capacity for booze. He never touched a drop while in training, but come Saturday night, the spigot was always on. It was Noonan who led the way to his favorite water-holes, downing boilermakers, straight shots of rye with a beer chaser. Come Sunday morning, buddies held him out a window on the second floor of his house and let the dry heaves begin. Whenever he got plastered in a bar, he usually launched into "Danny Boy." By the wee hours, he was maudlin and ready to be dragged home.

Five-feet five and one hundred twenty pounds with his overcoat on, Noonan was one of those countless Irishmen with skin the color of sugar and his bony body a ripple of sinew. His thin, angular face was a red glow behind a rapier-like nose. Nagy remembered with pleasure the first time Timmie had come to their house for a dinner of pierogi. Timmie had been bowled over by Steve's mother's living room. The chairs and sofa were covered with a heavy see-through plastic and Steve's mother told Timmie that if he entered the room, he must first remove his shoes. The room, devoid of any decoration save one crucifix, appeared at first glance like a sterile city morgue. "My mother only uses the living room for weddings, christenings, and funerals," Steve told Timmie. "We actually live in the back of our house in the kitchen." Halfway to the kitchen, Noonan smelled the spices and fresh bread of a perpetually cooking Sophie Nagy. Timmie stared at a heavy blue and white porcelain stove. A large oak table sat in the center of the kitchen with a bright red light fixture over it.

Sophie Nagy was a short, chunky woman whose arms were strong and heavy, whose legs were bowed as she waddled from side to side. Her cheery countenance was in direct contrast to that of her moody husband. A silent, frowning man, Frank Nagy was both sad and angry at the unholy influence of the labor movement on his son. Now a truce had been formed because of Rainy, Steve's girl. She was the buffer between the two, and a friendly, light-hearted, soothing influence.

As the three young men sat in a booth at Little Joe's, Benny got on his soap box again about plant conditions. The friendship between Nagy and Kowalski had grown from the years before when they were students together in Emerson Junior High School. It lay adjacent to Northern, the high school, and they had watched many times the scrimmages of the varsity football squad. By the time they were in their sophomore year at Northern, they both made the first team. Benny was a tough pulling guard and Steve a quick-running halfback. For three years under Coach Virgil Heston, Kowalski opened holes in the opposing line and Nagy darted through. The combination of the big Polock and the speedy Hungarian helped Virgil win his conference and go on to win his first State Class A High School Championship. Benny and Steve always eagerly awaited the big Thanksgiving game at the downtown Atwood Stadium with their arch-rival Flint Central. Eighteen thousand rabid fans made it the crown jewel of the season.

Trudy came over after a while and told them the latest Polish jokes. As she did, Benny put his arms around her playfully and they kidded one another. Steve looked at Benny and thought of that last game at Atwood in their senior year. In a tight, bruising game that day, Benny had been the difference. Recovering a fumble on Central's ten yard line, he blasted a hole on the first play and Steve walked in with the only score. As they showered under the stands after the game, Benny walked over to where Steve was soaping himself. "Look," he pointed to his right buttocks where a bite mark was turning blue. "Some guy from Central couldn't wait for Thanksgiving dinner."

The conversation at Little Joe's became desultory and Steve threw some beer money on the table. "I'm out of here. Rainy and I'll meet you at Knickerbocker's tonight."

"Things any better with your old man?" Noonan inquired.

"Not so you'd notice. If I stay away from shop-talk, I'm okay. The minute I get into it, I'm dead."

* * *

Back in high school, if Steve didn't have practice or got out of it early enough, he headed for the downtown library. The old limestone building, streaked with water stains, stood on the edge of the city park. He felt it was a haven for those unfortunate souls that slept in its doorways, hugging the stone-cold corners and inheriting the many cubbyholes in the building to seek the library's warmth. At closing time, with the insistence of a steely-eyed librarian who Steve avoided, they shuffled, one-by-one into the elements to take up their seedy paths, unwanted and uncared for. He always had a few coins for them. He felt guilty at their state in life and sometimes wondered if his fate led in that direction.

In his junior year at Northern, he fell in love with literature. He'd enrolled in an American Literature course taught by a tiny, peppery spinster, Mabel Terry. A kind, sympathetic, lively woman, five-feet one inch in height, she'd devoted the better part of her life to teaching. Miss Terry was a demanding instructor who quickly whetted Steve's interest in books and good writing. Regularly she made lists of literature she recommended, and with these lists, explained what she admired about the books and their authors.

Mabel Terry was attracted to Steve by an early paper he handed in. She realized his capacity for arranging his thoughts well on paper. He wrote succinctly and beautifully for an eleventh grader. One day after class she said to him, "Stephen, I want you to visit me any day you can in the afternoon, anytime after four."

"I'd like that, Miss Terry, but I have football scrimmage until four."

"Come when you can, Stephen. Five won't be too late."

He went over one day after practice. She offered him some tea and her homemade cookies. "I want to show you some contemporary writing that I think you'll enjoy." She took a book off a table and read excerpts from a short story by Saroyan. The story was entitled "The Daring Young Man on the Flying Trapeze," a story of a young man's failure and his approaching death.

When she finished reading and put her glasses down, she commented, "This is fine writing, Stephen. It has captured the imagination of people from all over the world. Saroyan is young, in his thirties. To me, his writing is fresh and sharp and tight. Let me read you the finishing lines. They have a certain beauty."

> Then swiftly, neatly, with the grace
> of the young man on the trapeze, he was gone
>   from his body.
> For an eternal moment he was all things at once;
> the bird, the fish, the rodent, the reptile, the man.
> An ocean of print undulated endlessly
>   before him.
> The city burned, the herded crowd rioted,
> The earth circled away, and knowing that, he did to.

He turned his lost face away to the empty sky
and became dreamless, unalive, perfect . . .

Mabel Terry glanced at the strong young man sitting across from her. For a moment, she felt herself becoming warm. She hoped she wasn't red in the face. It had been ages since, in her college days, she'd been touched and thrilled by a young lover but it had come to naught. She straightened herself in her chair and thought, *This young man has promise. He can go far if I help steer him down the right path.* She wondered whether he was condemned by circumstances to be a laborer in the auto plants. He seemed so fired up to read, to learn, and to write.

The teacher and the pupil visited for awhile until he finally thanked her and said he was due home. She invited him to come again any afternoon and promised she'd introduce him to more fine writing.

The next day in school, Mabel Terry spied Virgil Heston in the faculty lunchroom. Her mind had been on the Nagy boy and she decided to confide in Virgil about Nagy's talent. She knew that Virgil had one ambition, to win the State football championship. Nothing would stand in the way of that.

"Virgil," she said, as he downed his second cup of coffee; "Virgil," she repeated, getting him to acknowledge her presence. "You have a student of mine who you're teaching the rudiments of football. I understand he's as good at football as he is at English."

Virgil Heston turned and looked at this little woman whom he'd scarcely even spoken to. He tolerated her because she wasn't all fluff and yack-yack. Mabel knew Heston as a single-minded, rough-hewn man, given to occasional swearing. He was a man who, she felt, lacked the requisite skills to teach the important subjects like math or science or a language. With the teaching code the schools followed, he had to teach one other subject. It was a weak social studies anyone in his class could breeze through.

"Who you talking about, Mabel?"

"I'm speaking about Stephen Nagy."

"Oh, yeah. He's a good one. He'll make All State if he doesn't get hurt. He's fast and strong and . . ."

"He's also my most promising student in American Literature. Someday he'll be a great writer. Don't make him an automaton!"

"A what?"

"Look it up in Webster, Virgil."

Mabel Terry sailed out of the lunch room.

* * *

An inner yearning drew Steve to the old library downtown. He usually sat at a table near the stacks and let his literary wanderings take him on journeys of the mind. In them he roamed, picked, plucked, culled, and stored choices of books and choices of authors, guided by Mabel Terry's recommendations. As he read more and more, it made him wonder what particular spark caused people to write. He thought of all the men and women in unknown villages, tucked away in places he'd never heard of, some of them deep in the recesses of the land, in the valleys and on the great plains and the deep forests and the rolling hills, people who in quiet contemplation wove ideas for all those that came after them.

In his tattered blue notebook he recorded endless notations, passages, paragraphs, sentences, and quotations. These he read and reread late at night as he lay up in his room. The day came when he outgrew his first blue book. Before long his growing collection of writings and jottings became staggering in scope. He categorized everything and saw it steadily accumulate into volumes in hard cover notebooks he carefully labeled. The more he read, the greater his appetite for reading and writing grew.

By his senior year in Northern, he had picked the bones clean of those works that had excited him to the core. He embraced the works of some of the great contemporary writers: Thomas Wolfe, Faulkner, Hemingway, Dos Passos, Saroyan, and Steinbeck. His obsession for words on the printed page became a passion. One passage from Look Homeward, Angel by Wolfe, that unruly, gargantuan man from the hills and hollows of North Carolina, became his favorite. He kept the passage in his wallet, taking it out and reading it over and over until it was part of him.

> A stone, a leaf, an unfound door;
> of a stone, a leaf, a door

And of all the forgotten faces.
Naked and alone we come into exile.
In her dark womb we did not know our
        mother's face;
From the prison of her flesh
have we come into the unspeakable
and incommunicable prison of this earth.
Which of us has known his brother?
Which of us has looked into his father's heart?
Which of us has not remained forever
        prison-pent?
Which of us is not forever a stranger
        and alone?

Young Steve Nagy was overwhelmed by the haunting beauty of the words and the thought of his own life, of his torn relationship with an uncommunicative father. And he thought of his dear mother who walked every day to St. Joseph to light a candle.

The sadness and eloquence of Wolfe's words touched on some profound, universal truth and it pervaded Steve's thoughts. Its intensity and depth made him want to write as Wolfe wrote. It created in his psyche a feeling of loneliness and a deep well of wanting; wanting to share his inner most feelings with someone. It couldn't be Benny Kowalski or Timmie Noonan or Trudy or Charley Maxwell. It couldn't be his mother or his father. None of them would understand his feelings, his emotional highs as he read the great passages and thought about them. There wasn't anyone he could turn to, to share his deepest feelings.

* * *

One day Mabel Terry told Steve to look up two stories by Hemingway. "See if you can find 'Big Two-Hearted River' and 'Death in the Afternoon.' Both will help you. Then we'll talk about them. In what I've seen of your writing, I feel you're reaching for something. You'll find it if you keep on. Hemingway has a capacity to compress emotion without describing it. His perceptions are keen and he burns away anything that isn't essential to the telling."

This afternoon as she poured tea and passed her griddle-fried cornbread, the doorbell rang. When he answered it, a pretty girl with bright red hair and freckles said, "Hello." Miss Terry introduced him to Ellen Sue Rainney and she took a chair near them.

"Now, Stephen," Mabel said, "you've been reading the selections on Hemingway. Give us your impression."

Steve glanced at Ellen Sue, and a little embarrassed, started.

"Well, there was a forward by a writer named Maddox Ford. He said that few things were more complex than Hemingway's simplicity. I liked that."

"Did you mark any passages?"

Steve opened a dog-eared blue notebook and he read a passage. "The river shallow ahead entering the woods, curving into the woods, shallow, light glittering, big water-smooth rocks, cedars among the banks and white birches."

"Beautiful, isn't it?" Mabel said. " 'Big Two-Hearted River' has some passages that are pure delight. That's why I selected it. In that story, a man has come home from the war and goes to his old fishing grounds. Without even mentioning the war, you're aware of his feelings about what he has gone through. How about the other selection?"

" 'Death in the Afternoon,' " Steve said.

"What did you find?"

"Tremendous energy. The motion of the bullfight."

Mabel Terry stood up and offered Ellen Sue some tea and cornbread.

"There's a passage in that story where Hemingway talks about his standards of writing," she said. She went over to a bookcase and ran her hands over a number of books and pulled out one, thumbing through it. "You'll enjoy this, I think."

" 'If a writer of prose knows enough about what he is writing about, he may omit things he knows, and the reader, if the writer is writing truly enough, will have a feeling of these things as strongly as though the writer had stated them.' "

Miss Terry glanced at her two guests and thumbed another page.

" 'The dignity of movement of an iceberg is due to only one-eighth of it being above water. A writer who omits things because he doesn't know them, only makes hollow places in his writing. A writer who appreciated the seriousness of writing so little that he is anxious to make people see he is formally educated, cultured or well-bred is merely a popinjay. This too remember: a serious writer may be a hawk or a buzzard or even a popinjay, but a solemn writer is always a bloody owl.' "

"The metaphor of the iceberg is good," Ellen Sue chimed in.

"It's a marvelous example of the man's writing," Miss Terry exclaimed. "When I read this story, I was right there in that bullfight ring. I felt the fright, I smelled the smells, and I was paralyzed when the bull made his pass."

As Steve spoke again to his mentor, Ellen Sue carefully listened and was impressed. She'd seen him before on the gridiron. It was only the back of his head she glimpsed in American Lit. He seemed nice. Without a lot of male ego sticking out all over him like some of the jocks who gave her the long stare. She hoped they'd meet again.

Steve thought about the redhead on his way home. He liked what he saw. She didn't rattle on like some girls he'd met. Her hair was pretty. Maybe she'd go out with him.

* * *

Her full name was Ellen Sue Rainney. Folks called her Rainy. She was a willowy, freckle-faced redhead from the hills of western Virginia. Her daddy brought the family north when work ran out. When Steve asked her about her life in the south she said, "The soil just seemed to turn against us hard-dirt farmers. So Daddy brought us up here. He got work at Buick in the stamping plant." When Steve asked her where she came from in the South, she laughed and said, "I came from way back in the 'hollers.' That's why my skin is so dark. Maybe you heard that old saying, 'Put it where the sun don't shine.' "

Steve was taken aback by her open, bawdy manner. She had seemed so quiet and reserved at Mabel Terry's. Yet what she sometimes said seemed natural and inoffensive. She was fun to be with and her cheery manner brought sunshine into his life. She had lovely hazel eyes and her skin was olive dark, her hair flame-red. They bumped into each other at the old library a few weeks after they met at Miss Terry's. Both were in the stacks looking for selections by Faulkner so they sat at a table in an alcove and talked, their books scattered on the table.

In a sudden inspiration, Steven opened one of his worn notebooks and showed her a passage from <u>The Sound and the Fury</u> by Faulkner. In it, Faulkner described a Negro church in the rural south. The preacher played the parishioners like a pipe organ, powerfully bringing them to an emotional crescendo, letting them see Jesus in their midst. As Steve spoke and read to her, Ellen Sue found herself listening to this earnest, enthusiastic young man, and a sensual arousal stirred in her. It was the first man she had felt this way about and she felt warmth surge in her body. She felt she had to cover up her feelings and said to him, "How'd you get started in your love of literature?"

"Same as you," he answered. "Mabel Terry." As he said it, his eyes never left her face and he felt a deep stirring inside. He wanted to tell her what he'd been thinking about in the library before they met and she saw the look on his face.

"What is it? You look like you want to tell me something."

"I come down here from school, Rainy, and a lot of things go through my head."

"Like what?"

"Well, I don't know . . . I want to put down on paper all the things that run through my mind. Before you came in, I read a poem. By Wendell Berry. A farmer from Kentucky."

Steve showed her the poem he'd put down in his notebook.

"It's an excerpt from a poem called 'Boone.' "

> In winter the river hides its flowing under the
> ice bearing interminable down; the black crow
> flies into the black night;
> the bones of the old dead echo for the house fires.

"Umm," she said. "I like that." She tingled and felt flushed.

Suddenly he leaned over and said to her, "Until now, the only person I could talk to was Miss Terry. Now I have you." His face was warm and he felt drawn to her.

"You see," he went on, "the river. It's under the ice. It's powerful. It's always moving. It's like life, Rainy. It's all around you. You take it for granted. Then you realize you're part of something much bigger, something grander than anything you've ever experienced."

Emotion flooded through him and his voice cracked. She reached over and touched his hand. "I know," she said.

He felt close to her and he wanted to take her in his arms and hold her. Then he went on.

"The part about the crow, Rainy. I want to feel like that black crow flying on a dark night. I want to feel it. I start thinking of things that are black; like the robes of Father Ferency at St. Josephs, like a black man standing in a dark room with the lights off. I see these images and I want to write about them. The man in the room. The lights out. He stands there and he stares out the window at the black night. The winds howl and they sweep in an open window."

Steve's heart thumped and his hands started to sweat. She took one of his hands and said, "It's a new world for you. You're like a little boy with a shiny penny in his hand. He's at the candy store and he sees jawbreakers and sticky hats and licorice sticks and he wants them all."

She smiled up at him and continued to hold his hand.

"He faces one of life's sweet dilemmas."

Rainy put her face close to his and a wicked grin came over her face. "It's like the midget that married the fat lady. On their wedding night he said to her, 'Acres and acres, and they're all mine.' " Rainy laughed as her freckles bobbed up and down.

There's that ragged streak, Steve thought. *She's different from anyone I ever met; different and lovable.*

* * *

Steve and Benny sat in Little Joe's late one afternoon.

"You're nuts about her, aren't you?" Benny asked.

Steve laughed and admitted, "You're goddamn right I am. I'm crazy about her!"

Ellen Sue and Steve were now a twosome and they met whenever they could. They talked of many things, things they couldn't talk to anyone else about. It was what they both wanted and needed and it seemed providential that this beautiful redhead had come into his life. There was one problem that kept coming up. She was flesh and blood and it put his body in turmoil. He wanted Ellen Sue.

One weekend they sat by the stacks in the old library and he suddenly said to her, "Will you go to mass with me on Sunday? I want you to meet Father Ferency."

Steve saw terror form in her eyes and she didn't speak for a moment.

"What is it?" he asked.

She put her hands in his lap and slowly said, "I'm afraid. I don't know."

He'd never seen her like this. He sat for a moment without saying anything, holding her hands. Finally she said, "I've never gone back. Something happened." She took her hands away and turned away from him, and he could tell she was crying softly.

He didn't know what to do, so he did nothing, waiting. Finally, she turned to him and said, "I don't go to church. I had an experience. Down home."

"An experience. What kind of an experience?"

She shuddered and was silent.

"Do you want to tell me?"

"I . . . I guess so. I don't like to think about it. I was seven. My folks took me to my first prayer meeting one night. It'd been snowing and we had to walk. It was a long walk, maybe a mile or more. My daddy, my mother, sister Evaline and me."

"I didn't know you had a sister."

"She was eleven."

"Like you, red hair?"

Rainy said "No" with a sad expression on her face.

"I walked alongside her," she said. "I had brand new patent leather shoes and a red taffeta dress my mother bought me and my coat over it. She made most of my clothes, but this came from Clarksburg, the nearest town nine miles away. It was my first dress she ever bought for me. There was a big full-length mirror in the store and I twirled in front of it and Evaline teased me. She had a new dress too.

"We walked down a path that started at the back of our forty and we crossed this ridge that hid the church from view. We were joined by other families coming over the ridge. From the top, we saw the whole valley and the church spire. There must have been thirty of us, walking down the mountain. It was coming on dusk and lights began to twinkle in the valley. People all had flashlights. The snow fell softly and my feet were wet. Evaline poked me in the back and made fun of me and I poked her back.

"The church was a white frame building with a tall, narrow steeple. All the lights were on and we went in and sat in a pew near the front. The preacher was a tall, gangly redhead and he got right into it; preaching hellfire and damnation. He peered over his thin gold spectacles that hung down over his nose and ears. He shouted at us. Then his voice fell away and he wept, tears running down his face. I sat up to hear what he said as he whispered through his tears with his voice real soft. Then his voice came back strong and it rose until it hit the rafters. He harangued us about the sins of the flesh and proclaimed that Jesus was right there in our midst. Jesus saw all our evil doings and we were all miserable sinners. He exhorted us to change our evil ways and to follow the true Christ. His eyes stared at me and they were wild-looking, like a yellow bobcat! His hair was the color of fire and I squirmed in my pew. I was scared to death. I twitched and cried and Evaline held me while the preacher kept on going. His words swooped up one side of the aisle and down the other and then he cried again. He took off his gold spectacles, took out a big red handkerchief and he wiped them, then his eyes. Then he talked low again, like he was confiding in us.

"At one point I remember he screamed and raved and spittle formed on his chin and ran down his face. It was disgusting. His eyeglasses fell further down his nose. He took his hands and ran them through his hair."

"I can see why you were scared," Steve said.

"I really was. Then he went into this long monologue, something like, 'Jesus, Jesus, Lord God Almighty, God of all the Hosts . . . Jesus, save these miserable sinners; save these children from the great fire that burns, that great consuming fire of eternal hell! Bring these poor sinners, these creatures of desire and lust and temptation back into the fold, bring them back into your everlasting arms! Save them from the horrible flames that will ravage them throughout all eternity! Save them, Jesus!'

"I wanted to crawl into a hole, Stephen. I shrank closer to Evaline and gripped her hands. I looked over at my daddy and my mom. Their eyes were glazed like they were in a trance. They looked like they'd jump out of their clothes if the preacher asked them to.

"That's when the door to the church opened and some rough, burly people came stomping up the aisle toward the altar. They carried live snakes around their necks and the snakes coiled and hissed and looked at me. They weren't your little old garter snake variety, but big diamondback rattlers that buzzed. I heard them and saw their evil faces and I was petrified with fear and I wet my pants."

Steve laughed as he held her. She didn't think it was funny.

"A woman in front of me screamed and fell on the floor out of her pew. I thought the snakes had bitten her and I lost it. I threw up all over everything, my coat, my new dress, and my shoes." Rainy shook as she said the words.

"What an experience," Steve commented.

She looked at him with a weak smile and continued, "For years after that, I had terrible dreams. Snakes came after me and I'd wake up screaming. My folks finally took me to a clinic in Morgantown."

He wanted to say something to comfort her as she looked off into space. "It was such a beautiful dress. I never wore it again."

They left the library and started down the street toward his car. "I'd still like to have you meet Father Ferency," he said.

She mused a moment as if she hadn't heard him and said, "I dearly loved that ridge above the valley. Evaline and I played on it in the summertime. We were close as sisters. In the spring, we picked chokeberries on the ridge."

"Like a raspberry?"

"Not really. The fruit is red and black, sometimes purple. It's bitter. Momma added sugar and something else and they were wonderful when cooked. I remember one day when we picked them; the leaves had a beautiful green sheen and the fruit was bright and clean and sparkly. We picked a wicker basket full and Momma made jelly."

"Where's your sister now?"

"We lost her, Stephen." She stopped to cry with her head down. After awhile, she wiped her face with a handkerchief. "We loved her very much. Two years before we came north, she got cancer. One day after school, she came up to our bedroom and she had this funny look on her face." Rainy choked up, then settled herself, and went on. "She took one of my hands and put it on the back of her neck. I felt this hard lump. I was scared and I had a hard time not showing it. We went downstairs where Momma was making supper. She showed Momma. Momma was calm and said it wasn't anything to worry about. When Daddy came in from the barn, Momma took him aside.

"Next day we took the bus to Morgantown. They took x-rays and put Evaline in the hospital. We didn't hear for three days. Didn't have a phone. Neighbors did. Daddy came back from the neighbor's and said we had to go to town.

"She was nineteen. So beautiful and wonderful. Never came home. In a month she was gone. I still see her eyes staring at me from the ward."

They were both silent. They sat in Steve's car for a few moments and didn't say a word. They knew their life together was just beginning.

* * *

A few weeks later on Sunday, December 7th, 1941, Rainy agreed to go to mass with Steve. On their way to the church he told her, "I was an altar boy under Father Ferency. His first name is Hippolyte."

"What was that like?" she asked.

"He trained me. We have maybe one hundred and fifty Hungarian families in the church. I started when I was ten. Took evening devotions. The novenas lasted half an hour and I had to kneel for over twenty minutes. Then I helped serve mass. I put charcoal in the thurifier, took the top off, lighted it. I stared at the fourteen stations of the cross. I had to study Latin which I hated and I had to memorize all the responses. Had nine weeks of novenas. We met once a week, the altar boys. We prayed to a saint. I had to memorize the Act of Contrition and the Act of Hope. I smelled the incense burning, saw the gold in the mosaics, looked at the figure of Christ with his hands stretched out. Then I watched Father Hippolyte genuflect before a

91

crucifix and hold aloft the chalice. When the service was finally over, I put out the candles, washed the cruets, and hung my cassock and surplice in a closet."

"So you're a Catholic," she remarked. "I couldn't be one. You may as well know that."

"I understand," he said as they entered the ancient church on Hickory Street. They attended an early mass seated in the last row of the pews where she could make a quick exit if she had to. Rainy loved the mustiness of the church in "Little Europe" and the soft reflection of the lighted candles on the rough walls and the smell of incense in the censers.

"Funny thing," he said, "in the old days they didn't have pews. The service was two hours long and a bearcat on everyone. If you were a boy, you stood with your father on the left side. If you were a girl, you stood with your mother on the right side. Then when they finally raised enough money for pews, the service was cut to an hour and a half."

Rainy tried to follow the mass in the book and was befuddled by the sudden rising and sitting. After the mass, they met Father Ferency.

"Anything new on your scholarship, Steve?" the father asked.

"Father, Coach told me the other day I should hear soon. I signed the papers and he wrote a personal letter to Duffy Daugherty, the coach at Michigan State."

"What about your friend Benny?"

"He's talking to the Army. They think he'd make good officer material."

Father Ferency handed Rainy a small book. He knew they were in the first stages of love. "Miss Rainney," he said, "this is a little treasure of a book by Kahlil Gibran. It says things that come from the heart. I want you to have it because I am fond of Steve and I wish you both much happiness."

Rainy thanked the old priest and glanced at the book while they drove the fourteen blocks to the Nagy home. She noted that it was well-worn, with some passages marked, and with some beautiful illustrations.

Steve and Rainy sat in the warm kitchen with Mother and Father Nagy and enjoyed a dinner of Hungarian goulash, egg noodles, and crescents with levkar fillings. Frank Nagy brought up some homemade beer from the basement. The radio was on in the kitchen and a symphony was playing. Suddenly the music stopped and the voice of an announcer came on. There was a lot of static and Steve turned up the volume. The man was hard to hear and he repeated a message over and over. It sounded as if the man was crying: "The Japanese bombed Pearl Harbor in the Hawaiian Islands."

* * *

Little Joe's was packed, many servicemen sitting in booths, home on leave. Everyone's life had dramatically changed since that fateful day in December of 1941. The day after Pearl Harbor, Steve enlisted in the Army. "You got mebbe three months, mebbe more before you go," a sergeant in recruiting said. Benny Kowalski also waited his call and Noonan had already left for the service.

Steve and Rainy sat in a booth with Benny and his girl and Trudy sat beside them. Two bartenders had been hired to take care of the additional business that flowed in.

The news was bad. The Japanese advanced on all fronts and America now knew of the terrible price it had paid in the islands. Thousands of young American men lay at the bottom of the harbor in sealed battleships. Many more were in prison camps in the Far East. On the west coast of the United States, Japanese-Americans were being rounded up and forced to sell most of their possessions. They were being herded into camps in the desert away from the coast. At the same time, troop trains rolled west, their sections jammed with both soldiers and ammunition destined for Pacific action.

"You hear about the Nakamura family on Nebraska?" Benny asked.

"Yeah," Steve answered. "Somebody burned crosses on their lawn, smashed windows, and hurled rocks. Christ, we played against John. He was a good scat-back at Central. Didn't weigh over a hundred and forty. Somebody told me that the government turned him down when he tried to enlist. They classified him as 4F because he has some Japanese blood."

"I hear the family is leaving town. Wherever they go, they'll run into punks who'll make it tough for them," Benny said. He looked over at Rainy and Steve and smiled, "When you two getting hitched?" Trudy heard the question and hunched forward to hear the answer.

Steve had a pained look on his face. "Okay, you guys, Rainy and I have an understanding."

That was the signal for Trudy to put her two cents in. "You men are all alike. Your male ego gets in the way. Marry the girl. Let nature take its course. Quit trying to figure everything out to the T. Enjoy life; it's shorter than you think. Walter and I had some good years before he passed away. Don't play God, Steve." She patted him on the shoulder and went back behind the bar.

* * *

Nineteen hundred forty-three rolled around before Steve's orders came through. Rainy and he sat with his folks in the front parlor. All the plastic covers had been removed.

"What do you hear from Benny?" his father asked.

"Not much, Pop. He's in Africa with the 3rd Division. The last time I heard a couple of months ago, they were fighting Rommel in the mountains."

"And Noonan?"

"In tanks under Patton. Still a private. He must have screwed up and didn't get his stripes."

"What about you two? We gonna have a wedding before you go?"

"Jesus, Pop! I leave in ten days!"

"You gave her a ring a long time ago."

Rainy sat and enjoyed her future father-in-law's candor. She was playful around him and it made him feel good.

"Tell your Dad," Rainy said. "Tell him how we left it."

"For Christ sake, Rainy. That's not Pop's business."

"Seems to me it's family business," she replied. She warmed to the conversation, hoping against hope he'd change his mind and she'd be a war bride.

"Okay," Steve stated, "we're getting married when the war is over. The only difference is if I don't get a combat assignment and end up in a clerk's job. That's not going to happen. Now lay off."

Rainy remembered how they'd sat up half the night in the hotel in Detroit talking about her desire for marriage and she'd finally seen she couldn't budge Steve. The next day at home, she'd had dinner with the Nagys and before dinner had sat around with Mother Nagy in her kitchen and confided to Sophie of her many unsuccessful attempts. Sophie Nagy put her stubby arms around Rainy, her body smelling of washing machine soap and cabbage soup. They both had a good cry.

"I want his child, Mama. I love him so much. He's stubborn like a mule."

"Just like my man," Sophie said. "When they get their minds set, they don't change."

* * *

That afternoon in the parlor after dinner, Steve picked up the Flint Journal and read a front page story about the Japanese-American families forced into the desert internment camps. The article stated that the government had now come up with a plan for all Japanese-American males, seventeen and over. An all-Nisei regiment was forming and men could leave the internment camps and serve their country. Another article on the page questioned the wisdom of denying over one hundred and forty thousand people their freedom by placing them in the camps.

"Here we are," Steve commented, "fighting a war and we don't even trust our own people. It's tragic what they did to the Japanese-Americans on the west coast. Now we turn around and say to those young guys in these internment camps, 'We'll keep your parents cooped up and the rest of your family until the war is over, but you can come and fight for us now.' If I were those young men, I'd tell the government to go screw itself!"

"Never should have let them people in this country in the first place!" Steve's father announced abruptly.

Steve couldn't believe his ears. His anger mounted and as he exploded, Rainy said to herself, *Here we go again. It's like living with two bobcats.*

"That's bullshit!" Steve hollered. "They let you and mother in from Hungary. What's the difference?"

Rainy tried to stop him as he started to leave the parlor.

"Don't leave like this!" she pleaded.

Steve hollered again, "What have you got against those people?"

Frank Nagy rose from the sofa, his dander up.

"Listen to me, you hot-head. Those people are yellow-skinned. If they stayed where they belonged, this would never have happened!"

"I can't believe what I'm hearing!"

"You better believe it. They don't belong here. They all got slanted eyes and wear pigtails!"

Steve faced his father. "You know what you are? You're an ignorant son-of-a-bitch!"

Sophie Nagy's heart ached and she was in tears. This kind of talk would lose her son forever. Staring at her husband, her eyes pleaded him to stop. Frank Nagy didn't back down, didn't give an inch. Sophie turned to her son in supplication.

"We're outta here," Steve said. He kissed his mother and took Rainy strongly by the hand and they left.

* * *

A teary-eyed mother and a proud redhead said good-bye to Steve at the station on the south side of town. A troop train stood on the tracks, with people waving and shouting to loved ones, and young men looking at them from the windows of the train.

A silent middle-aged man sat fidgeting in his bedroom, his stomach churning and his head pounding. He got up from his rocker and stared at himself in the mirror. What he saw wasn't pleasing. He and his son hadn't settled anything. His hands shook as he held a short note and read it over and over.

>   Dear Pop,
>   You and I speak different languages. I don't know if we can ever speak the same language. I love you very much. Take care of Sophie and my Rainy. You and I have a lot to learn.
>
>   Your son,
>   Steve

96

Three Young Men: Steve

Section 1.03 Jimmy

"Big Fish! Big Fish!" Tony Watanabe yelled from the bow of the Sato II. In the gathering light, the rolling Pacific gleamed emerald-green. Sixty Nisei boats rode the waves as men in yellow slickers moved on slippery decks. As if on command, the tuna fleet formed in circles and moved in on the feeding fish. Men armed with long, stout bamboo poles cast bright-feathered jigs as tuna fed on a surface ripe with anchovy. With the heavy weight of the tuna, fishermen hooked their poles to a single line and hoisted together.

It was Sunday, December 5, 1941. The tuna fleet was out in force on the Sabbath. The catches had been enormous and Father Simeon Tanaka understood. In the early morning darkness, he blessed the crews and the fleet.

Toshio Sato smiled at his son, Jimmy, as his son opened the bow hatch. Tony Watanabe and Big John Matsu shouted friendly insults as they stood on the wet deck of the Sato II bringing in great coppery-blue tuna. The men's backs ached from the sheer weight they hoisted and the fish glistened in the growing patches of sunlight. Always the men were amazed at the slashing attack of the great fish and their gargantuan appetite. The contest between men and fish went on ceaselessly for hours as the tiny fleet drifted in the troughs, and the boats began to fill with tuna.

Big John Matsu grinned at Tony and raised his right arm in a familiar, obscene gesture. The middle finger on his right hand was extended and the other fingers and thumb curled down.

"Look out, tonight, old woman!" he shouted. "I'm after you!"

A day's good catch meant an evening of lovemaking on Terminal Island. Many a child born on the island had been conceived after a fruitful day on the sea.

Sunlight split the fog and in the striking light, a carpet of tuna lay between the circling boats. "You can walk on their backs!" Jimmy shouted to his father. The slickers of the men were wet with spray and their heavy boots squished into fish flesh.

Tony and Matsu hooked their poles and brought in massive, wriggling yellow-tails. The bodies of the fish were lustrous and iridescent and their bulk was dumped on the deck and transferred to the hatches. Tony and John reset their lines with yellow and orange jigs.

Toshio Sato spoke to his son. "I do not like what I hear."

"What do you hear, Father?"

"I've spoken to the elders. None of us trust the Japanese envoys the Emperor sent to Washington."

"I don't either," Jimmy answered. "The war party in Japan calls the shots. We may have to fight them someday."

"You mean war?" the old man asked, his features dark and grim.

"It could come to that," Jimmy declared.

Toshio Sato heard his son's words and they cast a pall on him as he sat holding the wheel. He thought of his years as a boy in Japan leading up to the time he had come to America. He saw his father holding a jeweled sword case and removing a sword from the case. His father taught young Toshio the ancient moves, moves sharp and clean, moves that made Toshio worship his father. It was the way of the Samurai, the sacred way, the way of the Satsuma clan. He thought of that day in 1901 when he left Japan for the states. His father presented the jeweled case and sword to him and he told him to hand it down to the first born male in the new country. Through the veil of time, Toshio again held the hand of his bride, Minniemata.

It had been a terrible time for them as they tried to sleep on the open deck of a rusted tramp steamer. Heavy storms swept over the ship as they held each other. When they finally landed in San Pedro, they had only sixty yen with them; one hundred and twenty dollars in U.S. money. He hired on as a tuna man and worked hard and saved his money. They watched their two children grow into adulthood. Then Minniemata had died. And in all those years, he had never been given what he wanted the most, the paper that said he was a citizen.

The fishing became intense as the bow and rear hatches filled. Salt air and the smell of tuna mingled with the odors of gasoline fumes and perspiration. Toshio momentarily left the wheel and worked with Tony and John, washing down the deck, loading the hatches and resetting the lures. Tony stood beside Toshio and spoke to him in a voice filled with elation and respect.

"Toshio-san, this is like the old days when the big fish stood on their tails and danced."

"We are honored by them," Toshio replied. "If we treat them with reverence, there will be many good days."

But there weren't any other good days. Shouts whipped across the water; gun shots echoed as neck muscles tightened. The many circles of boats broke off as strange voices rose on the wind. A sleek Coast Guard cutter bearing the flag of the United States broke through the murk, its siren wailing. A guardsman was seen on the deck firing a shot into the air. In the distance, another cutter bore down as a voice came through a bullhorn:

"This is an official order from the United States Government! This is an order. Form your boats into a single line and proceed to your docks at Terminal Island. When you arrive, berth your ship and do not leave it. Do not leave your ship. Do not take your catch to the cannery until officially notified by a Coast Guard officer. Do not leave your ship! I repeat. This is an official order from the United States Government!"

"Now it begins," Toshio muttered.

Three hundred tuna men in yellow slickers stared in wonderment and disbelief. Something terrible had happened to make the Coast Guard intercept them. Was it an earthquake? Had their homes been destroyed? Had the canneries caught fire with many lives lost? Was it something more sinister?

Sixty Nisei boats formed in line as blue-jacketed sailors manned machine guns and officers shouted into bullhorns. As Jimmy took the wheel from his father, his face drew dark and his shoulders tightened. Toshio stood silent near the bow, thinking the worst, and Tony and John stood grim-faced, locked in their thoughts.

Big John broke the silence. "What has happened?"

There was no reply.

Matsu turned to Toshio. "What do you think, Toshio-san?"

Toshio's face was tight. "I am afraid. Afraid for my people."

The boats began to move in a line to the east with the Coast Guard cutters behind them. Soon Catalina Island came into view. Its orange-colored Ferris wheel looked dull in the swirling fog. No one spoke on the Sato II. John Matsu stared at Tony Watanabe's heavily muscled back, his slicker streaked with ocean salt.

Terminal Island stood in the gloom. Crowds of people hugged the docks as boats slowed and moved into their slips. Coast Guard jeeps flashed blue lights and armed blue-jackets held the crowd back. Women wailed as they held their small children close.

Toshio's head was down and he muttered as he stood at the bow. Engines were cut and Matsu secured the Sato II to the dock. Blue-jackets walked the docks with rifles cradled in their arms. Women reached out to their men and were held back. Tony and Jimmy wiped down the twin engines and Matsu unloaded fish from the hatches into heavy wicker baskets. Jimmy and Tony joined him as Coast Guard officers walked down the line of boats. Each officer carried a clipboard and started to board the boats.

An officer looked down at the men on the Sato II.

"Who's in charge here?" he asked sharply.

"I am," snapped Jimmy.

"Pearl Harbor in Hawaii was attacked this morning by the Japanese."

* * *

The men on the Sato II were stunned. They looked up at the officer as Jimmy fought to recover his voice, "What are we to do?"

"I need your names and addresses and the names of each member of your household." The fishermen took turns giving him the information. "Take your fish to the cannery when I tell you to. When you're through at the cannery, go directly home. When you get there, stay inside. Turn your radio on to a Los Angeles station. Information will be given to you."

The officer addressed Jimmy. "Hand over your keys to the vessel and any papers. Give me the name of the vessel and I'll write out a receipt." After Jimmy had given the officer what he wanted and the officer had given Jimmy a written receipt, the officer turned abruptly and went to the next boat in line.

The men filled the baskets and closed the hatches. Toshio stood silently. Jimmy put an arm around him. "Father, Yoki is at the cannery. We must go."

Toshio wearily walked with the crew as they carried their baskets. Suddenly Matsu cried out, "I see her. I see Sarah." Jimmy looked down the long dockside and saw his wife standing in the crowd. She was taller than the other woman and was white. They had married five years before and celebrated by renting a car and driven down to the Mexican border where they spent four days and nights of unbridled passion. Jimmy waved to Sarah and indicated he'd meet her at the dock when they were through at the cannery. As they walked, the crew was joined by other fishermen carrying baskets.

Jimmy wondered what would happen next. If he lost his boat, they would only have their savings to fall back on. He couldn't believe what was happening. The tuna men were the lifeblood of the tuna industry. The canneries couldn't operate without them. Economics told him he'd get his boat back. He was aware of the enmity of some whites on the mainland to those of Japanese ancestry. A war with Japan meant nothing but misery and hardship for the islanders.

The cannery loomed ahead, its metal sides gray and rusting in the fog. Yoki Sato bent over a slick rubber mat that moved tuna to be gutted and sliced and packaged. Even after word had flashed through the cannery of the attack on Pearl Harbor, the lines still ran. The fish had to be processed or the cannery would lose thousands of dollars. Yoki bent her knees as she picked up a fish with a steel spike and gutted it with a sharp knife. She threw the entrails into a bucket and the good parts back on the line where others would strip the flesh and cut it. Her back and leg muscles ached and she thought of her mother, Minnie, who had worked beside her on the line until cancer had killed her. She missed her mother and her loving spirit and felt alone. Her girlhood friends were few as many had moved to the mainland for better jobs. Most of those left were trashy and spent all their time talking about their white lovers on the mainland. She loved Sarah who was like a sister to her, but Sarah was gone a lot of the time on photography assignments. Yoki patiently waited for the shift whistle so she could get her things from her locker and go home to her father's house. She'd call Sarah and they'd talk together about what had happened. Did it mean war? What would happen to the people on the island? To her father, to her, to Jimmy, to Sarah?

The crew of the Sato II stood in line at the cannery until it was their turn to weigh their fish and get a receipt. The fish were finally weighed in the baskets and then dumped into a vat running to the fish platform. Jimmy and his father walked down the line until they spied Yoki.

"Go home when the shift changes," Jimmy shouted over the noise of the line. "Father will be there."

Yoki hollered back, "What'll happen to Sarah?"

"She's at the docks," Jimmy yelled.

Father and son left the cannery and walked back to the long dock where Sarah stood. Jimmy went to her and held her.

"I must go," Toshio said. "I'll call the League and then the elders." The old man left his son and daughter-in-law and started up a dirt pathway toward his house. It led over a small rise and down to the bay facing Los Angeles. His house was modest and built out of frame with a tin roof, resting on stilts driven into the shoreline. He walked across a passageway which was over water when the tide came in. He opened the front door and entered the central room which had a large teakwood cabinet in a corner. He opened the cabinet door and lifted out a long, jeweled leather case. Unbuckling the case, he carefully removed a long samurai ceremonial sword that glistened in the light. He laid it on a table and picked up the telephone to dial.

"Japanese League, Frank Issei."

"Toshio Sato on Terminal."

"Are you home?"

"Yes, I came from the docks. The Coast Guard has taken all the boats."

"We know. We meet with them at four o'clock to get them released."

"You think it's temporary."

"We believe so. The tuna men are vital to the trade. The canneries need them. Whites never matched Terminal in production."

"What must I tell the other elders, Frank?"

"Calm everyone's fears. It will be a difficult time. Roosevelt meets tomorrow with the joint houses. He will declare war."

"Call me when you know more."

"I will. Many of our people have already been jailed. Two of our people are on their way to Washington as I speak. Anyone without citizenship papers will be scrutinized. You're still a subject of the Emperor. You swore allegiance to him. Advise the elders that the people must rid themselves of anything that appears as a weapon."

"Thank you, Frank. I'll call the elders. Tomorrow we meet in the Community Building. Can you be here?"

"I will have someone there. What time?"

"Eleven."

Toshio's hands started to shake as he put down the phone. Perspiration formed on his forehead and he felt weak. He sat for a moment and his eyes fell on the sword. A vision formed of his father handing it to him in their village. He picked up the sword and went outside and across the passageway. On the land overlooking the bay, he and Minniemata had made a garden. He strode into the garden and stopped before a small fish pond. He stared at the orange-colored fish safe in their home. He kicked at the soft earth near the pond and with a strong move, thrust the blade into the yielding soil until it was buried from sight. He wiped his hands on his soiled fishing clothes and looked where the sword was hidden.

"It will be safe here for my son."

He walked back across the passageway into his house and phoned the elders.

* * *

Three hundred bewildered and upset tuna men jammed the small Community Building the next day at eleven o'clock. They came through a heavy offshore gale in their boots and slickers and sat in folding chairs. Restless and unnerved, uncertain of themselves, they came for answers from the Japanese League, their representative in matters pertaining to the government, to fishing rights, the price of their fish at the canneries, and other issues vital to their livelihood. Many had heard rumors their boats were going to be sold to only white bidders, others that the authorities would soon be on the island to question them as to their patriotism or lack of.

The heat in the little building was stifling and the men were noisy. They were in no mood to sit and wait for answers. Sweat rolled down their faces and tempers flared. No one stood on the stage and it was fifteen minutes after eleven. Jimmy, Tony, and John sat together in a row.

"I got nothing," John said. "If we don't fish, I don't eat. I got about two weeks of savings. That's all."

The mood was one of pessimism and anger as Toshio Sato strode from one of the wings on the stage and stepped to the microphone. He was Chairman of the Tuna Men's Association on the island and the leading elder.

"Gentlemen, we're waiting for the League. Be patient. They promised to be here. Perhaps the ferry was late." Toshio took a seat at the back of the stage.

If this was a meeting of young men and their elders in Japan, it would have been one of strict obedience to their peers. Protocol would be followed and no one would speak unless asked to by an elder. Conformity and discipline had been drilled into the old Japanese and their children. But this was not the case at Terminal Island. These tuna men were U.S. born and considered themselves one hundred percent American, with American ideals and an American culture. True, their fathers were Issei (from the old country), but American values and ideas had taken over. These young men wanted answers, action, solutions and they wanted them pronto. Their livelihood was on the line and the League wasn't there. It was no time for formality or ancient tradition from a faraway land. Rumors flew around the room like startled birds. These men had families to raise and mouths to feed.

Toshio Sato was uncomfortable. Boots thumped the floor and men shouted. One man stood up and hollered, "The docks are off-limits. We can't get to our boats!" Another stood up and yelled, "I just came from the bank. You can only take out $100 a month. The manager told me the rest of my money was frozen by the government!"

Toshio stood up and started for the microphone as the front door opened and a rush of cool air blew through the building. A man in a top coat and a silk hat came down the aisle, his clothing a sharp contrast to the rough garb of the fishermen. He was invited upon the stage by Toshio, who shook his hand and helped him take his coat off. The man sat down in a chair at the back of the stage. Toshio came to the mike to announce, "Gentlemen, the representative from the League is here. This is Franklin Hirada. Give him the courtesy of your attention."

No one was more out of place than Frank Hirada. He was a tall, very thin, bespectacled man whose glasses hung precariously on a thin, soft nose. He had never set foot on Terminal Island. Dressed in a fine silk suit and carrying a very heavy briefcase, he felt ill at ease. His voice came over the microphone as high-pitched and nasal, almost effeminate. With no timbre in his voice and its high pitch, he immediately lost any effectiveness. The words that came out of his mouth were of little consequence, words about things that the men already knew.

"Our League has someone now in Washington. We will hear from him tomorrow. You must be patient until we know more. Please stay on your radios and keep everyone indoors. I don't know about your boats."

Hirada was shouted down by a man who shook his fist at him and hollered, "We pay you guys plenty. We can't wait for you to tell us what to do. We don't have our boats! We can't get our money!"

Completely unnerved, Hirada started to back up and shake. Toshio Sato stepped up to the microphone. "I am still in charge here," Toshio said in a stern voice.

Momentarily the men were stilled and Toshio asked Hirada if he had anything more to say. He answered meekly that he didn't. Angry shouts rose and Toshio quickly said, "Gentlemen, this meeting is adjourned. We will notify you of the next meeting." With that, he walked off the stage and left Frank Hirada sitting alone.

Pandemonium swept the hall as angry men stood and vented their feelings. Jimmy stayed and waited for his father. He said to him, "He told us nothing. Nothing at all. What do you make of it?"

The answer came from deep inside his father. "No one knows. I see much sorrow ahead. Come with me to the house. I buried the sword."

Jimmy knew how much the sword meant. "Where?"

"By the fish pond."

They walked into the garden and Toshio pointed to the place in the ground. "When this is all over some day, you can claim it. Now go to Sarah. She needs your strength."

As his father spoke the words, an image formed in Jimmy's mind. A tall, radiant white woman clothed in a yellow rain slicker, wearing fisherman's boots, walked down the docks and stood before the crew of the Sato II. She introduced herself and was helped aboard by John and Tony. Jimmy had been informed by the dock keeper a few days before that a photographer from the mainland had been assigned to the Sato II. The photographer was to take pictures for the Los Angeles Sun-Times. The pictures were to depict the life of a tuna man and an essay would accompany the photographs.

That was five years ago. After that day on the rolling Pacific, he had fallen in love with her. He had pursued her madly until she had accepted his bid to be her husband and she to be his bride.

That day five years ago had been the day Sarah Hogue had perfectly caught the scenes of the slashing tuna, the men with their poles hooked together as they brought in the great yellow-tails, those wriggling, coppery-blue fish that had been placed in the bow and rear hatches. It was a day of boiling seas and enormous anchovy masses. The great fish tore into them as the fleet drifted on the green-gold surfaces, surfaces that changed to emerald and blue-black when the clouds formed.

That was the beginning of his life with beautiful, talented Sarah, a life centered in his tiny shack on stilts, its roof streaked with sea salt. He found a woman who fulfilled his desires; a sensuous, beautiful, intelligent woman who taught him what every man should know about a woman, who was unafraid and untouched by the unending gossip of the female islanders who found it hard to accept a white woman in their midst. Those had been years of sacrifice for Sarah as she attempted to fit in to an unknown culture. Early on, she accepted her position as an outsider, and seemed to revel in it. He realized she had great talents with a lens and that from time to time, she would be miles away on some exotic assignment that added to her growing reputation as one of the finest women photographers in the country. Not once did he feel he was playing second fiddle. It became a marriage of two equal, independent, loving people. Sarah Hogue Sato became the darling of the tuna fleet, much to the chagrin of the lady islanders.

As he walked down the hill toward home, he wondered what might happen to their relationship as the darkness of war descended. He walked into the house and held her in his arms. She said to him, "There's talk in the Times of shipping all those of Japanese blood back to Japan."

He replied laughingly, "Christ, Sarah, they don't have enough ships!" She broke into tears and sat for a moment with him. Then she composed herself and handed him the mainland papers. A headline read "U.S. FLEET SUNK AT PEARL HARBOR." Under the heading was a sub-heading that read, "JAPS FEARED LANDING IN LOS ANGELES." Below this was a wire service feature that said "ALL PEOPLE OF JAPANESE BLOOD SHOULD BE IMMEDIATELY DEPORTED."

Jimmy read the headlines again. The phone rang and it was Matsu.

"The boats are gone, Jim."

"You know for sure, John?"

"Dock keeper told me they moved 'em across the bay to San Pedro."

* * *

Shock and dismay spread across the island. The boats were gone, and with them, the livelihood of the tuna men. People were grief stricken and openly wept.

"Better get out the Nikon," Sarah said. "I'll get another assignment. We're in better shape than a lot of people. I'll go to the mainland tomorrow and see my boss."

Sarah went into their tiny kitchen and pulled out a bottle of bourbon. She made them both a drink. She brought them back and handed one to Jimmy. The phone rang and it was Jimmy's father.

"Don't worry about money. I put some in a safe place, not a bank. Have you read the Herald today? The government is thinking of moving all Japanese families away from the coast. I have to hang up, I'm calling the elders for the next meeting."

Jimmy was used to his father's manner of speaking over the phone. One short sentence followed another. Rarely did his father allow any interruption of his thinking processes. As Jimmy hung up, a chill hit him.

"Things are happening too fast," he said.

* * *

Sarah's mind whirled as she sipped her bourbon. She'd been raised in an orphanage in Los Angeles and hadn't known her parents. When in junior high school, she had been given a Brownie camera by a friendly teacher. It soon possessed her life. By the time she graduated from high school, she was the president of her Camera Club at school and had won a local newspaper contest with her photographs of faces of people at the Los Angeles Zoo. From then on, she photographed anything and everything and hired on as a staff photographer at the Sun-Times when she was twenty. The camera was her stock in trade and she developed a reputation for excellent work.

As she sat with her Nisei husband, she asked herself many questions. *What's going to happen to us? To the islanders? Will they put Jimmy's father in prison because he's Japanese and the leading elder on the island? Because he owes allegiance to the Emperor? Will I lose my husband? Will he be taken from me?* She became sick to her stomach and her mind raced. She nestled closer to Jimmy and he brushed some tears from her face and said, "What the fuck are they thinking of, Sarah? They need us. The canneries need us. We're the best fishermen on the west coast. Without us, the canneries will run dry. The whites can't tuna fish. Time and again they've tried. Our catches are three to one to theirs. It's crazy! I gotta think that somebody with horse sense is gonna straighten this thing out!"

* * *

No favorable news came from the mainland. The people on the island were sorely pressed without their boats. The Los Angeles papers poured venom on the Japanese race and all descendants. It was time for the second meeting of the League. Tony and Jimmy walked together to the Community Building.

"I was in San Pedro yesterday," Tony said. "I got a lot of bad looks from people. Then I got the same answer from my bank. One hundred dollars per month. I talked to my tailor on Pacific Street. He said his business is nonexistent. He told me he heard that some white thugs beat up on a Japanese tomato farmer."

The tuna men came into the Community Building and six elders occupied the stage plus Frank Tanaka, the President of the Japanese League. The men liked Tanaka. At one time he had been a tuna man before being elected to the League. He was known for his no-nonsense manner. Frank Tanaka was a strong, muscular man of sixty with powerful forearms and a wildly sprouting mustache and short-cropped, bristly salt-and-pepper hair. He quickly came to the microphone when introduced by Toshio Sato. The instant he spoke, the tuna men knew they were doomed.

Tanaka grabbed the mike with two heavily callused hands and said, "We lost the battle in Washington. Three of us were there for four days. We saw our senator, our Congressman, and we met with White House staff and the President. Our remarks were like throwing rose petals over a dam. There is widespread, unwarranted malice being manufactured by many prominent people here on the west coast. They've convinced our government, your government, that all those of Japanese descent and all those Japanese without papers should be rooted out and moved from the coast."

Again Tanaka gripped the mike as if he would break it in two.

"Our arguments stressing the very essential need of our services from the tuna industry to those in the rice and beans and tomato fields . . . all fell on deaf ears. Their own government statistics which we cited time and again show the overwhelming superiority of our work forces. Those statistics didn't sway anyone. They've made up their minds. When I brought out the proven fact, the obvious fact, that none of our people in Hawaii are being jailed or even touched, they didn't want to talk about that. The obvious economic fact is that Hawaii is greatly dependent upon the Japanese farmer. That fact was rolled under the rug.

"Now, gentlemen, listen to me. You will be receiving a communiqué within a few days. It will say this: in fourteen days from the end of the month, you will have to sell most of your possessions. Your house, your furniture, your boat gear. You'll put everything that you can save into two suitcases per family member. Sheets, pillowcases, toilet articles, small kitchen utensils, and clothing. You will then proceed by the ferry to the mainland at L.A. You'll check into a Relocation Building and get a tag for your meals until you arrive at some destination. From there, you'll march to Union Station and board a train. You'll be taken to some desert compound and live behind barbed wire in cramped quarters. You'll exist under armed guard, in buildings provided by your government.

"Call me any name you want to, gentlemen. We fought for you. Fought like tigers and it didn't mean doodly squat. We tried to keep the boats under our economic pleas for the fishing industry. They're going to be sold to white bidders only in San Pedro and the industry can go to hell. The only thing we achieved and it was like a small tip on a bad day. You can take out more than $100 per month but they haven't told us yet how much it will be. Big deal. Shoot your questions at me now."

No one spoke as a pall fell over the room. It was as if condemned men had taken their last walk and felt the straps being put on them as they waited for the first voltage shocks to hit their bodies.

Jimmy saw that his father's face was ashen. After a long silence in which no boots hit the floor and no taunts came from the tuna men, Tony Watanabe stood up and asked to be heard. Watanabe represented all that was great in the fishermen. He was powerful, with a chest that thrust out and hands that could rip a man apart. His face was red-brown from the years at sea. Tony came to the front and stood below the mike. "I don't need that thing," he declared. "Everyone here knows me and can hear me." He turned so he faced Tanaka and said, "You're one of us, Frank. We're Americans here. Someday this will pass and in the meantime, we're gonna hold our heads high. You got any more advice for us?"

Tanaka's answer was terse. "Look your family in the eye. Act like men. No one can do more than that."

There were no other questions raised and Toshio adjourned the meeting. The days that lay ahead were like the uncompromising fog of the ocean in the early morning, when tramp steamers strayed from their lanes and bore down on tuna boats, sending boats and crews to a watery grave.

* * *

When Sarah met Jimmy at the door, her heart sank. From his manner, she knew nothing good had come from the meeting. "Let's go up the hill and see Father Nomo," she said. She put on a heavy jacket and they climbed to the highest point on the island where the church sat. The small, board and batten, one story building reminded her of the little churches of New England, all neat and clean, with white steeples pointing up to a cobalt sky. It was here on the island they had been married by the old priest who they hoped to see.

As they entered the church which was always open, Sarah thought back to her wedding five years before. Minniemata had been alive and had given her a lace shawl. She had worn it when she and Toshio had come to America at the turn of the century. After the ceremony, the tuna men had hoisted Sarah on their shoulders and put her in an old black palanquin and pulled the young married couple once around the island. Then they had watched from the high promontory as the congregation walked down to the bay. They had immersed themselves in the cold sea and took salt and threw it over their shoulders. It was an ancient custom signifying the cleansing of everyone's souls.

Father Tanishi Nomo stood near the altar and he put his short, stubby arms around Sarah and asked them to pray with him. Many times over the years he had blessed the boats and crews before they went out on the green Pacific. He knew now that the years ahead would require his best effort as war cast its shadow on everyone.

"I pray for your family, Jim, and for the safety of all those who are true believers in our everlasting God. Our God moves in strange ways and we must put our trust in Him for the eventual outcome of these days that lie ahead. May the two of you be kept in his open arms and may the day come when you can raise a family in happiness and peace."

* * *

After leaving the old priest, they walked to his father's house where Yoki met them at the door. "I don't know what to put in my suitcase for our journey," she said. "Father has told me about our departure. I won't leave the Manyusho behind. It's too sacred to the family." The Manyusho was a story book of Japan that had come down through the centuries and it was worshipped by the people. Sarah remembered how Minniemata had taken a verse from the great book and had read it at the wedding ceremony.

"Yoki," she said. "Let's you and me figure out what is best to take and what to get rid of. Let's not wait until the day comes." She put her arm around her little sister-in-law and they held each other.

A week went by on Terminal Island with nothing but bad news. Life went on but with little hope. An article in the Sun-Times claimed that the fishermen on Terminal Island knew all the harbor depths by using sophisticated sounding devices, that they had communicated this information to the Japanese Navy for an eventual landing. This was ludicrous. The fishermen did not have the money for such devices. They relied on ordinary ropes marked to determine the depths to help them avoid shoals on their way out the cut to the Pacific. Another story, much more disturbing, was that the government was preparing thirteen relocation camps deep in the western desert. They were for all Japanese families and their descendants.

Early one morning as Sarah prepared breakfast she said, "I'm going with you when we leave, Jimmy. I don't want to be away from you on assignments."

"They're not after you, Sarah," he replied. "They won't allow whites. From what Tanaka said, it'll be like living on a postage stamp, sleeping on straw pallets, not having any running water in the buildings. Father had a long talk with him after our meeting. Our people will suffer greatly. That's where you could help if you got in to these camps and told the story with your camera."

As the sun rose over Terminal, Sarah took the ferry to the mainland. About the same time, a number of military personnel came by ferry to the island and posted notices on buildings and telephone poles. The message told the same story that Frank Tanaka had given the fishermen. Hearts were once more saddened and many women ran crying through the pathways. Jimmy pulled a fresh notice off a building. The Japanese residents on the island had fourteen days from the end of the month to sell their homes, their furniture, their accumulated boat gear, and to pack two suitcases per person. The formal language read:

    a. Bedding and linens (not mattresses) for each member of the family.
    b. Toilet articles for each member of the family.
    c. Extra clothing for each member.
    d. Sufficient knives, forks, spoons, plates, bowls, and cups for each member of the family.
    e. Essential personal effects for each member.

The date of departure was set for May 14th, 1942.

By early afternoon of the day the notices were posted, white buyers descended upon the island like vultures. Real estate men and used furniture and used appliance dealers all aimed for a killing. A knock came upon Jimmy's door shortly after noon. The real estate man offered four thousand dollars in cash for his home. This was one-third of its value and he turned the man down curtly. A few minutes later another man was at his door and he was offered one thousand dollars for his furniture and appliances. Again he ushered the man out without a word. He figured he'd check around and see what others were offered. He called his father.

"Father, have the scalpers been around?"

"Of course. I can get thirty cents on the dollar."

"Same here."

The front door opened and Sarah stormed in. Her features were angry. Her voice went up three notches.

"I've seen everything now!" she declared. She took off her coat and hat and stamped her feet.

"What happened?"

"I got to the elevator on the first floor of the Times. I walked by a host of people, some I've had lunch with, worked with. I got the brush off. No one waved, no one said a word. One girl turned her face away. I got off on ten, met Frank Water's secretary who I've known for years. She didn't say 'Hello' or anything else. When I asked for Frank, she informed me that he couldn't see me. I was in shock! I couldn't believe the change in that building."

Sarah broke down and sobbed in Jimmy's arms.

* * *

The end of April came and with it, the fourteen days to get ready to leave the island. The fourteen days were a nightmare. Buyers badgered people to sell. As the days went by, the prices they quoted held up. People gave up and settled, one after the other. House after house went for what the buyers offered. Grown men cried as they signed the papers. Families visited neighbors trying to assuage their sadness as they compared notes on what to take and how to pack. Many sat on their stoops and wailed.

A few days before the dreaded day of exodus, the phone rang at Toshio Sato's. Frank Tanaka was on the line.

"Toshio-san, are you well?"

"As well as can be expected, Frank. What can you tell me?"

"The FBI will call on you tomorrow. They'll inform you of the embarkation plans. I must say good-bye to you. I have been called to Washington. Take care of yourself, Toshio-san."

Toshio's heart was heavy. As he stood up, Yoki entered with her boyfriend, Fred Imatsu. "Father," Yoki said, "Fred wishes to speak with you." Young Fred Imatsu had a look of disgust on his face.

"Mr. Sato-san, please look at this letter from the War Department."

Toshio took the letter and sat down near a lamp. He adjusted his gold spectacles on the bridge of his nose. He slowly read the contents. The letter indicated that Fred Imatsu was no longer eligible for military service. It did not indicate why. "I volunteered for service before Pearl Harbor!" the boy said indignantly.

He handed the letter back to the young man. "I know," Toshio answered. "Your father told me how proud he was."

Toshio asked the young man to sit down in his living room. He pointed to the open sword case sitting in his cabinet. Fred Imatsu looked across the room at the cabinet and did not understand.

"I had to bury my prized sword, given to me by my father. It will not be possessed by anyone until this war is over. Then my son can dig it up and have it." He looked the boy in the face. "You and I face a bitter fact. I was not born here. Because of it, I cannot claim citizenship. I cannot have the paper that says I belong here, to this country which I love. You, who have offered to serve this country, where you were born, this country you love, cannot do so. The government has decided not to let any person of Japanese lineage into the armed forces."

Toshio walked over to the cabinet and brought out the jeweled case. He held it as if it were a fresh-born child. "No explanation will satisfy either of us. We must live with what we cannot change. Only time and the surge of powerful events will change matters. In the meantime, you must be stout of heart. You must face up to that which you cannot change."

Toshio tenderly put the sword case on a teakwood table. "Be proud, young man. Time is on our side. Be whole in spirit."

* * *

Yoki Sato looked at the open suitcase on her bed. It was fully packed including her greatest possession, the Manyusho. She turned and stared at herself in a mirror over a chest of drawers and her eyes rested on a small cloth doll. It had strands of golden hair and wore a tattered red dress and tiny black shoes. She had won it on the mainland at a carnival with her boyfriend, Fred Imatsu. It was a prize among several cheap prizes at the back of a booth and the barker urged her to try her luck with three rubber balls. They were to be thrown at the mouth of a grinning clown cutout. Freddie gave the man three dollars and she picked up the rubber balls. The first two fell aimlessly but the third ran straight and true into the clown's mouth. A bell rang and the clown lit up. She had her choice of any prize. She picked the doll with the golden hair and christened it "Minnie" after her mother.

"Minnie" stared at her from the dresser top. She picked up the doll and held it close. She looked around the room to see if anyone was watching her. Satisfied that no one was, she thrust "Minnie" into the bottom of her suitcase.

* * *

A knock came at the front door. Yoki opened it and stood looking up at two tall, blonde white men who wore identical gray suits. One presented her with his identification as being from the FBI. "You are here for my father," she said. "Come in and I will get him." She led them into the living room. She excused herself and presently Toshio appeared. They introduced themselves and Toshio asked them if they would like some tea. They both deferred and continued to stand.

"Mr. Sato," one of them said, "you are well-respected on the island. We are here to tell you that on May 14th, the ferry services will run from six in the morning until all people are off the island. Please inform everyone of this. As everyone leaves the ferry in Los Angeles, they will see a yellow brick building at the end of the wharf. A large sign will read RELOCATION HEADQUARTERS. Your people will file in and give their name and address. Each person will be given cards that are to be used for your rations until you arrive at your destination. From this building, everyone will walk to the Union Station which is four blocks from the wharf. Military police and soldiers will be with everyone from the ferry boat until you are in the station and on board a train. Soldiers will accompany you to the final destination. Do you have any questions, Mr. Sato?"

Toshio replied, "No, gentlemen, it has been made clear. My people will be ready. Thank you for coming."

The two men in the identical gray suits turned and left.

* * *

The dreaded day arrived, and with it, a hard, driving rain that pelted the people as they came down the many pathways to the ferry docks. As the ferry bumped the docks, the people shuffled in with their suitcases. They huddled together on the hard seats as solid sheets of water erased the horizon. Toshio Sato sat with his daughter and her boyfriend. Next to them were the Imatsu family and Jimmy and Sarah. The Watanabe family sat with John Matsu and his wife. The ferry was hot and crowded. Many women cried as they took a last look at the island disappearing in the gloom.

Only the small children enjoyed themselves. They played their games around the ferry as their anxious mothers tried to keep them near. One of the great virtues of youth is its buoyancy and they refused to have sad faces.

Toshio still keenly felt the loss of Minniemata and thanked his God that she didn't have to suffer this experience. He cast a glance at his daughter and was pleased that her happy disposition would stand in well when they faced the coming hardships.

When the ferry landed at Los Angeles, a short trip of only forty minutes, the people picked up their baggage and held on to their small children as they started down the wharf to the building marked RELOCATION CENTER. As they walked along, cries rang out from whites along the wharf, cries of "Dirty Japs" and "Dirty Yellow-Bellies." Some felt the slap of ripe tomatoes striking their outer garments. Armed soldiers kept the crowd at bay. One man threw something and was knocked down by the butt of a rifle. Ugly words and driving rain added to their misery and terrified children now kept close to their parents. Suddenly a cry went up, "There's a white woman! She's walking with them!" Sarah felt something hit her face. She raised her hand to find part of an egg sliding down her face and neck and into her clothing. Jimmy tried to control his temper and attempted to shield Sarah from the crowd growing on the wharf.

The long line of people filled the wharf as they moved into the building and were met by soldiers sitting at desks. They were asked to open their suitcases so the soldiers could search for contraband. Sarah stood with Jimmy in front of a tough, burly sergeant who said, "Lady, you don't belong here."

She answered with disdain and dignity, "I'm with my husband, and I'm staying with him."

Eleven hundred people picked up cards and the long line proceeded the four blocks to Union Station. Again, a hostile crowd taunted them and was held back by the soldiers. Jimmy said to his father, "I can carry one of those bags."

His father replied, "I am still capable."

Toshio's face was wet with driving rain, but he appeared calm and composed. Union Station loomed ahead. The great, leviathan structure stood darkened by perpetual smoke and soot as its yellow-green overhead lights threw eerie shadows on the walkers. A train stood in the station, its engines discharging clouds of spume as engineers checked bearings, oiled wheels, and examined couplings. Soldiers led the people to the train whose windows were darkened. They slowly mounted the steps of the cars and moved toward seats visible only by tiny overhead lights. The air in the train was dry and stuffy as the people piled their suitcases in the overhead racks. Coats and outer garments were stripped off as people tried to stand the blast of heat. Children began their games in the aisles. Whenever the children came to the end of a car when it was coupled, they were met by armed soldiers who made them go back. The children stared at the soldiers and one little boy saluted, which brought a smile to a tight-lipped private. This was the soldier's third trip east to a way-station in the desert. It would be repeated several times.

When the train was loaded, wheels ground and steam built up and a gradual movement took place as the train left Union Station headed east. Sarah felt sick in the stifling heat and found a long line of women waiting at the bathrooms. She took her seat again as the train picked up speed. Soon soldiers began to hand out sacks with food to those with cards. Jimmy bit into a tough beef sandwich on stale white bread and put it back in the bag. He bit into an apple and made that his meal. He thought of his mother and how good her meals were and how she loved to prepare them back on the island. There was the sour an odorous takuan (a radish pickle), the sharp tang of seaweed, the pungent and salty soy sauce with delicious seafood dishes, usually the fish fried in deep rape seed oil, followed by sukiyaki, his favorite which Minnie made with strips of beef and vegetables broiled in a sweet soy sauce. He wondered what kind of food they'd be getting out somewhere in the desert. He took another bite out of the apple and thought of his mother again, how after her funeral the women on the island brought in platter after platter of rice balls and seaweed and macaroni salad and tea; how his father, by an old custom, wouldn't let the family eat any fish or meat for forty-nine days. Then he saw his mother being sewn into a muslin kimono with leggings and foot strappings and a cloth for her head, how the coffin had been placed in their living room with a small muslin bag at her side and all the people stepped up to the coffin to put coins in the bag.

The heat in the train was terrible and everyone wet handkerchiefs with water from a faucet in the bathroom. Toshio sat with his eyes closed and remembered the many good days on the island and out on the sea. After a while, he stood up and walked through the cars and talked to everyone, trying to make them as comfortable as possible.

Occasionally the train slowed and moved to a siding to let troop trains roll westward to embarkation points on the west coast. After a while, the people heard the wheels grind as the long train moved out into the main line and continued its journey. Only by their watches did the people know that night had come. Mothers knew it from the repeated crying of small children running out of patience with their games in the aisles.

At eight the next morning the train began to slow down and finally rolled to a stop. Shouts could be heard. People rubbed their eyes from a tired, sleepless night among uncontrollable fetid odors. There was a stir and fresh air seeped into the coaches as doors were opened and soldiers moved about. People reached for their bags and began to file out into bright sunlight that stung their eyes. Stretching as far as one could see was a brown plain filled with blowing tumbleweeds and sage. In the distance a purple mountain range appeared below an immense azure sky. Above the far mountain range appeared formations of storm clouds. It was then that the heat off the desert land came in waves. With it came the acrid, musty smell of the land. Across the track stood a single adobe building of no consequence with a sign on it that read DESPERADO STATION—U.S. GOVERNMENT. Coming down from the north in the direction of the mountains was a line of busses, yellow-orange in color. A cloud of dust was in their wake and as the busses came closer to the little station, the people made out names on the sides of the busses. Names such as Yuma County Consolidated Schools and Tio Grande Consolidated School. Sarah wondered what state they were in and figured it must be either Arizona or New Mexico.

The first busses came to a halt near the train and soldiers began to usher the passengers into them. Sarah and Jimmy stepped up into a bus past a fat Indian driver with a sweatband in his greasy hair whose jaw held a plug of tobacco. He spit it occasionally into a spittoon by his feet. As each bus filled, it took off in a southerly direction. After going about a mile, turned eastward on a two-laned macadam road. On each side of the road were wire fences which bore metal signs which read PROPERTY OF THE UNITED STATES GOVERNMENT. Yoki and her father sat near them and she suddenly exclaimed, "There's a jackrabbit!" It was huge in size and bounded into a hole in the ground. Black and white magpies sat on fence posts and a line of yellow cottonwood trees followed a dried up stream bed. Once in a while, a dust devil whipped in curls across the desert and quickly disappeared. Five miles down the road the busses ran until outlines of long, low buildings emerged and they were surrounded by guard towers. Soon the people saw soldiers in the towers and saw the buildings to be tar-papered and ugly. As the busses drew near, an entrance gate appeared and over it a sign that read DESPERADO CAMP #13 - U.S. GOVT. Barbed-wire enclosures stretched around the perimeter of the installation. The busses emptied and the people stood with their suitcases in front of a yellow frame building that had a sign reading ADMINISTRATION-HEADQUARTERS.

A very tall, unusually thin officer appeared from the building and stepped up on a small stand that had been erected. Silver bars of a captain stood on the shoulders of his uniform. Those in the front rows could see the captain was not well. His face was gaunt and very yellow in color as if he had jaundice. His uniform, though, was immaculate, and on his breast were many service multi-colored bars. He picked up a bullhorn that was on the stand.

"My name is Ingersoll. I'm your Commandant at Desperado. Shortly you will be shown to your barracks. By this time next month, this camp will have close to ten thousand internees. You will find when you go into your barracks that living spaces are lined out. Each unit is about twenty feet square. This is where you will live as a family." The captain stopped for a moment and his body was wracked with a heavy cough. His face turned red and he pulled out a handkerchief and covered his face. Then he went on. "There are no toilets or running water in the barracks. Each line of barracks has a mess hall, toilet and bath and laundry facility at the east end of their row. You will find the barracks unpartitioned. My men will help you with blankets and ropes which can be hung from the ceiling beams and will make some semblance of privacy. You will find straw pallets for sleeping." Again he stopped and was seized by a heavy cough. He turned his body away from the onlookers. For a minute or two he was silent and then said, "By three this afternoon, I expect the people in each barracks to select a Barracks Manager. This person will represent you in all dealings with me and my men. He will be directly responsible for your well-being and the upkeep of your barracks and the grounds around it. I want that Block Manager to report to me by three o'clock." Here again, the captain stopped and waited before he spoke. "When you have unpacked and soldiers have helped you with the blankets, you are allowed to be in any of your buildings at the end of the row. Food will be provided three times a day. Twice a day you will exercise on the grounds, once in the morning and once in the afternoon. My assistant is Lieutenant Holiday and he will speak to only the Block Managers. Now, I have one piece of advice. I don't like it here any more than you. It may be a long war. Forget about trying to leave. It's fourteen miles to the nearest town across a hostile desert. My men will now show you to your quarters."

As the captain stepped down, he motioned to a soldier. "Sergeant Wills, there's a white woman in the fourth row. Bring her to my office."

Sarah was approached by the sergeant and Jimmy said, "Do you want me to come with you?"

"No," she answered, "I can handle it."

The Sato family entered an enormous barracks, empty except for piles of straw pallets and other piles of blankets and rope. Soldiers asked the people to pick sections which were marked by blue chalk on the floor. Then they showed everyone how to lash blankets to the rafters and, with ropes and holes cut into the blankets, make a semblance of a partition. While this was going on and children were running the length and breadth of the barracks, Sarah stood in front of Captain Tom Ingersoll.

"Please sit down," he said. "I apologize for my cough. It's not contagious. My outfit came from Panama where we've been with the Coast Guard for years. If we didn't pick up malaria, we got everything else." Sarah saw clearly how his skin had been ravaged. "My boys are like me too," he said.

Sarah sat and said nothing. The captain offered her a cigarette which she refused as he lit one for himself. His cough started. He put the cigarette in an ash tray and said, "I suppose you're married to one of these people?" His comment wasn't unfriendly but indifferent.

"Yes," she said, "I'm the wife of James Sato."

"You make a problem for me," he answered. "We're to accept only those with Japanese blood."

"I'm sure you can make an exception," she said smiling.

"No, I can't. It'd take a letter from the War Department. You imagine how long that'd take?"

"I'm staying with my husband."

"No. You're not. If you need a little money, I can help you. Other than that, you'll be out of here this afternoon on your way to Santa Fe. Or my men can take you to the nearest rail center below there a few miles."

Sarah realized she couldn't budge the captain and said, "If I leave, what visitation rights do I have?"

"Thursdays. Two to four."

"I'll go to Santa Fe. I've been there before in my work."

"What's that?" he asked.

"I'm a photographer. I was with the Sun-Times in L.A."

"Okay. I've got one contact in Santa Fe. Friend of my brother. Edgar Hulling. He's a museum director. We'll drop you off there. I'll call him. You have lunch with your husband and then come back here. You need money?"

"Thank you, no. I'm all right. I appreciate your kindness."

"Glad to do it, Mrs. Sato. I didn't ask for this cotton-picking job."

* * *

The family gathered around Sarah while she packed a suitcase. The pillow cases and sheets and silver she left, and kept only some clothing and toilet articles. Then she walked with Jimmy, his father and Yoki to the mess hall.

The mid-day meal was a disaster. It was tough roast beef, with soggy mashed potatoes, a gluey tapioca, and hot tea. To the people from Terminal, it turned their stomachs. Most stared at their plates and touched little but the potatoes and tea. After living lives on fish and fresh fruit and vegetables, this kind of food would not stay in their stomachs. The beef on the train had been unsavory and this was no improvement. After staring at their plates, most of the islanders got up and went back to the barracks. They had let their feelings known to Toshio Sato. It would be the first thing on his list when he met with the captain at three o'clock.

As Sarah said good-bye, tears streaked Yoki's face. Sarah said she'd be back the next week on Thursday and not to worry. The old man shook hands with her and counseled her to be brave. He then thrust some American dollars in her hand and she tried to refuse them but he insisted. Jimmy walked with her to the Administration Building and said his good-bye as they kissed in front of the soldiers. Ten minutes later, a jeep drove out the gate with Sarah staring back at Desperado and its tar-papered barracks.

At three o'clock, Toshio Sato found himself in the Administration Building with six other men, all named Block Managers, all with the weight of trying to help their people with many requests for better living conditions. After once again listening to complaints which Tom Ingersoll had heard before, it was Toshio's turn to speak.

"Commandant," Toshio started, "this food cannot continue. If it does we will be sick or starve, one or the other."

"What do you suggest?" Ingersoll shot back.

"My people eat very little carbohydrates. Our diet has always been fresh fruit, vegetables, and fish from the sea. That is our diet. That is what we need."

Ingersoll studied the little man in front of him. His eyes were heavily lidded, his arms dark-brown and strong, his manner that of great composure and authority.

"Mr. Sato," Ingersoll said, "Your candor is refreshing, but we have a problem. We get our provisions from Army warehouses twice a week. They're trucked in. We have no real refrigeration facilities here, except in one small building. Until that is ironed out, I take what I receive. You put down on paper a two week diet and I'll see what can be done."

The old man nodded. "Sir, may I make a suggestion?"

"What is it?"

"Much land is here. If we had equipment. Shovels, hoses, a small tractor, we could grow much of our own food. This land is harsh, but I have seen some of the miracles my people have done in the valleys in California. It would also be a blessing, because we would have something to do."

"You mean on this land?" Ingersoll asked.

"It can be done. There are gardeners among our people. More will be coming, I'm sure. Give us a chance."

* * *

In the meantime, the people at Desperado tried to put order in their lives. Teachers were found; the mess hall became a school in the early morning hours. There were few books, no writing materials, no blackboards and the teachers had to rely on themselves. Yoki brought her Manyusho. It was a source of learning. Games for the children were organized and mothers joined in to provide supervision of the games and play time. Exercise time twice a day was a morale builder as it took people from their cramped quarters out into the New Mexico sun and provided an element of health lacking when it came to the unpalatable food. The changes came, and they were few at first, for there was still the frustration and anger because they weren't in their own environment. The physical discomfort of straw pallets, the overwhelming abundance of dust from the desert that blew in the sides of the thin, tar-papered buildings, the bitterness and boredom and ever-present thought of the government, their government, treating them like third class citizens, all these things were in their minds. The people were psychologically bruised and puzzled at what had happened to them. Many blamed the Japanese League and felt the League had sold out to the government.

One thing helped the people; the government set up a system of payments for work. An unskilled laborer was paid $12 per month, a skilled laborer $16, and certain classes of professionals, like doctors, $18. With these minuscule payments, all of which were saved, the people began to bring in from the outside some needed things. Sewing machines which the women made good use of for curtains for the barracks, dresses, slips, tablecloths, and many other essentials. Typewriters were purchased and a monthly newspaper followed. Each time supplies came in, money went out through the government quartermaster for what the people needed. The problem of the howling winds and the dust was finally overcome. Under guard,

124

the people cut timber from the mountains and sawed it and applied it to the thin framing of the tar-papered barracks.

Meanwhile, in Santa Fe, Sarah arrived in the bustling city and entered the museum with her one suitcase and her few items of clothing. Edgar Hulling greeted her and said, "Mrs. Sato, I hope you won't mind what I've done. I have an interview for you at our Cerillos Art School. I've arranged for a room for you at the LaFonda Hotel until you can get your bearings. Tomorrow at nine, I'm taking you to the Cerillos Indian School. They want to consider you as a teacher of photography. They've lost staff to the war effort and need someone."

Sarah managed to say, "Mr. Hulling, I can't thank you enough. I'll pay you back every cent. I do need a job. You make me feel wonderful. When I think of how the Sun-times treated me after Pearl Harbor, you would have thought because I married Jimmy, that I had become a traitor and the enemy."

"Mrs. Sato," he remarked, "I've fought most of my adult life for the advancement of the Indian. You don't have to tell me about prejudice and mistreatment. When I think of the internees, I say our government will be haunted someday by what they've done."

* * *

Thursday rolled around and at two in the afternoon, Sarah found herself at the gates of Desperado with a rented car. She asked to see the captain and was ushered into his office.

"I wanted to thank you for your help," she said.

"My pleasure," replied Tom Ingersoll. "By the way, what are you doing these days?"

"I'm on staff at the Cerillos Indian School as a photographer. If the Army approves, I'm photographing here and at Tula #12. I'm to depict the lives of the internees."

"Not bad," he replied. "I have no objection."

"What's going on outside the gate?" she asked.

"I figured your father-in-law had a good idea. We got an old plow and they're gonna raise their own food. It saves on our rations and improves morale. Plus it makes me look good. When the crops come in, they'll do the cooking."

Sarah was escorted to the barracks and she was pleased to see the improvements. Tables had been made and chairs and partitions were being put in by some of the fishermen. On the outside of the building, lathe had been added and the dust of yesterday was a thing of the past. Toshio greeted her with a smile and Yoki hugged her and then father and daughter left Jimmy and Sarah. She came to him and he disrobed her. They sank into the straw pallets laid together and made furious love. It reminded her of their first night in his tin-roofed shack by the bay on the island when heavy rain sent hail-like bullets on the tin roof and they lay there finally sated and deliriously happy.

After a while, Jimmy asked, "How is Santa Fe?"

She replied warmly, "I have a job. I'm staff photographer for the Indian Art School. If the Army approves, I have an assignment to photograph here and at Tula #12, another internee camp."

"And if the Army does approve?" he asked as he held her close and moved his hands lovingly over her breasts.

"That'll mean more time here with you."

Sarah opened her purse and handed him a Santa Fe paper she had folded up. "I wanted you to see this. I'm afraid I might lose you because of it."

On the front page of the Santa Fe Clarion was a news story about a new regiment that was being formed in Hawaii of all Japanese-American young men. It was called the 442nd Combat Brigade.

"Why should I join them?" Jimmy answered. "Not after what the government has done."

They dressed and walked outside the barracks where the people were engaged in calisthenics. Yoki saw them and walked over with her father. Jimmy showed the article to his father and asked him what he thought.

Toshio squinted at the paper and his face took on a look of sadness. "If this is true," he said, "it is the right thing to do."

"After what they've done to us?" Jimmy answered, bewildered by his father's answer.

"Of course," his father said, and walked back to exercise.

The rebuke bothered Jimmy and he was silent. Sarah took his hand and they went back in the barracks.

* * *

Almost a year went by, with Sarah seeing Jimmy every Thursday. Her letter of approval had never been received by the Cerillos Art School and she was mystified. Captain Tom Ingersoll was no longer at Desperado and had been ordered to active duty in the 3rd Division, a crack outfit in Africa fighting Rommel. His successor, a First Lieutenant Ordway, with Quartermaster experience, was glad to let things ride as they were as long as morale was good and his wife could be seen in Santa Fe on the weekends.

Sarah was happily employed at Cerillos and had rapidly become known for her teaching skills and her vivid photographs of the New Mexico desert at sundown.

At Desperado, the first crops were showing. Luscious red tomatoes, snap beans, celery, and onions. The miracle of crops grown on the barren soil had been as Toshio had said. It gave many of his people something to do and they would soon reap the rewards. In the meantime, because of the far-sightedness of Tom Ingersoll and his faith in Toshio Sato, crops both in and out of the compound were close to picking. It was an unusual sight to see the people standing in patches of green in the desert. It was even more incongruous to see soldiers standing over them with rifles.

More and more the barracks were assuming homelike qualities. Running water had been introduced to the buildings and flush toilets. A newspaper now appeared from a printing press obtained, paid for by the tiny wages earned each month. A small bank now stood in the corner of one of the mess halls with deposits handled by the Army. Much had been achieved, much approved under Ingersoll's leadership, but the fact remained: there was no freedom. The people still stood behind barbed wire.

Once when Sarah was in for a few hours on Thursday, she picked up the camp paper and saw a poem by Yoki Sato.

> The stranger
> does not speak to me.
> I do not know his thoughts
> I see his face, his eyes, his mouth,

But cannot read his soul.

* * *

In the eleventh month, an Army command car came through the gates. A meeting had been set up for that day between an Army spokesman and the young men at Desperado. Jimmy and Tony and John sat together in the mess hall. It was easily noticed that some men from the barracks were not there. It was the mood of many including Jimmy that they had been treated poorly and would not serve in any Army outfit.

A husky major with combat ribbons spoke from a makeshift stage. As he explained about the 442nd Combat Brigade of all Japanese-Americans, he was rudely heckled from the audience. "Why should we listen to you? You're free to leave. We aren't!" someone yelled. Another took up the refrain and men stamped their feet. The major had been treated like this before at other meetings of internees and he waited for the din to die down.

"All right," he challenged, "I'd think you want to show the world the stuff you're made of. To show your pride against the enemy." There was another shout and he waited. "This is your chance. If you don't take it, your children and your grandchildren will regret it as much as you! I want to tell you what President Roosevelt said when the 442nd was formed. He said, 'The principle of which this country was founded and by which it has always been governed is that Americanism is a matter of mind and heart. Americanism is not, and never was, a matter of race and ancestry. Every American citizen should be given the opportunity to serve this country wherever his skills will make the greatest contribution—production, agriculture, government service, or other work essential to the war effort.' "

The major finished by saying, "I'm here until five o'clock. This is the time to sign up. I wouldn't want to sit here on my ass the rest of the war and let outsiders think you deserved this punishment. I'd want to do something. This is your chance." With that, he stepped off the stage.

Jimmy and Tony and Big John got up from their chairs.

"What do you think, guys?" Matsu asked.

"I'm ready," Tony said. "Anything's better than staying here."

Jimmy didn't say a word. The two friends of his waited for him to say something. "What about it?" Tony asked.

"I'm not eager, but I'll go," Jimmy finally said. "My father made me feel like a coward."

The three of them walked to the front of the mess hall where the major sat at a desk, where a line had formed. In a half an hour, they were inducted into the Army as members of the 442nd Combat Brigade.

* * *

Two weeks later, notices came through the mail to one hundred and three men interned at Desperado. On the following Tuesday in the morning, busses would leave Desperado filled with young men on their way to a training camp. With many mixed feelings about the impending departure of these men who were leaving wives and sweethearts and, in many cases, families, it became the obligation of the people to give them a sendoff. Toshio Sato and the other Block Managers appeared before a genial First Lieutenant Ordway and asked the question, "Can we, with our limited funds, send someone into Santa Fe in search of saki and rice cakes and other foods to make the night before they leave a celebration?"

Ordway's answer went half-way toward what they hoped for.

"You give me a list of what you want and I'll give you a receipt for whatever money you have to spend, and I'll have two of my men scour the town for you. Regulations won't let me release any of you. You understand that."

Money came from young and old and Ordway sent his men. They came back that night with saki and rice cakes and soy sauce and marinated pickles and a collection of tiny American flags. With what the old mama Japanese cooks had to work with plus the provisions from Santa Fe, preparations were made for a party. As the time came for the party, many of the families felt strange. The one hundred and three inductees represented only about one-third of those qualified to serve. It was obvious that the majority of the people did not feel they owed the government any duty after the way they had been treated. And yet, many of those same people, as the time came near for the men to leave, began to search their consciences and wonder.

Sarah was well aware of Jimmy's impending departure because of her weekly visit. While sad, she knew it was the right thing to do, and felt good about it. Yoki had a difficult time because of her young lover who had volunteered. Fred Imatsu and Yoki spent as much time together in the last few days and promised they'd get married as soon as the war was over. It was all Yoki could hope for and she accepted it. She felt bad for her sister-in-law because Sarah couldn't get permission to attend the party. First Lieutenant Ordway would not let her enter the gates on a Monday and wouldn't go against his orders on visiting days.

Monday night came and the mess hall was filled to overflowing. With much speech-making and saki that flowed, one hundred and three inductees made the most of the evening. Big John Matsu and Tony Watanabe were roaring drunk. Tony got up on a table and sang. Drowned out by his friends and neighbors, he led a chorus of "Banzai's" before he passed out with his wife wailing. Tiny American flags waved from every table and families sat together until after midnight. Each man was given some plum seed for good health and a picture of a tiger because he is said to always come home. Finally the wives and sweethearts of these men, many of them the fishermen from Terminal Island, pulled and tugged and led their men into their straw pallets. For many of the men, it would be their last time as the gods of war took them into battle.

Toshio Sato awoke early the next morning as was his custom. He peeked behind a flimsy partition and saw his only son still sleeping. Behind another partition was his daughter, Yoki. He walked outside the barracks which he had been doing each morning before anyone else arose because of his job as Head Groundskeeper. Usually he peered carefully at all of the grounds and paths between the buildings to see that there were no stray papers or cigarette butts so that the commandant would be pleased. This morning his time was spent in thinking about his son and the terrible days that might lie ahead. More than once he found himself imagining receiving a telegram that his son had been killed in defense of his country. More than once he remembered saying to Jimmy that it was a man's duty to serve his country. Now the time was coming to say good-bye.

Jimmy Sato woke up and his stomach was queasy. He couldn't sleep any more so he dressed. He peered in to see whether his father was sleeping and knew he wouldn't be, that he'd be out inspecting the grounds. Jimmy walked outside and found his father sitting on a stoop. Father and son sat together. Neither spoke.

Jimmy put his arm around his father and Toshio said, "We all must do what is right. It gives me great pain to see you leave. You are a good son and you have made me proud."

Toshio Sato stood up and walked down toward the parade ground so that his son would not see him cry.

* * *

Flags waved from many hands and tears were shed and proud men boarded busses. Yoki Sato kissed Fred Imatsu and put a piece of paper in his hand. "Don't read it until you've gone," she said. Fred boarded the bus, looking back at his sweetheart.

Jimmy Sato, Tony Watanabe, and Big John Matsu took their last look at Desperado and headed into World War II.

Chapter 2 — Shelby

Eight men formed Charley squad in Able Platoon: Campione, Nagy, Nunzio, Heske, Robin, Woods, Tabas and Wheeling. They slept in the same dirty yellow pine barracks, took chow together, took close-order drill together on the parade field, fired next to each other on the rifle range.

Balding, red-faced First Sergeant John J. Moriarity made it abundantly clear to them on their first day in camp. They were going to live together and maybe die together and they better know each other in the squad like they knew their wives or sweethearts. Ahead of them lay eight tough, demanding weeks of Basic Training and he, John J. Moriarity, would be breathing down their necks. He would chew them out, up and down and sideways and spit them out like watermelon seeds whenever and wherever it fit his pleasure.

John J. Moriarity was a grizzled veteran of thirty years in the Army. A fast-talking, loud-mouthed Shanty Irishman who'd earned his first stripes at the Battle of Belleau Woods in northern France in 1918 at the age of 18, he'd advanced through the ranks of foot soldiers to his top post as a non-commissioned officer. Early on, he made his decision to be a tough, no-nonsense, nasty bastard, come hell or high water. He'd seen it all, lived it all, seen men fresh and green become a piece of hamburger meat in seconds from incoming shellfire, seen bodies torn and bloody on barbed wire, seen healthy, strong men reduced to gibbering idiots from shell-shock, seen the ever-present lice, the scurrying rats, and the dysentery until the trenches were nothing but mud and shit. Now he had been ordered to wet-nurse a bunch of sad-assed, numb-nuts who couldn't tell one end of a rifle from the other, to make men out of them. To mold them into ruthless fighting machines who would function as a unit, trained to kill, and kill again.

Shelby, Mississippi was the pride of the south, the largest infantry base below the Mason-Dixon line, located deep in rain-drenched, mosquito-ridden, snake-infested swampland. John J. Moriarity stared belligerently at Able platoon. He said to himself, *I'll spit out these raw recruits and feed them to the gators. I'll take these sorry-looking greenhorns and I'll be an ass-eating, mean, son-of-a-bitch, somebody they'll remember the rest of their days!*

The day the troop train rolled into Shelby from St. Louis, Steve Nagy had a uniform and shoes thrown at him by a gum-chewing corporal. He chowed down tepid pork and beans and watered-down coffee, and found himself in the squad in the hot sun of Mississippi learning close-order drill. He was issued a M-1 Grand rifle packed in cosmoline that he had to clean and disassemble and reassemble under the watchful eyes of John J. Moriarity. He was issued a bunk in a barracks and loaded down with sheets and blankets and pillows, and learned how to properly stow his gear in a dull green footlocker with his name and rank stenciled on it. From there he trudged to another barracks where he was treated to a poorly threaded eight millimeter film covering the terrible consequences of venereal disease with graphic, nauseating pictures.

One hour before lights out, a fight broke out when Bobby Nunzio made a wisecrack about the Chicago Cubs and John Heske decked him. Nunzio lay on the floor in the barracks with blood streaming down his face and Heske shouting, "You fucking fag, you speak to me once again and I'll tear your asshole out and make you eat it!" One day in the heat and smell of Mississippi, and the men of Charley squad had formed a distaste for Nunzio. He had succeeded in creating that dislike in that short time. It started with his bragging about his job in civilian life, that of an automobile salesman in Detroit. To anyone who would listen, he quickly established himself as the top salesman and referred to the "rich" in Grosse Pointe and Bloomfield Hills who relied upon him for a good deal, better than anyone else. Then when it came time for the usual jokes that circulated around the barracks, Bobby Nunzio had to try to top everyone with off-color stories involving sex in which the subject matter was gross and the teller became gross. It was easy to tell that he considered himself superior to everyone else in the barracks, that he should have been given a much better deal by the powers-that-be, than that of a lowly private in the infantry. In the time span of one day, Bobby Nunzio was unwanted and unloved.

Moriarity pulled Heske away from Nunzio like plucking a daisy from a flower-strewn field. He then deposited him rudely alongside Nunzio. Less than a day in Shelby and the squad had the scoop on Moriarity; that he'd been in more than one barroom brawl; that his scarred face and overripe nose had witnessed more than his share of knock-down fights.

John Heske's bunk was on one side of Nagy's. In Nagy, he found an outlet for his dislike of Bobby Nunzio and of the First Sergeant. Heske was from the south side of Chicago, where he'd driven a cab. He had a strange, grating, nasal twang when he opened his mouth. He'd reach up to comb his greasy hair full of brilliantine while he boasted about his fights in the Golden Gloves fighting as a lightweight. Heske's rat-shaped face was divided laterally by a pencil-thin black mustache. His mouth was filled with a cigarette that hung there precipitously, ready to fall at any minute. Two fingers of his right hand were yellow-brown from nicotine stains.

"You work the south side of Chi, you got a tough deal. Jigaboos. Mean bastards. Cut yer throat for a fin. You wanna job in Chi, you see your ward bosses, the heelers. You gotta grease palms. How you think I drive cab for fifteen years?" Heske pulled out his rat-tail comb and ran it through his greasy hair.

It took one day on the range for the men of Able platoon to find out Walter "Cock" Robin was the best marksman. He'd hit thirty straight without a miss. Walter was the oldest man in the barracks at the age of thirty-seven. Most were in their twenties, some younger. Walter was like a brood hen with chicks. His hands were monstrous, like two great bear paws, heavily callused and cracked. He was a farmer from southern Illinois along the Mississippi. When he shook hands, it was like having your hands rubbed with rough sandpaper. Spitting out a barracks window with his tobacco cud, he possessed a foul mouth that could disturb a burlesque comedian. Robin kept obscene photographs taped to the bottom of his foot locker, proudly showing them to the young soldiers.

Cock stared at an effeminate-looking Jimmy Woods who lay on his bunk, his nose buried in a comic book. "Hear your sister's a good lay, Woods." It didn't matter that Woods had no sister. The remark had been heard in the barracks and Robin had made his point. Jimmy Woods turned on his side.

Woods was a loner. He didn't fit, didn't seem to care if he fit. Didn't care what was going on. You knew he'd fail Moriarity's inspections. His boots were unshined, bunk not tight enough to flip a quarter, uniform hanging on him like a scarecrow in a cornfield. Nagy figured he was a misfit, not a candidate for war as an infantryman. Steve felt he should have been put in quartermaster as a clerk or in the mess hall. It wasn't that the men disliked Woods. It didn't seem right that he should be picked to ram a bayonet down a kraut or a Jap.

The first night in Shelby, Able was aware of Henry Tabas. Tattooed on his back between his shoulder blades was an American flag with a green snake curled around it. When Henry twitched his shoulders, the snake leaped out at the men, his fangs gleaming. "Where'd you have that tattoo done?" Robin asked.

"Some time ago," Henry answered. "Some broad told me it was a work of art. I asked her if she'd like to see the rest of my canvas." Tabas belly-laughed and was christened "Snake" by foul-mouthed Cock Robin.

The first time Nagy met Henry Tabas he said to himself, *There's a killer.* Tabas had cold, flat eyes that drilled through you. Nagy heard it said that he'd been the chief mechanic for the Sells-Floto Circus. Somebody else said Tabas had been part of a heist in the west, had served time. Whatever the truth, Henry was a cool customer. In addition, he was a wizard at fixing things. He fixed Steve's watch when it stopped, fixed a leak in the john that Moriarity couldn't get the locals to tackle, fixed the guts of Moriarity's jeep when the motor pool kept sending it back. All agreed that Snake Tabas would be a good man in a firefight.

As for Nunzio, nobody had anything good to say. Sucking around Moriarity, trying to butter him up, most figured Nunzio jerked off. When Campione and Nagy went to Moriarity and asked for another man as their ammo carrier, having been given Nunzio, Moriarity wouldn't budge. "Live with the prick," he said, "maybe he'll get knocked off and I'll get you someone else."

The story teller in the squad was gangly Kyle Wheeling from West Virginia, down along the slow-flowing Catawba. There was nothing he liked better than to get a bunch in the barracks and go into his act. "Boys," he'd say, "them fish in the Catawba are dern right lazier than a hog in a mud waddle." He'd laugh and say, "I got this little 'ole place along the river. Know'd a cat'd be there, jes lyin' there, lettin' juice bugs float down to him. I put my hand down in that water and I feel for him, nice and soft, just like a girlie's titties. I stroke him like you stroke a woman, nice and slow, know what I mean, boys?" Kyle looked around until he knew everybody had heard him and then said, "Pulled him right outta the river. That fish was sweeter than sin."

Wheeling pulled out a chaw of tobacco and handed some to Cock Robin, then rolled it in his mouth. He opened a barracks window and shot out a brown-green stream.

"Tell you about my momma, boys. About her soap. Made it when the moon was a sliver. Burnt blackjack wood in the fireplace. Had to be green." Kyle looked around again to make sure he had his audience. "Them ashes made the lye fire the soap. She put me to watering those hoppers to run the lye. You had to pour the water real slow like. If you poured the water too fast, it's run them ashes right outta your lye. Then we took guts of fresh-killed hogs, split them, washed them, hung them up to dry. Lordy, that made the best soap you ever seen." Kyle shot out another stream of tobacco.

"Momma had an old timey trick. Took a feather to tell when the soap was strong enough. Put sassafras in the soap. That sassafras root made your clothes smell like a baby's bottom."

"What did you do about worms?" Cock answered. "All our farm kids had worms coming out their ass." Cock now had everyone's attention. "One time my belly was killing me from worms. Doctor comes and tells Momma about wormweed. Stinks bad . . . worsen skunk or bad pussy." Cock looked around with a lecherous grin.

"What did you do?" Heske asked.

"Momma took a handful of wormweed, put it in a half pint of molasses, cooked it until it was like candy. Fixed the pan of molasses with wormweed. We ate it. I let her go in the back forty and had worms coming out of me a mile long!"

Everyone roared. Cock was happy.

"Same with flies," Kyle Wheeling countered, recapturing his audience. He got up and let another stream out the window. "We got a weed, grows along the river. Kills flies. Momma put this weed in a bucket, mixed molasses with it, took a poke of cornbread, took off the crust, put it to fit that bucket. Cut a hole in that cornbread crust. That dad-blamed fly lit on that cornbread, smelt the molasses, went down that cotton-pickin' hole. That old scent cold-cocked him!"

Heske looked at Wheeling. "How'd your momma take to you chewing tobacco?

Kyle squinted, took another gouge in the tobacco. "Shoot, he replied, wiping the leaves off his chin, "who you think taught me?"

Alberto Campione was the mystery man, its least talkative. Three words out of the man they called "Runner" was like dry-run days in the oil fields. He stood six foot-three, weighed two hundred pounds, was hard as the packed clay of Mississippi. He regularly ran sprints on the parade ground after dismissal from drill. In the short sprints, and in the mile, no one touched him. To Nagy, who was considered second to Campione in speed and strength, the Indian was a marvel in physical bearing and grace. Nagy wondered how Campione would do on the obstacle course run. Some thought Alberto might break the long standing time record set in World War I.

In the barracks when not on duty, Campione spent his time drawing with charcoal pencils. His sketches of some of the men in the platoon he gave without any conversation. The sketches exhibited his skill at drawing eyebrows, the nose, the eyes of a man, the twist of his mouth, the way the man's hair lay. The one given to Heske made him feel like he was looking in a mirror.

Several of the men noted Campione's sadness. They figured that was the reason he drank. When the weekends came, he and Nagy headed for Maybelle's, one of the local bars, where the big Indian drank boilermakers, coming back to camp loaded. Where he kept a bottle in the barracks was a hot topic for conversation. Moriarity hadn't caught him on inspections. Most figured Moriarity would wise up or Alberto's kidneys would be floating.

Nagy tried to draw Campione out in their conversations, to get him to talk about his life on the mesa. It came in short sentences at Maybelle's after a few drinks. Nagy knew something disturbed Campione, couldn't figure out what it was.

As the rains made life miserable and snakes took to the high ground, the men of Able marched and trained. They ate the same nauseating food, watched the same training films, suffered the same inspections from their unloved First Sergeant. They broke their rifles down, cleaned them, reassembled them, wrote letters to their wives and sweethearts, waited for the letters to come.

In his free time, Steve made word-pictures of camp life in a diary he started. He thought of his old man and their harsh words, figured Frank would still be in Plant 10, by the river, lifting flywheels, heaving them on the belt. The light in the plant would be blue-gray, the air heavy with steel dust and welding sparks. He imagined his father walking home up St. Johns Street, opening the front gate, Sophie helping him as he shook from the job.

* * *

Saturday afternoon. Alberto and Steve walked out the main gate at Shelby on a pass. They didn't have to be back until Sunday night. There wasn't a good-sized town for miles around, so they headed for their favorite watering hole across the highway at Maybelle's.

Maybelle was a hunk of woman in her late fifties, standing five feet ten, weighing close to two hundred pounds, with bright reddish-orange hair. Both of her fleshy arms bore tattoos of bluebirds and cardinals in flight. When she wiped her bar counter down, the birds took off.

Maybelle treated her soldier boys like visiting dignitaries. Her growing popularity assured a full house on weekends. Since Campione had started to come in regularly, she had chosen him to center her affections. This Saturday was no exception. Steve and Alberto sat in their favorite booth by a front window where they witnessed the camp gate comings and goings and the heavy traffic coming down U.S. Highway Four. They ordered and Maybelle winked at Alberto. Once more, Nagy tried to get Alberto to talk about his life back on the mesa.

"Got a steady girl, Runner?"

"No."

"Funny," Steve said, "you get more letters than I do. Who writes all the letters to you, your folks?"

"No. A friend of mine. Was with him in school in Santa Fe. He's in England. Tail-gunner on a B-17."

"I figured you had lots of women."

Alberto sighed, "I messed things up." He stared out the window. Nagy figured he'd never know what happened. He nursed his beer while Alberto had a boilermaker.

Nagy figured if the war didn't kill Campione, his liver would. He thought a minute, then asked, "What do you mean, messed up?"

The answer came slowly. "There was a woman. In Santa Fe." Alberto stared out the window and was silent. Then he turned back to Nagy. "A white woman."

Steve was hooked like a fish on a strong line. He waited until Alberto continued. "She's a teacher. In her thirties." There was a painful silence. "I fell in love. She's married. To a Jap. A Japanese-American. He's in one of those camps in the desert."

Steve shifted his weight in the booth, looking directly at his friend.

"I got plastered one night. I found I couldn't have her and I hit the booze. They say I tried to rape her. I don't believe that. They put me in jail. I got out by going in the Army."

"They dropped the charges?" Steve asked.

Alberto nodded, looked away, his manner sad. Nothing more was said. He looked as if his whole world had crumbled. He put his arms on the table and buried his head in his arms.

Nagy tried to ease things. "Rainy is still pissed at me. She wanted to get married before I left. I told her we'd have to wait until I got back."

Alberto had his head down and Steve walked up to the bar and ordered another beer and a boilermaker for Alberto. He took them back to the booth and nudged Campione. "Here, drown your sorrows."

Campione sat up, took the drink and downed it. Then he said, "You know that place they call Rushmore. Where they have the carvings on the mountain of the presidents?"

"Yeah. They finished it a while ago. I saw it in a newsreel."

Campione's eyes seemed to come alive. "I want to find a mountain."

"A mountain?"

"I want to put my father's face on a mountain."

"You're a sculptor?" Nagy asked in surprise.

"I worked for a sculptor. He taught me."

Nagy hailed a waitress for more drinks. Campione added, "I owe it to my father."

"I don't follow you," Nagy said.

Alberto's first finger made circles on his glass of beer. "I disobeyed my people, the clan. I wanted them to buy some tractors and back-hoes from the whites so we could repair our irrigation ditches in the valley. They were all broken and hard-packed by the sun. The clan turned it down. They won't do business with the whites. I got angry, made some protests, was punished."

"What did they do to you?"

"Horsewhipped me in the kiva."

"Jesus!"

"I have to make it up to my father. He stuck up for me."

140

"Horsewhipping? That's god-damned cruel! Sounds like the dark ages, not the 40's."

"I got through it. When the war's over, that's my goal. To find a mountain and sculpt my father's face on it."

"That's a hell of a project, Runner."

"It'll take years and plenty of money. I won't know how to start."

"Your father sounds like someone I'd like to meet. My father hates my guts."

"Because of that strike?"

"That and me as a union organizer."

They stared out the window. Alberto turned and fiddled with his glass of half-filled beer. Then he said, "You go to church back home?"

"Yeah, I'm Catholic."

Alberto reached in his pocket and brought out a little carved bear that glistened in the light.

"Where'd you get that?" Nagy asked.

"It's a fetish. An old woman gave it to me many years ago." He handed it to Steve and Steve felt the smooth, cold stone and its well-rubbed curves. He handed it back to Alberto.

"Carry it all the time?"

"Since I was eight."

There was silence again as they stared out the window.

"We have a church on the mesa," Alberto volunteered.

As he spoke the words, Snake, Tabas and Kyle Wheeling came over with a pitcher of beer and joined them.

"What's the beer for?" Nagy asked.

"Runner beat Cock on the range yesterday," Snake answered. "We thought the cock sucker was invincible."

"Snake's taking bets on Runner," Wheeling said. "Thinks he'll be first in the company next week on the obstacle course."

"Wouldn't bet against it," Nagy replied.

"They got live ammo, boys," Wheeling said. "You keep your cotton-pickin' ass down or you don't wipe it for a month!" He laughed, showing his teeth browned from the wad of tobacco in his mouth.

"Maybe that peckerhead Nunzio will get hit!" Snake exclaimed. "I hate that prick. You see him sucking up to Moriarity!"

"Runner and I have to live with him. Moriarity won't give us a better ammo man," Nagy responded.

"Make you a bet, Steve. Bet he ain't around by the end of Basic," Snake offered.

* * *

First Sergeant John Moriarity stood six inches from Jimmy Woods' nose, his quick, snapping bark ripping Woods up and down. He kicked Woods' footlocker with his foot. He took Woods' bunk with both hands, lifted it and threw it the length of the barracks. He examined Jimmy's scuffed boots like an IRS auditor checking a suspect income tax return, threw both of them in the direction of the bunk. Most in the platoon knew what came next. Woods would spend the rest of the day and half the night on his hands and knees in the latrine, cleaning urinals with a toothbrush.

To Jimmy Woods' credit, he stood straight and took Moriarity's abuse. Those near Woods witnessed a face angelic, that of a boy-man living in his own world, a world unpopulated by loud-mouthed, overbearing Top Sergeants; a world without barracks and rifles and shined boots and tightly-made bunks; someplace serene, faraway, far removed from a muddy yellow barracks in Mississippi.

"You listening, Woods?"

"Yes, sir, First Sergeant."

John J. Moriarity's acne-scarred, booze-ridden face flamed crimson.

"How many times I tell you not to address me as 'Sir'?"

"Many times, First Sergeant."

"What did I ask you before that?"

"If I was listening, First Sergeant."

"What did I say before that?"

"You said I was so stupid I forgot to wipe my ass."

"And before that?"

"You said I was yanking my crank."

Woods couldn't win. Each time it happened, Moriarity took it out on the rest of Able. Nagy told himself if Moriarity kept it up, somebody would take a potshot at him some day.

* * *

The talk of live ammunition on the obstacle course made everyone edgy. With the course on the edge of a swamp, no one was thrilled with the thought of crawling under obstacles, of coming face-to-face with a timber rattler or a cottonmouth.

The morning of the run, Moriarity stood with the retinue of non-coms at the beginning of the course. They had stopwatches and egged on Able with catcalls and insults. The whistle blew and Nagy leaped forward. He zig-zagged through the oversized, frayed truck tires embedded in deep sand, then grabbed the thick ropes hanging down from a twenty foot-high barrier. He climbed steadily, his strong legs pressing against the boards and his upper arm strength carrying him up and over the top to fall heavily on the other side in deep sand. As he fell, a large form blew by him as Alberto was going full bore.

Runner Campione flew over the barrier with little effort and took a lead on Nagy and the rest of the pack. Nagy sweat like a stuck pig and breathed hard as he lay in the sand. He felt like lying there forever and telling the United States Army to go fuck itself. He got to his feet and followed a disappearing Campione toward the water pits strung over with barbed wire, bullets zinging overhead. The water was crotch-high. He found himself drenched in it as he crawled as low as he could under the wire. Behind Steve came the rest of the platoon. One man was down in the water refusing to move. Moriarity stood over him shouting, "Move! Move!

You dumb-ass! I'll break you in little pieces, Nunzio! I'll tear your fucking ass off, make you eat it with a spoon!"

Bobby Nunzio felt his sphincter muscles go and he smelled the shit and urine in his pants. Trying to crawl, he began crying. Moriarity stood over him bellowing with rage, forcing Nunzio to crawl along to the finish line where he collapsed in the sand, his body racked with sobs.

Nagy stood at the finish line catching his breath as a dozen men surrounded Alberto and congratulated him. A new record had been set! Eight minutes and forty seconds, a full thirty seconds off the old time set in 1917.

Nearby, Bobby Nunzio lay crying in his excrement, Moriarity standing over him in disgust. The men of Able stared at Nunzio. John Heske thought to himself, *What a sad sack of shit.*

* * *

Mail call.

Steve Nagy eagerly tore open the latest letter from Rainy. He saw the many xxxxx's at the beginning and the end and was pleased to learn that Rainy had gone back to see Father Ferency. She had spent over an hour with him talking about what she hoped would be her life with Steve when he came back. She also mentioned that she'd taken dinner with his folks and that his father was in a good mood. Steve and Alberto walked back to the barracks together and Alberto handed him a thin blue V-mail letter from overseas. "This is from my buddy in England." Steve took the letter and lay down on his bunk.

RUNNER—You old sonofabitch. You're in the Army now, you're not behind the plow; you'll never get rich, you sonofabitch, you're in the Army now! Hey, buddy, I feel sorry for you. I told you to join the Air Corps and you didn't listen. That's understandable. You never did listen. Look how you took to the booze when I warned you. Hey, you can't believe how cushey I got it, with real, honest-to-gosh pillows to lay my head on. And talk about the chow! None of that ersatz stuff you're eating. Real live eggs, not that putrid green stuff you get—ham and sides of bacon and great pancakes and all the other goodies. You made a mistake, buddy. I told you about my bird. Her name is Diana Maypole, and I'm going to marry her if I can get through this war in one piece.

Lately I ain't too thrilled with our missions. All daylight stuff deep into Krautland without any escorts. It ain't no fun and games no more. We're bombing the shit out of the heinies but their Focke-Wulf and ME-109's are all over us and my guns get red-hot. When we finally scramble back to Merry Olde England, minus some good guys that got it, we get into the biggest crap game you ever seen. Twenty dollar bills light our cigars.

Hey, Runner. You better write to Sarah and tell her how sorry you are for screwing up her life. Then, for Christ sake, forget her! There's lots of good stash out there waiting for you. With your gonads, you could charm a snake.

Your buddy,
The invisible one
Dennis Charbonneau

* * *

"What's the 'invisible' bit about?" Steve asked.

Alberto shrugged his shoulders and sat down and said, "One day back in our dorm at St. Catherines, Dennis said to me, 'One thing about the service; you can be invisible. For a fucking Sioux from Pine Ridge, it's the way to go. Nobody gives a doodly-damn who you were, who you are, or where you came from. When you get in, Runner, don't volunteer for anything. Just lie low. Ride it out and stay in the rear ranks. You'll have more fun and more freedom. Don't let them put any stripes on you. The minute you get stripes, you get responsibility. That's nothing but grief and horseshit in the white man's world. Stay in the background.' "

"You believe that?" Nagy asked.

"So far I do," Alberto answered. "When I see a shitface like Moriarity in authority, I want no part of it."

"Well," Steve said, "this is where I have problems."

"What do you mean?" Alberto asked.

"What if I hadn't gotten involved that time with my union, just let things pass. If everybody felt that way that night in the plant, we wouldn't have struck. Those dies would have gone elsewhere. I suppose if you believe in something, you can't be on the outside looking in.

It doesn't work that way. You gotta get involved to make things better. I don't know if I buy that invisible bit, Runner. Look at it this way. We got a war to fight and a war to win. Somebody has to lead, to direct men so they do the maximum good at the right time. And yet . . ."

"And yet, what?"

"Oh, I don't know. I think back to the strike. I still don't know if we accomplished anything. We got the town down on us, a lot of men lost their jobs, cars didn't sell. I'm mixed up on the subject. I guess I'm just jawing, Runner."

"No," Alberto said, "I don't know myself."

* * *

Equipped with full packs and rifles, Able marched along the red clay roads of Mississippi. The air was steaming hot with thunder clouds forming. Two more weeks of Basic and they'd be out of there, heading to an embarkation point and into the reality of war. In the six weeks since arriving at Shelby, boys had become men and the men of Able felt sharper, cockier, stronger, and felt like kicking ass. Tough days were ahead. They were getting ready for the big show, the real thing.

Able came to a rise in the ground, with the heat steaming off the hard-packed clay. An outfit marched toward them, battle flags waving. Little soldiers stepped along in perfect formation, their eyes straight ahead, their uniforms pressed, their guns held in the proper position.

"It's the Japs!" someone yelled.

"God-damnit!" Moriarity shouted, "keep it down! I'll tell you when to open your yaps! When I say to keep it down, I mean it! You sad-assed excuses for combat infantrymen are gonna start right now and DOUBLE-TIME! That's what I said. DOUBLE-TIME! I'll show you who's boss of this platoon. I'm gonna run your sorry asses all the way back to the company!

"Nunzio!" he yelled. "I'm lookin' at you, boy. Keep your eyes straight ahead. Hold that rifle up where it belongs."

Able had heard about the outfit coming toward them, the 442nd Combat Brigade. An all Japanese-American outfit, attached to the 36th Division, they were supposed to be billeted at the northern end of Shelby. They ran their own show.

The 442nd swept by, the words GO FOR BROKE stenciled on their helmets. The little soldiers carried full packs and looked sharp. None of them could have weighed over one hundred and thirty pounds. They shook the red clay of Mississippi from their boots as they passed by.

* * *

Saturday night at Maybelle's.

The joint was loaded with GI's and locals. Maybelle had simple, enforced rules for her barmaids: no heavy lipstick, the hair short and clean, no screwing with her soldier boys. To her suppliers, the message was clear: the best booze money could buy. To her bartenders: no watered drinks.

When Nagy and Campione walked in, she put her arms around Alberto. She congratulated him for his winning time on the obstacle course, the news of which had traveled over the 36th Division. She handed him an unopened bottle of her best 100 proof Wild Turkey Bourbon.

"On me, soldier-boy," she declared with a grin.

"That's all he needs," Nagy said softly, but Maybelle caught the drift. She stuck her face up to Nagy. With a growl she stated, "Listen, Nagy, I ain't his nursemaid. Let him enjoy it. Where you boys are going, you're gonna wish you had more of it."

Runner planted a kiss on Maybelle as he uncapped the bottle. This brought the house down, with men yelling and clapping and coming over to congratulate Alberto. Maybelle thought to herself, *If anyone else kissed me like that, I'd cold-cock him.*

Alberto and Steve sat down as the front door opened and two soldiers walked in. The place went dead. They were from the 442nd, had never been in Maybelle's before. Nagy figured they must have their own watering holes up the highway. You had to give the old broad credit. She stepped up to them and welcomed them to her saloon. They sat down in a booth, with all eyes on them in their freshly pressed Class A uniforms. The two men ordered drinks and proceeded to play a game of cards. As Nagy turned back to Campione to make a comment about the Japanese-Americans, Runner suddenly said, "I had a strange dream."

"What kind of a dream?" Steve asked.

"I lay in a pool of water in a woods. It was dark. All the trees had their bark stripped by shellfire. The water was red."

"Jesus, Runner, you're making me uncomfortable."

Campione answered by saying, "I want to be buried up in the churchyard."

Alberto's words were buried like a corpse in a graveyard by sudden shouts carrying over the barroom; angry, continued shouts.

"God-damned, dirty, mother-fucking Japs!"

Three obese, thick-bearded men in soiled overalls yelled at the two Japanese-American soldiers, cursing and shouting. One of them bellowed, "You yellow-bellied bastards!"

"Don't you lousy, good-for-nothing punks threaten any of my soldier-boys!" Maybelle yelled as she banged her billy club on the bar and started toward them. One of the bearded men headed for Maybelle and hollered, "Old woman, I'm gonna teach you a lesson!" Showing his dirty, decayed teeth and a wide gap in his mouth, he grabbed her arm before she could swing the club. As he did, Runner said to Nagy, "Take care of Maybelle." Alberto jumped from their booth and ran toward the two toughs yelling at the two Nisei.

Nagy faced the man holding Maybelle by the arm.

"One more move, fat boy," Steve announced, "and I'll break your arm."

"Fuck you, Yankee," the man yelled and spit in Steve's face.

Nagy grabbed him and yanked him off his feet. The sound of a shoulder tearing was like the crack of a rifle. The man slumped to the floor in pain. Steve looked to where Alberto stood by the booth of the other bearded men. They had grabbed one of the Nisei, scattering red-backed cards across the barroom floor. Alberto took the two men, one in each hand, and lifted them from their seats and banged their heads together. The sound was like a watermelon falling off a speeding truck, the men sitting like empty sacks on the floor. By then, there was plenty of help and nearby soldiers dumped the three troublemakers out the alley door. In the distance a siren screeched and Maybelle roared, "The sheriff's on his way. They won't be coming in here for a while."

Nagy invited the two Nisei to join them at their booth. The smaller of the two said, "I'm Jim Sato. This is Tony Watanabe." The two soldiers picked up their scattered cards and joined Alberto and Steve.

Maybelle yelled, "Drinks on the house!" As she did, she waved her arms and the birds flew.

Sato stared at Alberto and asked, "You're the one that set the obstacle course record, aren't you? We heard about it. Congratulations." Alberto nodded, but was silent. The four men shook hands.

"We're grateful to you for what you did," Sato said.

"You get this kind of shit, don't you?" asked Nagy.

"Enough of it," Sato answered as he picked up his drink.

"Regiment won't let us fight back," Watanabe said. "If we get into fights over this kind of thing, they'll break us up and send us back to where we came from."

"In our case," Sato said, "we'd have to go back to Desperado, a relocation camp in the desert."

"I heard about those places," Nagy acknowledged.

Sato stared out the window. He had a small, egg-shaped face with narrow eyes. His nose was thin and ended close to his top lip. His chin stuck out like an angry challenge. He turned in his seat and faced Alberto and Steve. "Sometimes we wonder who the real enemy is." The sadness Nagy saw in Sato's eyes was the same sadness he saw in Alberto. Campione hadn't uttered a word since the two Japanese-American soldiers sat down.

"Where you from in the States?" Nagy asked.

"Terminal Island. That's off San Pedro and Los Angeles."

"What did you do out there?"

"We were tuna fishermen," Watanabe replied. "The day of Pearl Harbor, the Coast Guard made us go to shore and took our boats away. We never saw them again."

"Then they put you in those camps?"

"More a prison than a camp," Sato shot back. "For over a year. Our families are still there."

"Jim, we'd better get a move on," Tony said. "Thanks again you guys. Best of luck to you." They shook hands again and started to leave. Other GIs said good-bye to them and they left. Alberto stared at their backs.

"See the smaller one, the one called Sato," Alberto said.

"Yeah?"

"His wife is Sarah. The woman I told you about. Who I'm supposed to have tried to rape. The white woman in Santa Fe."

* * *

Able platoon was out on the swamp range firing at a tow target. It was a huge area the government had taken over from the locals. The prices paid were being contested by those who had lived on the land for generations and there was a lot of bad blood. Many of the local people were up in arms about what they felt was shabby treatment. Nagy heard the story from Maybelle who said that Uncle Sam had booted out some hard-scrabble people and paid them peanuts for their land. They had to take their meager possessions and find new places to live. It reminded Steve of what Alberto had told him one day at Maybelle's, how the Spanish had run off some of his ancestors from their sacred land. It pissed Nagy off when Moriarity referred to those dispossessed as "swamp rats." It was another reason why the men of Able hated their First Sergeant.

Nagy had finished firing when it was Nunzio's turn. Nunzio stepped to the line, his eyes half-crossed like a kid about to be slapped by his mother. He was scared and sweat poured over him. Those who watched him saw his body shake.

In firing tracers at a tow-target pulled by a small plane, you waited for the Piper Cub to come over the tree-line hauling the red streamer on a long heavy wire, and you fired at the streamer. The night before in the barracks, Robin said to Steve, "It's like shooting pheasants. You move the gun barrel out and give your target a lot of lead. Then you let the red sleeve come into your slugs. Go with the flow, Steve."

The plane turned parallel to the firers with the red sleeve floating in the breeze. Nunzio pulled the trigger on the machine gun set in the sand and slugs flew up between the plane and the target. His shooting was erratic and moving toward the plane. The red sleeve was being led too much as the arc of the slugs soared toward the plane.

"The bastard's shooting at the plane!" Heske yelled. He ran forward and jumped on Nunzio and pulled him from the gun. Nunzio broke loose from Heske as men yelled at him, tried to stop him, as he ran out forward and in front of other firers shooting at the tow-target. Someone hit Nunzio and knocked him down.

Moriarity hollered, "Quit firing! Get back!" Moriarity bent over Bobby Nunzio and shouted, "God damned sonofabitch!" As the firing ceased, men rushed to Nunzio. They put him on a stretcher as he shook and loaded him into an ambulance. The unit sped off the range to the base hospital.

When Able platoon returned to the barracks, Nunzio's gear was gone, his footlocker empty, his mattress rolled up on his bunk.

* * *

Able was in its final inter-platoon shoot-out against Dog platoon. Two weeks before, it lost to Charley platoon by twenty points. Most of those in Able held Woods responsible. His poor marksmanship was obvious as Maggie's Drawers waved over his unscathed targets. Cock Robin led all shooters, with Runner a close second. It didn't offset Woods' poor showing. A new man was now in the squad, Pepe Ramos, replacing Nunzio, whose name was never mentioned again. John Heske muttered before Able went to the range, "Ain't no way Woods' gonna improve."

"Mebbe we help him," Ramos suggested. Heske listened to Ramos because they had both fought in the Gloves.

"All right," Moriarity bellowed, "give me sixteen firers. Line up and count off. Go up to the weapons shack and get your piece. Double time! Move out!"

Sixteen men from Able ran down to the mustard-colored weapons shack where a pimple-faced corporal issued them rifles and they raced back to Moriarity. He stood behind a table as they loaded their rounds. Jimmy Woods gritted his teeth as he pushed each bullet down into the steel plate forcing the rounds into position to fire.

"What's the matter, Woods," Moriarity shouted, "don't you know how to load your ammo?"

"I got it, First Sergeant."

"Get up there then."

"You got fifty rounds," Moriarity hollered. "These targets are pop-up targets; they're up for only three seconds! Move out now!"

Nagy went to Foxhole #16 and the rest of the men of Able were spread out over the range.

"Keep the muzzle pointed down-range at all times! Moriarity yelled. "Scorers, get your men in position. Raise your heads when ready."

Moriarity bellowed again, "Hey, 12. You're holding up the show. Get into position!"

Seconds later, Woods' scorer raised his clipboard.

"Twelve's ready, Sarge."

"Load one magazine of ten rounds," Moriarity barked. "Firers, unlock your weapons. You got targets at fifty, one hundred, one-fifty, and three hundred meters."

Nagy waited for any movement, any sharp reflection. His throat was dry and his finger itched on the trigger. There was a bright flash and he heard shots and he was caught off guard. He squeezed the trigger and missed. Then he closed his mind to all sounds and fired as the targets bobbed up and down like figures in a wild dance. Finally he rolled over and stood up in his fire pit.

"Thirty-one out of forty," his scorer said.

Cock Robin stood next to him in Pit #15 with a pained expression on his face.

"How'd you do?" Nagy asked.

152

"Missed one," Cock said as he frowned and pulled out a plug of tobacco and put it in his mouth."

"You little shit-face!" Moriarity raged, his voice carrying over the firing range. He stood over Jimmy Woods, his face black with anger. "I ain't never had anyone as bad as you, Woods. Christ, man! What if that was forty krauts comin' at you? You'd be a hunk of meat by now. Am I gettin' to you Woods?"

Woods' answer was a flat, typical response. "Yes, First Sergeant." His face was undisturbed, dreamlike.

"I gotta do somethin', boy. You're gonna stay out here with Robin and Campione until they teach you somethin'. I dunno. I just dunno. Rest of you men, turn your weapons in. Close order drill at 1400. Dismissed."

"What about our scores, Sarge?" Wheeling asked.

"I'll have 'em at chow. Dog takes the range now and they'll chew you up."

At chow that evening, Moriarity stood over Woods. "You birds are hopeless. Dog took you by forty points."

* * *

Alberto had been drinking since mail call. He stood by his bunk with a bottle in his hand. If Moriarity or one of his non-coms walked in, Campione would be up a creek. It was as if the big Indian didn't care whether he was caught or not. Campione turned to Nagy and handed him a letter. "Read this," he said in a surly voice.

"I don't want to read your mail, Runner."

Nagy was pushed back roughly on his bunk and Alberto's voice became belligerent. "Read it." Nagy took the half-crumpled letter that Campione thrust at him and straightened it out and lay back on his bunk.

Dear Alberto,

I'm sorry to have to write to you that Dennis was killed. He and his crew were coming back from a mission when the plane crashed in an attempted emergency landing near their base in England.

I received a telephone call from his brother in Pine Ridge, South Dakota. He said that if I could reach you to tell you that Dennis considered you his best friend.

Alberto, you and I had the privilege of knowing Dennis. He was a marvelous person, a free spirit, one who spoke his mind, and believed his people were entitled to more than they were receiving. I knew I couldn't tame that spirit while he was at St. Catherines. He was a very special person who we came to know and respect for his individuality and to love him for it. I am very sorry and it leaves a void here that will never be filled.

We are very busy in our school year. The track team took first place honors in Gallup and next week they go to Montrose. I think of you often and what you meant to our school and to me personally. Your drawings have been framed and are in place in the dining hall. They attract many wonderful comments.

Alberto, when this terrible war is over and you come back to Acoma, I want to help you on your quest. So does Frederick Creekwater. Before he left for government work in the east, he spoke about you, and said he'd help you find your mountain. So will I.

May God be with you and give you strength in the hard days ahead.

Sister Margaret

* * *

Roll call.

"Tabas" - "Yo."

"Nagy." - "Yo."

"Wheeling." - "Here."

Woods." - "Here, First Sergeant."

"Robin." - "Yo."

"Campione." - "Campione." - "Where's Campione?"

"Heske." - "Here."

"Ramos." - "Yo."

"Where's Campione?"

"He's sick, Sarge," Nagy yelled.

"What do you mean he's sick? He ain't on sick call."

"He's in the latrine, Sarge."

Moriarity dismissed the platoon and strode into the barracks of Able. Alberto lay on the floor in a corner of the latrine, rolled up into a ball, his hair matted, his body and uniform stinking of whisky and puke. Moriarity hollered, "Nagy? You and Tabas! Clean this piece of shit up and bring him to my office. Drag him if you have to!"

Nagy and Tabas worked on Campione, trying to clean him up. It was like working in a sewer, the smell making them retch. They held him up and he swung at them and threw up on Nagy. They tried again and he slid from them and lay face down on the cold floor. Finally they got him up and stripped his clothes off and held him in a shower. They called for Wheeling and Robin to hold him while they managed to clean him and get clean clothes for themselves. Campione kept mumbling and falling. Nagy had Heske find some clean clothes of Alberto's. With the help of most of the squad, they half-dragged Alberto into Moriarity's office. There they held Campione while they listened to a diatribe released with venom by a red-faced Top Sergeant.

"God-damn it, Campione. Old man Carwile was going to put you in for OCS! I wouldn't send you as far as the PX. What in holy hell got into you. What do you have to say for yourself?"

Alberto heard some of Moriarity's invective and his words came out slurred and garbled as he said, "My friend." He slumped down again and Nagy and Tabas had to hold him up.

"What's that? What do you mean, your friend?"

Nagy interrupted Moriarity. "He got a letter, Sarge. He made me read it. His best friend was killed overseas."

Moriarity peered at the drunken hulk in front of him. "So your best friend was killed. You think you're the only one that lost friends in this war? You think what we're trying to do is fun and games?

Moriarity came around in front of his desk and stuck his thick-veined nose in Alberto's face. "God!" he bellowed, "you smell like a fucking sewer! You think because you lost someone in this war, you got the right to screw off, to act like a baby? Do you? You think I enjoy babying an asshole like you?" Inches from Campione and saliva dripping from his chin, he yelled, "Let me tell you something, mister! Where we're going, and mighty damn soon, you'll get your act together in a hurry or get your head blown off!"

Campione slumped and farted as Moriarity bellowed, "You think because you made a record, I'm gonna treat you better than anybody else. You got another think coming. You think you're the first Indian I ever had in my command who couldn't hold his booze? Think again. You people all got problems. None of you can handle the stuff. I'll tell you something else, Campione. You ain't gonna make stripes until hell freezes over! You listen and you listen good. You stop your drinking now! That's an order. You straighten up or I'll have your ass every fucking day. Now . . . we're moving out and you ain't gonna have time for anything but fighting!

"Get him the fuck outta my sight!"

Chapter 3 — Combat

Section 1.04 Rapido

Four star General Mark "Wayne" Clark towered over everyone else in the map room in the villa in Caserta, Italy. He'd just flown in from Cairo from a meeting with Eisenhower, Churchill, and Alexander. He brought back the battle plans for the invasion by sea of Anzio, the little port town on the west coast of Italy behind German lines. If the Allies could establish a beachhead there, it would pave the way to the gates of Rome.

Part of this broad plan called for a strong attack on the 5th Army front in order to hold down the troops of Kesselring's crack German divisions, to keep them occupied which would help guarantee the landing on the coast below Rome.

General Clark had already spoken to Geoffrey Keyes, his II Corps commander. They'd agreed on the 36th Division bearing the brunt of the upcoming battle against the Germans. Now it was time to confront his old friend and fellow South Carolinian, Brigadier General Addison B. Carwile, commander of the 36th.

General Carwile had a distinguished combat record with troops. His 36th had been mauled at Salerno in the original invasion of Italy where they'd rallied on the beaches and fought off several German tank attacks. Known as a keen strategist and a brave and resourceful leader of men, Carwile had come up through the ranks in World War I. He was considered a soldier's soldier. General Clark also knew of his friend's affinity for 14 year old scotch. He made sure a case had been flown in from Scotland.

Clark waited for Keyes and Carwile while he studied the war map. He winced at what the 36th was up against, but he remembered what John J. Pershing had declared in 1918 when he committed troops in the famous Argonne battles. "When you have troops, you use them." Keyes and Carwile entered, saluted, and shook hands with Clark. A MP closed the door behind them and stood guard. Clark offered the generals a drink and came right to the point, striking the map of Italy with his knuckles.

"Churchill won the day in Cairo, gentlemen. Ike was lukewarm. On January 22nd, the Allies will attempt a landing at Anzio, behind Kesselring's solid line of fortifications. I hope Winston's charge of a 'tiger-in-their-midst' doesn't turn out to be a beached whale. As part of this overall plan, which I reluctantly agreed to, 5th Army gets a very tough nut to crack, along with our British pals to the east. They move on the 19th, we on the 20th. The 36th Division is spearhead on our front."

General Carwile took a shot glass and made himself a drink.

"The 36th crosses the Rapido here and here," Clark pointed. "The 141st upstream, north of San Angelo, the 143rd south of the town. Corps Artillery will be on Jerry's strong points and the crossings will have to be at night, because of the open plain. If we can hold down Kesselring in front of us until our boys make their end run at Anzio, our job is done. Questions?"

General Keyes remained silent, having said his piece to Clark hours before and it hadn't swayed Clark. Clark turned to Carwile.

"Wayne," Carwile began in a soft Southern accent which contained steel in it, "I don't know of a single case in all my knowledge of military history where an attempt to cross a river that's incorporated into the main line of resistance has succeeded. You know that Kesselring's boys manipulated the power dams upstream. They turned that area into a marsh. A great place to shoot mallards, not to exploit. I flew over it two days ago. Kesselring sits behind that marsh in his concrete bunkers and sandbagged roofs and hopes we'll try him. There are no roads across that muddy flat that will support troops. We'll have to carry our boats and cables and bridges about two miles to the river, all of which will be under enemy observation. Jerry cut down all the trees on both sides of the river. We'll have no cover. You got us crossing on a hairpin bend. It's so tight a place to cross, Jerry can fire in our rear."

Addison Carwile picked up the bottle of Gelenfiddich and poured himself a drink.

"As for Corps Artillery, why waste the ammo? Jerry is underground. He's in as tight as King Arthur was in Queen Guinevere's vagina. I've seen the aerial photographs of their positions." Carwile pointed to a place on the map. "Now, if I could span that stream here to the north where I could have a decent chance at a flank attack, I might take that high ground above Cassino. As it is, you're going to have a bloodbath on your hands!"

General Carwile looked at Clark for a response. He knew before he spoke that Clark had agreed to the take-off points at Cairo.

"My orders stand," Clark said.

Carwile downed his drink, saluted, and left the room.

* * *

The 36th moved back on the line, pushed through elements of the 34th Division. The 34th looked weary and beat-up, their eyes bloodshot, their faces showing exhaustion, terror, and dullness. These were men numbed by war, some of them sleepwalking, tired, trying to erase the stink and the blood and carnage for a few days before they went up again to the line.

Able platoon occupied an old irrigation ditch sandbagged by the 34th. Rats ran through it until they became names, GI's tired of gutting them with their bayonets. Ever-present in the lines were lice and unwashed bodies. Fetid odors blended with the pervasive smell of cordite and the whump of incoming shells.

It was mid-January of '44. The country along the little Rapido River had been flooded by the Germans to make the river crossing more difficult. Looking out over the sandbagged parapet of the ditch, all Able platoon saw was two miles of marshland brown with winter, covered with a light snow. Patrols moved at night as combat engineers spent the daylight hours searching for mines in the marsh. Two GI's from Baker platoon on patrol had shuh mines leave them with a ticket back to the States minus a foot each.

Nagy thought of the old squad from Shelby. Campione, himself, Nunzio, Heske, Robin, Woods, Tabas, and Wheeler. Pepe Ramos took Nunzio's place; made corporal before they hit Salerno. After Salerno, when the 36th held the beaches against the tanks, Pepe made sergeant and platoon leader. He got the Silver Star for turning back the krauts in a night action he led. Jimmy Woods got the DSC for knocking out a machine gun position. Woods came of age on the beachhead at Salerno; now was assistant platoon leader. Even Moriarity congratulated Woods after that action.

All in all, Nagy thought, we've been lucky. Nobody in the squad was in a body bag. Not much doing that morning. Few shells from Jerry, answered by 105's. Ramos came up the ditch to Steve. "Got our orders. You ain't gonna like this one."

"What's up, Pepe?" Steve asked.

"The 141st and 143rd gonna cross the river two nights from now. We gotta lug boats through the marsh. Those boats weigh over four hundred pounds!"

"There's no cover by the river," Steve said. "I been on patrol up to the river. All the trees are down. Jerry cut 'em down. I'll bet he has mortars sighted there. We'll be dead meat!"

* * *

General Carwile made sure the battle plans were given to the 36th officers in the line. Unhappy as he was with his orders, he'd follow them, see that the chain of command moved the word down to the NCO's. He couldn't countermand the order for the II Corps Artillery fire, so he spoke to his key artillery officers about targeting German troop movements in the open if the 36th got across the river. As pessimistic as he was, he kept his thoughts to himself. He'd said his piece to Clark and it didn't work.

The night before the 20th, combat engineers cleared mine-free approaches to the river, marking the routes with tape. Their mission was to guide the infantry to the river bank and help launch the wooden boats and the rubber rafts. The plan called for putting up footbridges across the river as soon as the river banks weren't under small arms fire. Then they'd build larger bridges for heavier units to cross.

At 8:30 the night of the 20th, Able platoon started out across the two miles to the river across the marsh. Jerry was ready for them. From the time Able started, they were under shell fire. By the time the fifteen hundred men of the 141st regiment got to the river, a third of their boats lay useless, shattered by shell fire. Baker platoon alongside Able lost twenty men in five minutes.

Able got to the river, moved out in rubber rafts. The fog was so thick you couldn't see the far bank, fifty feet away. Star shells burst, lighting up the sky. Towers of water shot up as rafts were blasted, men screaming as they were flung into the river to drown. Kyle Wheeling and Moriarity were in the lead raft ahead of Campione and Nagy. Alberto saw their helmets and their shoulders. The raft shot up in the sky and disintegrated. Bits of flesh and metal and rubber disappeared. Alberto and Nagy made the far bank and dug in the mud. Men on both sides of them dug in and wouldn't move. Nagy and Ramos and Woods were up from the mud, urging men forward, kicking them when they didn't move. Most of the squad made it over the bank, into a shattered cornfield, the few stalks white as ghosts. Jerry fire answered from a deep belt of dugouts, concrete bunkers and slit trenches protected by barbed wire, booby traps and mines. Their defenses ran a zig-zag course that enabled the machine gunners to pour enfilading fire into the ranks of the 36th. Alberto fired his Browning time and time again at gray-clad forms in front of him until he ran out of clips. Woods stood up and ran forward, urging men to follow him. Ramos and Woods saw their line of men was too slim, too small to carry it any further. The German firepower was overwhelming. "Fall back, fall back!" they yelled as a thin line of men, crippled and devastated by overwhelming firepower, turned and ran for the river bank.

Alberto ran, gasping for breath, back to the river, his nerve's shot, his eyes popping, his mouth like cotton. The air was filled with the slam of steel. The dead were piled high along the river bank, their bodies like ripe plums.

Alberto fled into the water, his BAR* blown away, his right leg bleeding from a German slug before he hit the water. He made the other bank with Jerry coming out of fixed positions and firing at him. Rafts blew up and wooden boats were shattered and drifted. Cries rang out for "medic" and men took sulfa packets from the dead. Nagy and Alberto lay in the mud and stink on the near bank as they were pounded by elite German troops. The attack failed and other platoons took up the attack. The night became a grisly epic of brave men being beaten by superior strength.

Sometime during that searing torture to men's minds and bodies, two wounded GI's lay on the far bank, too injured to make it back across the river. Alberto could see them and hear their cries, the river only fifty feet across. *They aren't moving, but they're not dead. I hear their cries for help. I can't move. My leg's bleeding. I'm beat. I can't do it. I'm goin' to lie here. I can't make it to the other bank. I can't. Jerry's over there. I'm going to get killed.* Campione got on his feet, staggered as he waded into the icy water, and swam across as towers of water shot up. His weapon was gone, his helmet discarded. He reached out to the two men and dragged them down to the water's edge. Taking one over his shoulder, he carried him into the water and hauled him to the near side. The other man lay on the far bank, his cries answered by a medic who stood by him and treated his wounds. Suddenly the medic's body was lifted skyward and became bone and tissue, his body parts disappearing into the bloodied water. Alberto got to his feet again, staggered and unsteadily gained the water's edge, his leg bleeding profusely. He again swam to the far bank and pulled and moved and carried the other GI back to safety.

---

* Browning Automatic Rifle

Again the attack went forward and again it was thrown back. A thousand men of the 36th crossed the stream on the 20th and the 21st. Less than one hundred made it back.

In those two terrible days with time twisted and forgotten in the maelstrom of horror, a gasping, hurt Alberto Campione lay on the near bank. A medic gave him a shot of morphine and put a sulfa pack on his leg. Pepe Ramos and Steve Nagy carried him back to a forward aid station, where the big Indian lay in shock, his words incoherent.

One week later, he was back in Baker squad. Kyle Wheeling, the tobacco-chewing, story-telling farmer from the banks of the Catawba, was listed as "missing-in-action" and a new man, Private Herman Meyer, took his place. First Sergeant John J. Moriarity no longer strode and cursed the men of the 36th.

Addison Carwile spent his time at the aid stations and the field hospital, trying to comfort his men. When Geoffrey Keyes called, Carwile said, "Tell Clark I was right."

The general went back to his tent and cried.

Section 1.05 72 Hours

Sergeant Jimmy Sato woke up in a dark kitchen where he'd slept in his bedroll, the floor like iron and his back aching. An old woman stood brewing coffee. The strong aroma reminded him of the thick black brew they enjoyed on Terminal Island.

The woman was stout and short of build and her face was pock-marked and leathery, with several chin whiskers showing. She smelled fresh and clean as she crossed the room and sat in a rocker and started to knit. A ball of yarn trailed on the hard stone floor. Completely at ease, she seemed unconcerned with the soldiers that were billeted in her house. It was another day in her long life, as if the war had passed her by. Sato stood up slowly, moved his shoulder muscles, rubbed his tired eyes and spoke the few French words he knew.

With a smile, she put down her knitting and walked to a gray cupboard. Taking out two earthen crocks, she filled them with coffee and offered one to him. Then she pumped water into a limestone sink to clean her gnarled, arthritic hands. Through the many years, the water had etched itself into the sink, making a curved, smooth trough.

It took the 442nd five full days to drive the enemy out of Bruyeres. Street by street, house by house, cellar by cellar. Jerry made them pay dearly for every inch. Now the remnants of Charley Company lay in four old stone houses on a side street in the French town in Alsace. Sato relished this peaceful interlude knowing it wouldn't last. He wondered where the old woman's family was. Maybe all dead. Did she have sons and daughters? Did the sons fight the Boche? She slowly rocked and knitted and appeared serene. It was as if she said to him, "I'm here; in my own house. I was here when the Boche came in 1914. Before you were born. I'll be here when you're gone. I've lived my life here and I'm impervious to wars and battles and bloodshed. I'm much more important than armies or boundaries."

Sato thanked the old woman for the coffee and he walked to a window and peered out. In the distance to the north stood a high ridge, its view partially obscured by drifting mists, its uppermost edges crowned with fresh snow. Through a back window he saw a lone cow grazing in a green field dotted with patches of melting snow. The old house smelled of rutabaga and sour dentures. The ancient walls were faded gray-brown and water-streaked. Looking out the window, his thoughts went back to the battle.

Charley Company was part of the 2nd Battalion of the 442nd regiment. Second Battalion came in from the southwest, Charley in the lead. The 100th Battalion was on their left below the high ridge and the 1st Battalion was in reserve. Bruyeres was the first town in France assigned to the 442nd to liberate from the Germans.

GI's moved warily into the suburbs and the silence was eerie. Nothing stirred. Shutters were drawn, flags were gone, dogs didn't bark. Things didn't look right; the men of the 442nd felt it in their bones. They felt they were walking into a trap. The Go-for-Broke Battalions came on silently, hugging buildings. Corporal "Big John" Matsu was on point, his rifle ready.

They came to a town square, where water sprayed from a fountain, where figures in sculpture danced in the spray. Early morning light made tiny rainbows. It was a place for children to play, a place for lovers to stroll in the evening, arm-in-arm, their bodies close to one another, a place for grandparents to sit on benches and gossip in the cool of the evening. Where townsfolk gathered to hear minstrels strum or work puppets in front of red curtains. It was a place for love and laughter, a place where four streets came together to form a plaza.

On that day there was no serenity, no light-hearted lovers holding hands, no children playing, no grandparents gossiping. Three Tiger tanks clanked down two of those streets, their muzzles belching flame, their great bulk blotting out the sky, their obscene fury tearing men into shreds. Rocking blasts collapsed buildings and cries of "medic" rang out as men of Charley Company bled and died. Jimmy Sato yelled, "Bring up the bazookas!" moments before a wall crumpled in front of him. A small child ran from a house and was split in two. His blood ran in faint streaks into a gutter. Behind the hulking tanks came German infantry.

In the once-quiet plaza, great pillars of dust swirled into the skies as brick and mortar shattered and fell. Gray-blue cobblestones were stained and smeared with sinew and brains as an inferno of madness blew the French city apart. A vicious, unrelenting carnage of artillery and anti-tank weapons buried the once-proud city. Short, stocky yellow-faced men with Go-for-Broke stenciled on their helmets discovered immortality in a heartbeat. Big John Matsu had gone all the way from Terminal Island to Shelby to Salerno and bloody Cassino. He stood in the way of a Tiger burst which crumpled a building and sent him into eternity.

For four days the battle raged, with 1st Battalion of the 442nd having to come out of reserve and move past the crippled survivors of 2nd Battalion. It moved with the 100th and their outgunned but faster and more mobile Sherman tanks. Muzzle to muzzle, the tank battle seesawed back and forth on the eastern side of Bruyeres until it became a barren wasteland.

On the fifth day, the 100th pushed Jerry out of Bruyeres. Gray files of prisoners marched to the rear. Names like Matsu and Tanaka and Nakamura and Nagano would be forever tied to the French town in Alsace.

It was then that people came out of their cellars and shutters opened and flags flew and dogs barked. Children played in instant rubble and asked the little yellow-faced men for candy. Little slant-eyed men gave Bruyeres back to the French.

* * *

Jimmy Sato finished his coffee and thanked the old woman as the Lieutenant came into the stone house hollering, "Sato, roust your men! Charley's out of the line! Baker platoon has three days leave and we're going to Paris!"

One hour later, Baker platoon rolled west in trucks, past the ravaged town, across the Moselle River, through farm country where October's brown and drying corn stalks were in contrast to the rubble of Bruyeres. Down avenues of tall poplar trees glistening in the sunlight, down toward the enchanted City of Light that held out hopes and dreams and sanctuary for seventy-two hours.

It was late afternoon in the City of Light. Chestnut trees lined an autumn sky and wood smoke filled the air and you smelled the odor of charcoal braziers. The eternal city where couples drank and made love beside the river. Beautiful, radiant Paris, throwing off the country's war wounds. Paris on a seventy-two hours pass. A place to get drunk and get laid.

Late afternoon shadows formed on plane trees as soft light lingered on the boulevards. Sato grabbed a cab and went to the Place de Invalides. He stepped into that magnificent amphitheater with a throng of Parisians who stared down at the cavern of alabaster that was Napoleon's tomb. He was entranced by the sensuous, rust-colored resting place of France's greatest warrior. As he stood there in awe, Sarah Sato stared back at him from the cold stone. Her deep-set hazel eyes sparkled and her lips were moist with desire. Sarah's arms stretched out to him as he was taken aback by her image.

There hadn't been a woman since Sarah. Not in the paltry dives of Naples or the brothels of Rome. There'd been many nights when cheap vino had blotted out his vision of her. He remembered vividly their last night in a motel in Norfolk on his last leave. Their love had been both savage and tender and he now relived each moment.

With an effort, Jimmy walked away from the tomb and started toward the Seine. Cool autumn air hit his face as he viewed the great metropolis. A bistro stood on the corner, Parisians laughing and drinking, their faces close together, intimate. Jimmy entered the barroom and saw a bartender standing behind a high, zinc-topped barrier, green and yellow lights flashing from a jukebox.

He sprawled in a red booth and let his tired eyes wander around the room. There was no evidence here of the ravages of war. A few servicemen sat at the bar or lounged in booths, looking for women.

A tall brunette sat at the far end of the walnut bar. Her figure was trim and her hazel hair piled high. As he watched her, she turned lazily, cat-like, and her cold, mean eyes fastened on him. The look was fierce and possessive.

It was peaceful in the bistro. He wanted to sit back and let his belly out and watch the woman's legs. To forget the war, forget the fear, the utter exhaustion, the numbness that came over his body and his mind, the knowledge that in less than seventy-two hours he'd be back on the line. Hearing again the crump-crump-crump of battle, the rip of machine pistol fire, the strange moan of the battlefield and the whine of incoming mortar fire, the smell of cordite and the sickly sweet smell of the dead under black ponchos, their limbs grotesque, their bodies stiff in the snow. He knew that when he got back to the platoon, he'd have to write a V-mail to the widow of Big John Matsu. That would be hard to do. He and Tony and Big John had been like brothers from the days on the Sato II and through Shelby and Italy and now Big John was gone. Sato shivered as he thought of how transient life was.

The bartender suggested a drink called the Flamingo. One part cognac, one part bourbon, one part red wine. He drank it and ordered another.

The woman got off her stool and her legs were long and lazy. Her skirt opened as she cast a haughty look around the room.

She opened the door, turned half-way, fastened a cold stare on Jimmy Sato. He threw some crumpled francs on the long bar and hurried outside. The cold wind hit him and he shivered and stopped to light a cigarette. His hands shook as he took a drag.

She stood under a street lamp, picking at her handbag. Moving her lips seductively, she applied a carmen smear to her upper, then lower lips.

They walked arm and arm down a narrow street where she motioned him to follow her into an entrance. They stood in a walk-up, the hallway gloomy and uninviting, the wallpaper peeling and water-stained. A madame brought them some cheap cognac and he coughed as it burned his throat. They drank cognac until a room was cleared.

She sat on the bed and kicked off her shoes, her look detached and spiritless. She pointed to the patch on his uniform.

"You fight the Boche?" she said in French, her question matter-of-fact, listless.

He answered that he did.

She arched herself like a cat and lighted a galoise, her fingernail flicking the match. Unemotionally she replied, "I fuck the Boche. I fuck them all."

Section 1.06 The Ridge

Six hours had passed since 1st Battalion started from Belmont and climbed the firebreak up the ridge. Jerry had shelled the slope and the woods caught on fire, sending rolling smoke that semi-blinded the men as they climbed.

The II Corps had given the 1st Battalion the assignment of getting to the eastern terminus of the ridge, then to circle south to the valley, cutting off Jerry mountain troops, and making contact with the 442nd Brigade at Biffontaine. It meant going single-file in a deep woods without any semblance of a battle formation. To General Addison Carwile, it was a crazy plan, one in which Jerry could be lying in wait.

The general fretted. The II Corps called the shots again, putting one of his battalions on a suicide mission! Probably worked out on a map by a half-assed staff officer who'd never seen a firefight and had only been bloodied by bulging hemorrhoids.

Jerry was there someplace. The 1st could be in a meat grinder. It might be another Rapido. Carwile's close-cropped, graying hair stood on end as he waited word. He stood outside his headquarters with his aide and looked up at the western terminus of the thirty-six hundred foot ridge, one the Germans had held which overlooked the town of Bruyeres and the village to the east, Biffontaine. A runner handed a message to his aide who passed it to the general.

All hell had broken loose on the ridge! Jerry had mined the downward eastern slope where it began its descent to the valley and had zeroed mortars along the footpath. Striking from two directions, he'd scattered the men of the 1st like leaves. Elite mountain troops, fighting now in defense of the Fatherland, came out of the forest, running low and firing, blowing through the 1st like molten lava. They drove in strength through the long, thin line. As quickly as they came, they melted into the woods, leaving an obscenity of death in their wake.

After the first communication from Battalion, radio communication went dead. The general pulled out a chewed cigar from his breast pocket and shoved it in his mouth. His face was grim and dark. Fog covered the ridge and it started to sleet. The general ordered his other two battalions of the 141st regiment committed, both two kilometers away. He knew the 442nd Brigade was in Biffontaine, only a kilometer from the eastern end of the ridge. He stared at the ridge as his jaw tightened. He'd have to commit them.

* * *

First Battalion counted its dead and wounded as early morning seeped through the forest. Pepe Ramos' body lay in the woods as blue jays scolded and jawed in the trees. Ranking Sergeant Jimmy Woods stood looking down at Sergeant Steve Nagy in his foxhole.

"We can't get through to HQ Company. Wire's cut. Krauts were behind us on the trail. We got Division. Two battalions trying to bust through to us. Take Runner. Set up a perimeter defense. Spread the MG's, the BAR's. Pool everything; ammo, food, water. If we have to, we'll ask Division to put artillery on our perimeter when Jerry comes again. We got no officers standing."

Nagy looked out to where Campione was dug in. Runner had been the ultimate warrior when Jerry blew through them, ripping white-clad figures, knocking them down until Jerry disappeared into the woods. Nagy remembered how Alberto had talked about being "invisible," how he wanted to stay a dog-face private. Well, he had. He could have easily made his stripes, could have been top dog in the platoon, could have gone to OCS from Shelby.

Instead, he got plastered and Moriarity read the riot act before they shipped over. Then after he saved the two GI's on the far bank, and he was to be decorated with the Silver Star by General Carwile, MP's found him snockered to the gills in a bordello in Rome.

Nagy walked over to Campione. They slowly set up a perimeter around the pocket of surrounded men, giving the machine gun positions priority, making men divvy up their ammo and food and water. Going back afterwards, Campione said, "When they come again, we should strip the ones we kill. They got food on them."

"Does your church have any special burial rites?" Alberto asked.

"Like what?" Steve answered.

"In our Keresan religion, when a person dies, in order to be buried on the mesa, the body has to be in the ground by the fourth day."

"What's the four days for?"

"It's about the soul leaving the body."

"I never heard that one, Runner."

Nagy walked over to the slit trench he shared with a new man, Burting, who'd come to them after they crossed the Moselle. He was a big, raw-boned farm kid of nineteen.

"Sarge," he whispered.

"Yeah, kid?"

"They'll come again, won't they?"

"When they're ready."

Nagy struggled with his emotions, turning from young Burting. Jerry had them pinned down. He stared at the low fog and checked his clips. The rain fell again and was turning to sleet. Nagy's gut hurt and he knew it was fear. He tried to calm himself by breathing deeply. Woods and he were in charge now. If they didn't get help soon, they'd be dead meat. He waited for the krauts to come again.

* * *

The general woke up feeling uneasy. In a dream, he stood on the banks of a river, staring at the icy water. Men held out their arms to him as boats spun and capsized, sending men to their deaths. It was the Rapido assault back to haunt him. Clark wouldn't listen, wouldn't change the crossing site. Cairo called the shots and he wouldn't countermand orders. As a result, the body bags piled up. He and Keyes and Clark took a beating from the press. Then came the taking of Rome and the little ill-fated action on the Rapido was just a pimple in the ass of progress. Some pimple, he thought. Some ass.

Now he had another situation not of his choosing. He dressed hurriedly and walked down a dark hall to the map room. Major Harry Winters, his G-3, was using a pointer, showing staff the situation. In the Foret du Champ on a ridge, nine kilometers east of Belmont.

"First, 141st reached their objective yesterday at 1500. They were attacked in force and overrun. Of the original battalion, three hundred men are up there in pockets, cut-off. Headquarters Company was in the rear of the column and they fought their way back.

"Second, 141st, is here, in the valley to the north. Under heavy fire. Third was in reserve and went in at 1600 yesterday. They're in a firefight. Twenty minutes ago, a message came in from 1st. Jerry hit them again. They're low on everything. If necessary, they want direct artillery on their position."

"I'm going to Biffontaine, Harry," the general said. Cut the orders. I want the 442nd on that ridge. They're the closest."

"Any in reserve, General?" Winters asked.

"No."

Carwile turned to his aide. "Bring up the car. We'll stop first at Belmont. See who got off the ridge. Then go to Bruyeres and Biffontaine."

* * *

Addison Carwile stood over Lt. Colonel Bryce Callison, commander of the 1st Battalion. Callison lay on a litter with his head bandaged from a machine gun slug.

"General," Callison began, "I had three companies on that trail. Dog was in the lead and my headquarters in the rear. We had no choice at all in that woods. The only way we could advance was single file on that woodcutter's footpath. It took us forever to get to the end of the ridge. There was no way in that heavy woods to get any scouts out. Dog got there at 1500, and we got a message from them. They were set up, General. That whole end of the ridge was heavily mined. Jerry had a triple line of concertina wire twelve foot high blocking our way. His mortars were zeroed in on the path. He blew through us like shit through a goose!"

"What do you have left up there, and how long can they hold?"

"Most of Baker. Some of Charley. Not much of Dog. We fought our way back when we couldn't go forward. Couldn't get any messages through. Jerry was all over us!"

"Can they hold out?"

"Mebbe a couple of days. They carried cold rations for two days. They're short on ammo and water. We shouldn't have gone up there that way, General!"

Carwile bent down and shook hands with Callison. "Next time you see Geoffrey Keyes, you have my permission to tell him that. I'm committing the 442nd. They're closest to your boys."

* * *

The general and his aide started down a country road to Bruyeres. The sky was dark with snow and the road was heavy with mud. Lines of infantry, their heads down, moved on both sides of the road. The command car passed a mustard-colored German .88 piece. A yellow-haired, gray-green uniformed member of the Wehrmacht lay spread-eagled on its firing tube, maggots sucking at his eye sockets. A Sherman tank stood on a nearby bend in the road, its crew making coffee. On the edge of Bruyeres, two MP sergeants made them stop as they saluted and checked their ID's.

A guard saluted them at 442nd headquarters as they entered a room that smelled of coffee brewing and disinfectant. Colonel Fred Wynant, a tall West Point officer, started to rise and saluted with this executive officer. Wynant's desk consisted of a door ripped from its hinges and set on top of some ammo boxes. A communications wire ran through a broken window to a bare light bulb. Taped to the wall was a map. Heat came from a primus stove. The broken window was covered with a dark cloth and a tired, stained chaise lounge sat in the corner of the room, its bulk sagging like an old hound dog. Three scratched, brown folding chairs stood by Wynant.

"God-damn it, Fred," the general laughed, "you have all the comforts of home." He rubbed his hands by the stove and shook hands with both of them. Before Fred Wynant could accept the compliment, the general bored ahead.

"Fred, your forward lines are on the eastern edge of Biffontaine. What's left of the 1st, 141st are right here and they're getting the shit kicked out of them." The general pointed to the position on the map.

"Three hundred boys are up there. Cut-off. Second and 3rd are trying to reach them. They're both facing heavy fire from Jerry. You're going in. All three battalions. When can you get started?"

Fred Wynant had come up through the ranks and he knew his men and how to use them. It didn't take a genius to see that he was worn out. They'd taken Bruyeres and suffered badly.

"Tomorrow, General. We're beat-up. We're under strength. But we're closer. I see that."

"I can't let those boys go under," Carwile replied.

Wynant's face was up in the general's. "So we use them like they were used at Cassino, General?"

Carwile's dander was up. He knew how Wynant loved his Nisei, how they'd bled for him, how they'd been used as dog meat at Cassino in repeated attacks that failed. Now he was telling the colonel to have his men drive up a thirty-six hundred foot ridge in the face of an entrenched foe.

He took a deep breath and gazed steadily at the colonel who he admired very much.

"When you have troops, Fred, you use them."

* * *

The next morning at 0500, the 442nd moved out of Biffontaine. The ridge facing them to the north looked dark and menacing and Sato remarked to Tony Watanabe, "Lieutenant says a battalion of the 36th is up there surrounded."

"So we get the dirty stick again," Tony replied.

"You're smart for a tuna man."

Charley Company entered the forest on a rutty, mud-filled trail, passing ambulances and mess trucks waiting for survivors. Sato cursed the sleet and rain as he plodded on in the darkness. Sarah stared at him from the Place de Invalides and he felt sick. All he got from the platoon were grumbles. It was always the same story. When the white boys got in trouble with Jerry, who had to bail them out? Jimmy tried to remind his men that they'd taken Bruyeres without outside help. It didn't make any difference. They wanted to gripe. Gripe they did.

The footing was terrible. One foot forward and half a foot back. All he saw was the form in front of him as he staggered and slipped in the mud. All he heard were occasional early morning bird songs and the faint rustling of men's legs in wet-soaked wool uniforms.

All the NCO's had been told by their company commander that, from the coordinates, the embattled battalion was surrounded, was approximately one and a half kilometers from Biffontaine. Thinking of this as Jimmy slogged along, he knew that Jerry had to be close. Light crept into the forest, spreading its first rays on the upper edge. As the light spread, Jimmy saw the heavy growth of trees and knew that any minute, the enemy would hit them. Each large tree loomed along the trail like the enemy, its hostile form reaching out to kill.

Jerry hit them at 0600. White-clad troops were everywhere. Sato took a bullet in his right shoulder and he fell screaming. On his back, he located it, found it to be in the flesh, not deep. Gritting his teeth, he rose from the mud and fired at a form in front of him. The form disappeared. Another took its place. Jimmy's mouth went dry as he gasped for breath and fired again as the cry of "fix bayonets" rang out.

Men spread out on both sides of the trail and set cold steel at the end of their rifles. A white form hurled itself at Jimmy and was met by a bayonet that lodged in his flesh. The German and Sato were on the forest floor as Jimmy tried to pull his bayonet out of flesh. A sucking sound came from the soldier's lips and the enemy lay in the snow, his eyes staring up at Sato. He pulled the bayonet from the lifeless form and faced another white wraith charging toward him. Sato shot the soldier at close range and he fell on Jimmy, his life blood pumping into the earth. Jimmy found himself bleeding and unable to move. He lay with the weight of the man sprawled in death as the battle raged in the forest. All around him, men killed and were killed. Jimmy shook with pain from his shoulder and managed to roll the dead soldier off him and reach for his rifle.

Charley Company closed with the enemy and the battle raged on and off all morning and into the early afternoon. The German broke off, then came in waves. By late afternoon, the forest was littered with the dead and wounded, both friend and foe. Medics moved among the men as quiet finally settled over the deep woods. A medic bandaged Sato's shoulder and blessed darkness descended. Through the tall cedars could be heard the faint cries of the wounded. All that day, the 442nd moved less than four hundred yards.

The second and third days were copies of the first, with sorties by the German and answering fire from the 442nd. Runners were constantly on the move, bringing up ammunition and water.

"If we don't move Jerry soon, we won't make it," Tony said.

"I got six dead and four wounded in Baker," Jimmy responded.

The fourth day dawned as elements of the 442nd climbed rocky terrain infested with machine gun nests. Coal-skuttled troops from the Fatherland sent many Nisei to horrible deaths. Rooting out the German from defended positions was the ultimate price to pay.

Then Sato heard a cry coming from the rocky soil, a cry so intense and barbaric, he felt his ancestors rising from their graves! It was the ancient cry, the savage cry of "Banzai!" that swept Charley Company forward up the hill. Men rose from the unyielding ground, their bayonets fixed.

First a few men. Then a few more. A dozen . . . twenty . . . forty . . . sixty Nisei charging up a rough defile, driving forward with a call to take the ridge or die! Men climbed, scaled heights, had their guts blown away by crack German gunners, gasped for breath, choked in the dust and debris of battle, shrieked with rage and hate, and in an unforgettable charge, routed the enemy with their fury. A bunker suffered a direct hit, a flash of orange streaking the sky. Men moved past the bunker as black smoke boiled and white-clothed troops were cremated.

Sato was down with an enemy soldier wrestling with him, the two combatants rolling down the hill, their bodies ripped by the implacable soil, Sato's hands searching for the man's throat. Suddenly he was free with Tony Watanabe standing over the enemy, Tony's bayonet thrust into the mid-section of the German. Watanabe pulled the blade from the lifeless form as they stood in the maelstrom for a brief instant. Then they were climbing again with another bunker erupting in flame and gray-green clad figures running out.

Tony made a sucking sound as his body was stitched with machine pistol fire. He fell in the rocky soil as his voice rose. Shouting in his mother's tongue, he yelled, "Go! Go! Get those dirty sons of bitches! You bakatare! You bakatare!"

Jimmy Sato sat high up on the defile and cradled his friend as Tony whispered to him, "Kachin, itai, itai" (Mama, it hurts, it hurts).

* * *

The bloodied remnants of Charley Company stood on top of the ridge at 1500 hours. Sato looked down into a long, lush, green valley. His hands shook and tears flowed down his face. His closest friend was gone. Big John and Tony had paid the final price. The tears wouldn't stop. Sato sat for a moment with his hands covering his head. After a moment, he stood up and gathered his men and took a head count. Twenty were on the ridge. Thirty-six started out four days before.

A German soldier stood near them in a foxhole, his hands blown off, blood covering his face and arms and uniform. "Kamerad! Kamerad!" he pleaded (Comrade, comrade).

Sato walked by him.

* * *

Deep in the Foret du Champ, the exhausted and harried remnants of the 1st Battalion continued to hold out. During the fourth day of their virtual imprisonment, the wind came up. With it, the sound of grinding, racketing tank treads. Woods figured one more attack by Jerry and they'd have to call in the artillery. It would mean losing men, but it could be their last chance to get out.

Woods made his rounds and felt his strength leaving him. He had a single chocolate bar and half a canteen of water. As he made his rounds to make sure men weren't asleep on guard, he saw Heske stripping a dead German.

"Get the fuck back in your hole, Heske."

"I'm looking for food, Sarge."

"I don't give a shit. You find something, you share it. We ain't grave robbers. Pick up your piece and get in your hole. I'll rip your ass if I see you doing it again."

Woods stood face to face with Heske. The cab driver from Chicago got back in his foxhole, his face livid. As Woods walked away, he heard Heske say, "I'll get that little cocksucker yet."

Woods turned and faced Heske and said, "When we get out of this mess, you and me are gonna duke it out. Nobody calls me a cocksucker and gets away with it!"

Cock Robin stood by Campione as he finished something on a piece of paper and handed it to Runner.

"What's this for?" Campione asked, knowing what it was. Men gave you letters when they thought they weren't going to make it.

"For my wife."

"I'm not your nursemaid," Campione growled.

"Whose bright idea was it anyway, coming up this fucking trail?" Robin asked.

"Musta been Corps." Alberto set his BAR down and pulled out a half-used chaw of tobacco. "Old man Carwile ain't that stupid. Some jerk at Corps probably thought the whole thing up."

"Thanks for taking the letter." Robin's face was serious.

Alberto wiped his face with a hand.

"Here, you old coot, I got something for you." He reached into his pocket and produced a rumpled piece of waxey paper. It was part of a K ration cover, dark brown and crinkly.

"Got bored in Belmont. Nothing to drink. Did this before we started up the firebreak." He winked at Nagy standing by him and handed it to Robin who unfolded it.

Cock looked at the sketch. It was of two worn, heavily callused hands cradling a rifle. The hands were dark and thin white trails of dried, rough skin flowed along a dark sea. Cock turned his hands over, then back again.

"Them my hands, ain't they?"

"Sure are," Alberto responded as he stared at the farmer from Missouri.

"Knowed you were a drawer. All Injuns like that?"

"All white men shoot as well as you?" Runner retorted.

"Sure do thank you," Cock replied, folding the paper and putting it in his pocket.

"Willy, that's my son. He draws."

"Didn't know you had a son."

Embarrassment showed on Robin's face. "He's what they call 'touched.' They got a name for it. They call it mongoloid. I don't talk much about him."

Walter "Cock" Robin turned toward his hole in the earth. He had walked a few paces from Nagy and Campione when mortar fire lifted him and slammed his body into a tree. The explosion knocked both Nagy and Campione down as Robin's life blood seeped into the forest floor. Shells exploded and men dove for cover. Trees were mangled and torn, their bark stripped as clouds of birds rose in the air and the earth was scorched and seared. Steve Nagy felt a sharp pain in his left arm and blood ran down his hands. A medic cut the sleeve of his left arm and stopped the bleeding with a tourniquet. The left arm was torn from mortar fragmentation and he couldn't hold his BAR. John Heske worked the twin triggers of his machine gun as white-clad forms advanced through the trees. Young Burting advanced the clips as Heske fired. Alberto Campione tasted green bile from his rage as he skewered a blonde head coming full bore at him. Bodies lay in the snow as the 1st fought for its life.

* * *

The fifth day came to the encircled men. Fear and fatigue and cold and empty bellies began to break them. They fell asleep on guard, they hallucinated, they cried, they cursed the heavens, railed at the enemy, jawed at the Corps for putting them on the ridge, damned the fate that brought them to this spiny, rocky soil.

Heske wanted to give up. "Let's surrender when they come again," he said to Burting.

Woods heard about it and reamed him out. "There ain't any cowards in this outfit," he yelled. "You pull that and I'll shoot you!" Woods looked around at men in their slit trenches. "Any man that gives up, I'll shoot. We're gonna hold 'till we drop!"

Nagy marveled at Woods. He'd held them together along with Pepe Ramos. For a kid so green, so young, so unconcerned as he was at Shelby, always enduring Moriarity's wrath, he'd come a long way. He'd grown up fast at Salerno and turned into a first rate fighting man. Now he was the glue that held them together as they wondered what lay ahead, whether they'd be the next under the black tarps. Nagy stood in his hole. The latest kraut attack had been bad. Pepe Ramos and Cock Robin lay fifty feet away with other men of the 442nd. He saw Campione reach in his pocket and pull out his bear fetish and rub it. Nagy looked around and stared at the beleaguered men near him. They were smeared with mud and blood, their hair matted, their eyes half-closed. Some of them shook from cold and exhaustion and fear.

Near him stood steady, imperturbably "Snake" Tabas, working on his foxhole. His face was bandaged and his uniform bloodstained and torn, his eyes blank. Snake put his entrenching tool down and rolled over and urinated. The yellow stream floated over the bittersweet stench of the dead. Rumor had it Snake had been a con for some burglary on the west coast. If so, he must have made his peace. His was a cold serenity. Of all the men in the platoon, Nagy felt that Henry Tabas would be the last man standing.

As he watched the men, two P-47's nosed over the embattled ridge, trying to drop food and ammo. Two chutes opened like weary lilies on a summer day. They began to fall and drift as the wind picked up. They hung over the ridge, tantalizing the men of the 1st. Slowly they moved away toward the valley to the north and were lost from view. Men stood in their holes and ran the emotional gauntlet. Some swore, some cried. Some faces were blank with disbelief.

Nagy's hands shook as he lighted one of his few remaining cigarettes. His body ached to his bones from the cold and his left arm felt sharp, stabbing pain from the mortar wound. As he looked at the bandage on his left arm and felt the pain run down into his hand, he suddenly was reminded of what Runner had told him back in Maybelle's about the day the Spaniards had seized Acoma and had cut off the left hand of every male over fourteen. At the time, Nagy had listened to Alberto, but hadn't been convinced of the impact of his statement. Now, as he worried whether the mortar fragments had severed any ligaments, and wondered how soon he could expect to be taken to a field hospital or aid station, he thought about what Alberto had said. To every male over fourteen the Spaniards had severed a connection to life. The consequences for a generation must have been terrible.

Nagy rubbed his forehead with his remaining good right hand and ran through his matted hair. He had to keep his spirits up and his wits about him. Next to Woods, he was in charge. No officers remained, other than two with wounds. Every time he felt he couldn't make it, as if he wanted to run deep into the forest and lie down deep, dig himself in deep, deeper than anyone could possibly find him, it was then he thought of Rainy. He remembered the brief, but wonderful happiness they had shared. He kept repeating to himself, *Rainy, Rainy. I love you. I need your strength now. I feel I can't go on. I'm tired and cold and I can't think straight. All I think of is you and the good times. Like that day in the library. Remember? I had my notebook and you asked me to read what I'd put down. That poem by Wendell Berry, the one called "Boone."*

In winter the river hides its flowing
Under the ice bearing interminable down;
The black crow flies into the black night;
The bones of the old dead ache for the house fires.

And you said, "How beautiful." I said, "See, there is the river. Under the ice. It's powerful. It moves under the ice. It's like life, Rainy. It's all around us and we take it for granted.

Alberto "Runner" Campione peered with crust-filled, bleary eyes into the forest. Steve Nagy, his best friend, stood dug-in at his foxhole a few yards away. He was crying and no one saw him or heard him.

Jerry came at dusk, flitting past dark trees, running low, his machine pistols firing. The men of the 1st were too weak, too worn down, too outmanned. Woods radioed in the clear to Division. The message was simple. *We have run out of options. Put direct artillery on our perimeters and our forward positions. Now.* The coordinates were given.

Men hunkered down in their foxholes and waited for the directed hell to be released. Shells tunneled through the wet sky, blowing holes in coal-skuttle, helmeted troops of the Wehrmacht. White-clad bodies were hurled sky-high, torn and shredded. The enemy lay in the woods as twisted, mangled, deformed remnants of Germanic pride. Around them lay half-alive, bleeding, body-drained, shell-shocked men of the 36th.

* * *

Morning came on the sixth day on the ridge. Snake Tabas wearily stood examining the carnage. White uniformed bodies lay in front of him as he held his rifle with shaking hands. He couldn't help thinking where he had come from a couple of years before, how the fates were kind to him. He was back in Portland and Asa stood beside him in the rail yards. They'd found the Andrew Jackson bill in the corner of the boxcar which brought them from Spokane. Asa challenged him to take it and get tattooed. He wanted him to have a green snake tattooed on his back so that when he twitched his shoulders, the snake would bear its fangs. They'd been released from Dannemora after five years for the hold-up in Tacoma. Snake wiped his eyes with the bandage on his hand and saw someone standing in front of him. A little soldier with a rifle stood over him and said, "Been looking for you guys. Want a cigarette?"

Tabas took the cigarette and the soldier helped him light it. He got out of his hole and the two men embraced. Tabas wept openly and said softly, "You guys made it!" Other men from the 442nd came into sight and the weary survivors of the 1st found themselves being offered cigarettes and water. Some men shouted with joy, some danced a jig. Others uttered silent prayers.

"They look worse than we do," Nagy said to Campione.

"Took us four days to get to you," the little soldier said to Tabas. "I'm Hideo Tanaka."

"Tabas, Henry Tabas. Where you from?"

"Hawaii," the little Nisei answered.

"Hardly moved the first two days. Jerry hit us hard. We got some flame-throwers into their bunkers. Used the bayonet the last day." Tanaka took his helmet off, put his rifle down, ran his hands through his thick black hair. Then he rubbed his face. Nagy came up to him and the Nisei offered him a drink from his canteen.

Sergeant Jimmy Sato turned to his radioman and said, "Tell 'em we found 'em. Give 'em our coordinates. We need lots of help. We're beat up bad!"

Nagy eyed Sato. "Last time I saw you was back in Maybelle's at Shelby, remember?"

"That's right," he replied. He then saw Campione standing a few feet away. "That's your buddy, isn't it?"

Runner Campione recognized the little man with the sergeant's stripes sewn on his uniform, realized it was Sato, the husband of Sarah. He remembered the brief episode in Maybelle's, how the two little Japanese-American soldiers had sat with them in their booth and he'd had a good look at Sato. He again saw that thin nose and mustache that seemed to be penciled in. It hit him hard how this little man had been able to command the love and admiration of his Sarah. It made him suddenly sick to think of Sarah and how he had confessed his love, only to be told that she belonged to someone else. And here the two men faced each other in this alien place, thousands of miles from Sarah. It was like a slap in the face to realize that what he desired the most in this world was beyond his reach.

"Where your officers?" Nagy asked Sato.

"All dead," answered Sato. "I'm in charge."

As he spoke the words, the ominous, chilling sound of a tank was heard coming toward them. Its treads clanked as the sound increased in volume and Nagy yelled, "It's Jerry! Take cover!" Men ran for cover, running into their foxholes, attempting to get behind mangled and torn trees from the artillery barrage of the night before. The remnants of the 1st, 141st and men from the 442nd were mixed together like the fish of the sea as the shadow of a great shark loomed.

The monster tank rumbled on, its grinding motion rocking the forest. Trees shook and were torn sideways. The muzzle of the Tiger tank was like the eye of a vicious cyclops, swaying back and forth. Behind the German tank came white-suited infantry.

Alberto hollered, "Where's the bazooka?"

As his words formed, out of the forest ran a massive stag, its russet coat shining in the early morning light. The great beast glided into the open and moved to where Alberto stood holding a bazooka and two rockets. It stopped for a moment as Alberto reached out and touched its massive sides. With a great leap, it vanished in the forest.

Runner Campione stood in a clearing as the monster tank crashed toward him. His brief exultation at seeing the great stag was short-lived. He knew it was a sign for him. Only a direct hit on the gun muzzle of the tank could stop its belching destruction. He steadied himself on the flat ground, placed one of the two grenade rockets in the bazooka. As he did, the Tiger tank fired. John Heske's body was lifted and thrown into the sky and came down lifeless. Jimmy Woods' head was severed from his body and rolled on the cold ground. In his eyes shone an unanswered statement from the boy who read comic books at Shelby.

Alberto put the bazooka to his shoulder and fired. The muzzle of the tank exploded. As it did, Alberto was slammed violently to the ground by the burst of a machine gun firing from a hidden position. The tank ground to a halt as the men of the 36th and 442nd jumped from their holes in the ground and met the enemy.

* * *

The earth vibrated as Alberto lay in a wilderness of spruce and pine. Cold, driving rain pelted the earth as fire burned in his body. Part of his intestines bled into the ground from a gaping hole in his stomach. Steve Nagy, shaking with tears, cradled Alberto in his arms as deep pains shot through his left arm and hand. A corpsman gave Alberto a shot of morphine and thrust a sulfa tablet in his mouth. The big Indian coughed bile and blood as a blue jay scolded in the pines.

* * *

Weightless, Alberto "Runner" Campione floated above the dry New Mexico desert. He looked down upon the bronze ramparts of Acoma as golden sun pierced the cliffs and bittersweet air wafted on parched winds. His sisters stood by a horno, baking paper-bread. His mother, Maria, ground corn in a metate in the great room. Felipe Campione stood proudly beside a cottonwood fire as orange embers spit out and died in the sand. His father cut the heart out of a deer as he spoke of his distrust of the whites. He then hung the heart on a pole by their lean-to and reached into his faded jeans and produced a hazel-colored deer fetish.

"This was given to me by my father, Alberto. Now it is yours."

Father and son left the desert and climbed the rough steps leading to the mesa. They walked together to the Plaza and stepped down the sacred steps leading to the kiva in the ground. The old cacique greeted them as a warm fire glowed by the altar. Then they left the kiva and Alberto said good-bye to his family.

Sarah floated in front of him, her radiant black hair worked delicately into a bun. She took his hand and led him down a hallway. The scent of burning mesquite filled the air and a small fire burned in a grate. The fire illuminated several ceramic pieces which he recognized as the work of his mother, Maria. The shifting flames cast shadows which made the figures seem to dance.

Sarah led him to a window and pushed the shades aside. Her bedroom looked out upon a vast desert plain. A mountain rose in the distance. Staring down at Alberto from the facade of the mountain was a solemn Indian. The Indian's regal gaze swept across the desert in bold disregard of those who had wronged his people. He surveyed his spacious horizon as he was the last of his race and had inherited all he witnessed.

Circles of light filled the sky and Sarah beckoned to Alberto. A pale moon sailed through the night sky as darkness rolled over him.

Chapter 4 — Burial

Bright streaks of early morning light hit the copper-colored ramparts of the Acoma mesa. Thunderclouds lay on the western horizon as the heat rose in the desert. The native people stood at the foot of the great mesa and searched the road to the north for the military procession bringing Alberto Campione's body to its final resting place. Dust clouds formed on the horizon and coming into view was a line of vehicles on a single lane dirt road. Now the people saw the three gray-green vehicles and a yellow-orange school bus. As the bus came into view it had on its sides the famous black and red headdress of an Indian chief. This was the insignia of the St. Catherines Indian School in Santa Fe. The Army units and the bus slowed and came to a halt. From the first army vehicle a casket was unloaded by military personnel. It was quickly surrounded by leaders of the clan and the old cacique led the way. Two of the war chiefs and two selected elders hoisted the casket on their shoulders. They carried it up the well-worn, hand-hewn steps leading to the summit where they took it to the household of the Campione family.

The locals dressed in solemn black stood on each side of the steep steps to make way for the many honored guests. An elderly nun emerged from the bus followed by a number of teenage students. Then came a long-nosed Indian in a dark, hooded garment that swept the dust before him. Many recognized the famous sculptor, Frederick Creekwater, who came from the village of Madrid. From the military cars came two women and two soldiers. The soldiers had bright patches on their shoulders. One of them was from the 36th Texas Division and a much smaller soldier from the famous 442nd Combat Brigade made up of Japanese-Americans. The brigade was the most decorated unit in the American Army.

Both of the women were dressed in black. The tallest wore a lovely turquoise necklace that graced her body. The other woman had brilliant red hair that shone in the early morning light. The two women chatted quietly together as they mounted the steps to the mesa. Following the women were many dignitaries who were greeted warmly by the native people. The Governor of the State of New Mexico shook hands with many and was observed speaking to one of the United States Senators from the State of New Mexico. The burial party made its ascent up the rough steps which were strewn with fresh-cut spruce. The boughs carried a sweet morning scent. The visitors arrived at the summit and were guided through the dirt streets to the Campione house. The streets had been swept and strewn with spruce cuttings.

The family of Alberto Campione greeted their guests and invited them into the great room. The open casket stood in the center of the room. The family had washed the body and wrapped Alberto in a simple brown blanket. His head faced the east as was the custom and it was whitened with cornmeal. Alberto's father addressed everyone and asked them to touch the deceased's forehead. He explained that this was to tell his son's soul that they forgave his transgressions. Four gnarled mesquite prayer sticks painted black lay beside the body.

The Governor and the Senator first came to the casket and touched the deceased's forehead. They were followed by Sarah Sato and her husband, Sergeant James Sato. Sarah was watched intently by Alberto's mother and her two daughters. As Sarah gently touched Alberto, a chill ran up and down her spine. She thought of that first day in the museum in Santa Fe when Alberto's eyes had lighted up as he beheld the sculpture of Frederick Creekwater and he had said, "This is what I want to do with my life." She remembered how he had told her of his strange dream that kept coming back and how she had said, "It's a sign, Alberto. You will someday find that mountain and you will put your father's face on it." Then she thought of that terrible night when Alberto had gotten drunk and torn her dress, before the sheriff's department subdued him and put him in jail. And now she stood looking down at his mortal remains. She shivered slightly and hoped that no one had noticed it. This young man that had so much talent, who had so much to give to the world, to his people, to the art of sculpture. Now it was all over and he had come to rest with his people on the mesa. Sarah silently said a prayer and thanked her God for never revealing Alberto's love for her to her husband.

Jimmy Sato stood beside Sarah and thought of the time in basic training at Shelby when Alberto and his friend Steve had routed the rednecks. Then he had the vision of the battle on the ridge in which Alberto faced the Tiger tank.

Frederick Creekwater was next in line. Touching Alberto's forehead he remembered how Alberto had asked him in his shed in Madrid, "Do you know what the stone will be before you start?" and he had answered, "Alberto, in any form of art, there are hidden truths. They lie beneath the surface. You can't force them. You struggle; everybody struggles. The truth will come, Alberto. Slowly. The form emerges form the rock's sleep like a long dream."

Sergeant Steve Nagy stood with his girlfriend, Rainy. He looked down at his closest friend and a picture formed of those two terrible days on the Rapido. Pinned under heavy shellfire, gasping for breath, as Alberto lay on the bank next to Steve, he saw Alberto rise from the mud and mortar fire and dive into the icy waters. He swam to the opposite bank and brought back two wounded GI's. One at a time. At the time, the river was shelled heavily as the boats tried to cross. Then when it came time for General Carwile to pin a Silver Star on Alberto on the parade ground in Rome, Alberto was in a cat-house enjoying himself.

As Steve thought of Alberto, he felt he had to say something to those assembled in the great room. It came from his heart and it came slowly. "When there is a man like Alberto Campione," he said, "with so much vigor, so much life, so much promise, we must learn from his vision. He must be burned into our feelings and our memory like an angry fire. Many times he spoke to me of his people of Acoma. He wanted them to grow, to advance as a people, to reach mightily beyond their limiting boundaries. He had a dream. A wonderful dream. To put his own father's face upon a mountain. It was to make his father and his family and his people of Acoma proud of him, proud of the Keresan nation. We of the 36th Division and the 442nd Combat Brigade salute him for what he did for us."

When all the guests had paid their respects, the ancient village priest stood over the casket. His hair was below his shoulders as he uttered a prayer in native Keresan. When he was through, the war chiefs and the two elders picked up the casket. The cacique stood behind them with his long wooden staff and he sang an Indian song. It reminded Steve Nagy of a Gregorian chant he'd tried to sing when he was a choir boy under Father Ferency. The father of Alberto followed first in line behind the casket, followed by his wife and two daughters, their heads bowed.

Early morning light cast shadows on old San Estaban Rey as the funeral party entered the adobe church. When everyone was seated, the priest stood in front of the altar and spoke in the language of his people. He then blessed the remains of the son of Felipe and Maria Campione. Felipe Campione took his wife's hand and smiled at his two daughters. His son had come home and his greatness would live in Felipe's heart. The little boy that he had taken hunting and who had run with the great stag on Mount Hasasu had become a man who would always be remembered by the people of Acoma. Tears began to flow and his wife squeezed his hand.

The old priest finished and he motioned Sergeant Steve Nagy to come up in front of the altar. Steve left Rainey's side and walked to the altar. He opened a small black case and presented the Congressional Medal of Honor to the Campione family in memory of their son. As the nation's highest military award for valor and bravery, it was a fitting tribute to the memory of the Indian from Acoma.

* * *

Burial

In keeping with their custom and tradition, only the members of the clan and the Campione family witnessed the final act. The body, covered by a single sheet of muslin, was placed firmly in the grave in the old cemetery behind the church. It was put in feet-first so that Alberto's head was up, facing the east and the morning sun.

* * *

Maria Campione awoke before dawn and left her sleeping husband. She wanted to mourn for her son alone. She walked in the great room and found her blue bowl. Gently she removed the silver cross from her neck. It was done with the same deliberate ease as a woman undressing in front of her husband of forty years.

The air in the adobe house was stale. She must dust and clean before people came to pay their respects. The cross made a scraping sound as it slid down the sides of the bowl, and she smiled. It looked like Jesus on the waves of an unknown sea. A hand touched her shoulder. She turned and met her husband's kiss.

"I'm going out," he said.

Felipe Campione strode to the far eastern end of the mesa. The sun rose and the wind came up and orange dust billowed from the desert floor. He watched as a construction company laid earthen pipe for a new irrigation system.

The End

Author's Note

John M. Nakamura — Born 01/16/21

Died 04/05/45

During the research for this novel, my wife and I paid two visits to France and toured the battlefield near the village of Biffontaine. While there in 1985, I had the pleasure of meeting and spending some time with Henri Georges, who was then the mayor. He graciously accompanied us over the ground on the high ridge. He had been a boy of fourteen in October 1944 and he remembered distinctly standing outside his farmhouse with his father as they watched elements of the 442nd Combat Regiment fix bayonets and charge a hill position in the face of enemy fire. Henri Georges gave me copies of the French newspapers describing the great reunion in October of 1984 of many of the men from the 442nd and men from the 36th Division. This reunion commemorated the 40th anniversary of the battle which freed a battalion of the 36th that had been surrounded by the Germans and trapped for seven days. He also gave me a copy of the letter that United States Senator Daniel Inouye had written to the French government in which he congratulated the government for its recognition of the significance of the action on the high ridge. Also included in the papers given to me was a list of all those soldiers who had participated in those bloody days during World War II, the days in which the 442nd lost more of their own men than they saved in their valiant attempt on the ridge.

When we arrived back in the States in the fall of 1988, I wrote to Senator Inouye and informed him of what I was doing. He gave me a letter of introduction to Chester Tanaka who had written the book about the 442nd entitled <u>Go for Broke</u>. I met Tanaka in the museum in San Francisco which is a memorial to the 442nd. As we talked that day and Tanaka pointed to a large battle map of the Biffontaine action, he casually asked me where I hailed from.

"Flint, Michigan," I said.

"Did you ever know John Nakamura?" he asked.

"Yes," I said. "John and I were good friends. We played together in the Flint Junior College band in '39 and '40."

Tanaka paused a moment and looked at me.

"I'll tell you a true story. We were both at Biffontaine. I was his platoon leader. After there, we were sent down around Nice on rest and then served on the border near Italy. In the early spring of '45, the 442nd went back to Italy and we were fighting Germans again in the mountains far to the north. John came to me one night and we talked. He said he was going to be killed the next day. I told him I could take him out of the line for a couple of days and he wouldn't have it. He said it was his duty. The next day he was killed in a mortar barrage. John was a very good soldier."

The comments of Chester Tanaka stayed with me. When I arrived back in Flint, I told the story to my friends. About a year later, I noticed in the Flint Journal obits that Elsie Nakamura had died. She was John's mother and was over ninety at the time of her death. I called Evelyn Golden who knew Mrs. Nakamura and I told her the strange story. She said, "I'll meet you at the funeral. Afterwards I'll introduce you to John's brother and sister." After the funeral, I told the relatives about Tanaka's remarks about John. They were amazed.

The story doesn't end there. In October of 1992, I received a letter from Harley Krapohl, one of the friends of John. Enclosed with the letter was a sheet of information on John that Harley had obtained from the War Department. The following is an excerpt:

> John Nakamura was drafted in September 1942 and finished four weeks of basic training at Camp Crowder, Missouri. Before he was assigned to an Army unit, however, he was given an "honorable discharge" with the explanation that he had been "erroneously inducted." At that time it was not Army policy to draft young men of Japanese ancestry, even if they were native-born American citizens.
>
> After his discharge, John returned to the University of Michigan to work toward a master's degree. In June of 1943 he volunteered for the 442nd Regimental Combat team, composed of Japanese-American volunteers. He trained at Camp Shelby, Mississippi, and was sent overseas in June 1944.
>
> The 442nd was incorporated into the 5th Army and during the summer of 1944, the unit participated in the Italian campaign. In September 1944 the 442nd was pulled out of Italy and sent to southern France. As a unit of the 36th (Texas)

Division, they saw action in the Vosges Mountains. In October they were called on to aid a unit of the 36th Division that had been cut off by the enemy. In recognition of the rescue by the 442nd, the soldiers of the 36th Division declared all soldiers of the 442nd "Honorary Texans."

The rest of the winter of 1944-45 was spent in a holding action in the Maritime Alps. In the spring of 1945, the 442nd returned to Italy to take part in the last big drive of the Italian campaign. It was there that John was killed, on April 5, 1945, caught in an enemy mortar barrage.

———————

The following is an excerpt from the military newspaper *The Stars and Stripes*, dated April 9, 1945. John Nakamura had been interviewed a few days before he was killed. This is what he said:

When I was in France, I used to think of Italy. I used to think of that time we were thirsty and drank out of a stream and the next day, further up the stream, we found a couple of dead Jerries, a dead Italian lady who was pregnant, some dead goats and a dead cow—all of them had been in the water a long time. I also remember the 27 days from Grosseto to Pisa in which time there was no rain or a single cloud. Boy, that was good fighting weather. Now that I'm in Italy, all I can think about is Nice.

The reporter added that John had never missed a day of combat and had 175 actual combat days to his record.

Addendum

Why did so many Nisei volunteer for military service in World War II? Why did they fight so valiantly and in doing so compile the most outstanding record in the history of the United States Army? Why, indeed, as the 442nd "Go-for-Broke" Combat Regiment . . . when the right of habeas corpus guaranteed by the Constitution was being revoked after Pearl Harbor and they found themselves by the thousands with their parents and relatives in detention camps in the western desert of the United States? Why, indeed, since the Constitution guarantees that no person shall be deprived of life, liberty, or property without due process of law? Why, indeed, when their dignity was stripped away?

I have been asked these questions many times. I, myself, ask the same questions. The questions make me pause and think back to those terrible days when one hundred and thirty thousand Japanese-Americans were behind barbed wire in camps similar to Camp Desperado that the author uses in his novel <u>Alberto's Dream</u>. My answers come from personal knowledge and my own convictions.

The Nisei volunteered for several reasons. It is true they wanted to get away from the discomfort and boredom and hurt they felt being behind wires with rifles pointed at them from manned overhead towers. It was also true that there was peer pressure to stand up and fight for their country, no matter the indignities already suffered. I believe that the biggest factor was pride; pride in their heritage and their people; pride in their ability and resilience to overcome all obstacles, to show the world they were good Americans.

The novel <u>Alberto's Dream</u> tells the story of the Nisei and the 442nd Combat Regiment. Fictional characters bring together many cultures and their own brand of problems centering around indifference and prejudice. The author has woven a story enjoyable to read. It is well researched and presented, the forest battle above the little village of Biffontaine in France in the autumn of 1944 gripping and true.

Addendum

The battle was a focal one for the men of the 442nd, a harrowing experience for all those on the ridge, friend and foe, including those Nisei who came to the relief of a surrounded battalion of American troops of the 36th Division.

I commend the author for his literary achievement and for bringing the story of the battle-action to the reader.

Aloha,

DANIEL K. INOUYE
United States Senator

Bibliography

Armor, John and Peter Wright. <u>Manzanar</u>. New York: Times Books, 1988.

Art in New Mexico. <u>Paths to Taos and Santa Fe</u>. Abbeville Press and National Museum of American Art, Smithsonian Institute.

Atwell, Lester. <u>The Private</u>. New York: Popular Library, 1958.

Battery Press. <u>The Fighting 36th</u>.

Berendt, Joachim E. <u>The Jazz Book</u>. Westport, CT: Lawrence Hill, 1953.

Bosworth, Allen R. <u>America's Concentration Camps</u>. W. W. Norton Co.

Broadfoot, Barry. <u>Years of Sorrow, Years of Shame</u>. Toronto: Doubleday Canada Limited, 1977.

Burnette, Robert and John Koster. <u>The Road to Wounded Knee</u>. New York: Bantam, 1974.

Daniels, Norman. <u>Killer Tank</u>. New York: Prestige 1965.

Davis, Gordon. <u>The Sergeant-Doom River</u>. New York: Bantam, 1981.

DeLauer, Marjei. <u>Allan Houser</u>.

---. <u>American Indian Artist</u>. Allan Houser article.

Duus, Masayo U. <u>Unlikely Liberators</u>. University of Hawaii Press, 1987.

Evanoff, Michael. <u>St. Johns Street</u>.

Fine, Sidney. <u>Sit Down—The General Motors Strike of 1936-37</u>. Ann Arbor: The University of Michigan Press.

Bibliography

Forde, C.D. _A Creation Myth from Acoma Folklore_, 1930.

Garrett, James. _And Save Them for Pall Bearers_. 1958.

Gavin, James M. _On to Berlin_. New York: Bantam, 1978.

Greeley, Andrew. _Confessions of a Parish Priest_. New York: Prestige.

Gridley, Marion E. and Editors of Country Beautiful. _The Story of the Sioux_. New York: G. P. Putman's, 1972.

Hackworth, David H. and Julie Sherman. _About Face_. New York: Simon and Schuster, 1989.

Handbook of North American Indians. Smithsonian Institute.

Henderson, Bill. _The Dance Rituals of the Pueblo Indians_.

Hill, W. W. _An Ethnography of Santa Clara Pueblo_. Albuquerque: University of New Mexico Press, 1982.

Hosakawa, Bill and Robert A. Wilson. _East to America—A History of Japanese in the U.S._ New York: Morrow, 1980.

Hyde, George E. _A Sioux Chronicle_. University of Oklahoma Press, 1956.

Irwin, John Rice. _Alex Stewart—Portrait of a Pioneer_. West Chester, PA: Schiffer Publishing Lts.

Kalin, Harold. _Attack in the Forest_. New York: Prestige.

Kraus, Henry. _The Many and the Few_. Los Angeles: Plantin Press.

Leathers, Noel L. _The Japanese in America_. Minneapolis: Learner.

Bibliography

Locke, Raymond F. <u>The Book of the Navajo</u>. Mankind, 1976.

McGovern, Ann. <u>If You Lived with the Sioux Indians</u>. New York: Four Winds, 1972.

McPartland, Marian. <u>All in Good Time</u>. Oxford University Press, 1987.

Monroe, Jean G. and Ray Williamson. <u>They Dance in the Sky</u>. New York: Houghton Miflin, 1987.

Museum of Art of the American West. <u>Masterworks of the Taos Founders</u>.

Parsons. <u>Pueblo Indian Religion</u>. Chicago: University of Chicago Press.

Rifkin, Jeremy. <u>Time Wars</u>. New York: Simon & Schuster, 1987.

Shirey, Orville. <u>Americans—The Story of the 442nd Combat Team</u>. Infantry Journal, Inc., 1946.

Smith, Bradford. <u>Americans from Japan</u>. Lippincott, 1948.